MESSAGE FROM A KILLER

At the park, Tripp held her hand as they strolled along the river toward where the fair was still going strong. They'd only gone a short distance when Abby's phone rang. After glancing at the screen, she held it out for Tripp to see. "The caller ID is blocked. Should I answer it?"

He shrugged. "It's up to you. I'd let it go to voice mail. If it's important, they'll leave a message."

He was right, of course. It rang another eight or nine times before the phone finally went blessedly silent. With no little trepidation, she forced herself to check if whoever had been on the other end of the line had left a message. It was disappointing to see that they had. She didn't want to listen to what they had to say, but there was really no choice. If she deleted the transcript unheard, she'd spend a whole lot of time wondering if she'd done the right thing. Better to find out for sure. If it was a spam call, she could relax and send it to the trash.

Regardless, her sixth sense was sure she wouldn't like whatever the person had to say. She hit the play button and braced herself for the worst. The caller's voice sounded robotic rather than human, sending a shiver straight through her. The message was short, but terrifying just the same.

Ms. McCree, listen well. You should learn to keep your nose out of affairs that are none of your concern. You will come to regret it if you ~~don't to head this warning. Just~~ *ask Madam G what happ*~~ened because she didn't listen~~ *Wendy Larabie, too . . .*

T0014588

Books by Alexis Morgan

DEATH BY COMMITTEE

DEATH BY JACK-O-LANTERN

DEATH BY AUCTION

DEATH BY INTERMISSION

DEATH BY THE FINISH LINE

DEATH BY ARTS AND CRAFTS

Published by Kensington Publishing Corp.

Alexis Morgan

DEATH BY ARTS AND CRAFTS

An Abby McCree Mystery

Kensington Publishing Corp.
www.kensingtonbooks.com

KENSINGTON BOOKS are published by

Kensington Publishing Corp.
119 West 40th Street
New York, NY 10018

All Kensington titles, imprints, and distributed lines are available at special quantity discounts for bulk purchases for sales promotion, premiums, fund-raising, educational, or institutional use.

Special book excerpts or customized printings can also be created to fit specific needs. For details, write or phone the office of the Kensington Sales Manager: Attn.: Sales Department. Kensington Publishing Corp., 119 West 40th Street, New York, NY 10018. Phone: 1-800-221-2647.

The K and Teapot logo is a trademark of Kensington Publishing Corp.

First Printing: January 2023
ISBN: 978-1-4967-3968-1

ISBN: 978-1-4967-3969-8 (ebook)

10 9 8 7 6 5 4 3 2 1

Printed in the United States of America

Chapter 1

"Should we go see if Bridey needs help with her luggage?"

Abby McCree glanced at her companion and shook her head. "That's what I had planned to do, but she texted me specific instructions just before I left the house. I'm supposed to back into the driveway, make sure the passenger door is unlocked, and keep the engine running for a quick getaway. She promised she'd be right out."

Dayna frowned as she studied the house. "But didn't you say that she was really pregnant?"

"Yep, she's just over six months along."

If anything, Dayna looked even more confused. "Not that I've ever been pregnant myself, but should she be carrying anything heavy?"

Abby trusted that she would've said if she needed extra help. However, Dayna and Bridey hadn't yet met, while she and Dayna had been friends since college. In contrast, Abby and Bridey Kyser had only gotten to know each other after Abby moved to Snowberry Creek.

Today, the three of them were embarking on a mission on behalf of the town of Snowberry Creek. A short while ago, Abby had been coerced into becoming a member of the city council, and her first assignment was to act as liaison between the council and the committee organizing the town's very first arts and crafts fair.

The event was a week away, and all of the major pieces were in place. But in an unexpected move, the head of the committee and the mayor had approached Abby with a special request. They wanted her to spend a weekend visiting several other fairs to touch base with the artists scheduled to be part of the Snowberry Creek fair. She was to ask if they had any last-minute requests, hoping a little advance warning would help things go more smoothly.

Since several of the events were some distance from Snowberry Creek, the committee offered to foot the bill for a night in a hotel on Saturday night. Deciding it would be the perfect way to spend a summer weekend with friends, Abby had accepted the assignment but with a special demand of her own. She'd make her own reservation and submit receipts for reimbursement after agreeing on a reasonable price for the room charge. Anything that exceeded that amount would be her responsibility.

She had immediately upgraded the room to a suite and invited Dayna and Bridey to join her. The plan was to combine the work she needed to do for the committee with a fun getaway for the three of them. They'd visit two fairs on Saturday before checking into the hotel. Being pampered in the hotel's spa would be their reward for all their hard work. That would be followed by an expensive dinner and show at the casino next to the hotel.

A good time would be had by all. Well, if they ever actually got started.

Their schedule was pretty tight, and it was past time for them to hit the road with still no sign of the third member of their party. Abby was about to give up and go ring the doorbell when the front door opened. A very exasperated-looking Bridey stepped out on the porch with her husband, Seth, trailing right behind her. Bridey blocked his way and held out her hand. Seth reluctantly surrendered to the inevitable and handed over her suitcase. She grinned and gave him a quick kiss before hustling down the sidewalk to the car. After tossing her suitcase into the back seat, she dove in right behind it.

"Hit the gas, Abby, before he thinks of anything else I should've packed. The man means well, but I swear his hovering keeps getting worse. Despite the doctor assuring him that everything is fine, Seth keeps finding something new to worry about. He actually insisted I bring the baby monitor we bought. I'm supposed to set it up so that you can keep an eye on me all night long. Heck, I've had to limit his time online just to keep the hysteria to a minimum."

It was hard not to laugh. Just for grins, Abby revved the engine as if getting ready to tear off down the street. Then she waved at Seth and drove sedately out of the driveway. At least he was laughing as he disappeared back into the house.

"Ladies, we are finally on our way! Nothing but fun and excitement ahead for us."

Dayna and Bridey applauded wildly as she turned north toward their first stop. "Oh, I should introduce the two of you. Dayna Fisk, this is Bridey Kyser. Bridey owns Something's Brewing, the best coffee shop and bakery in the area. Dayna is a potter who does truly beautiful work. I have several of her pieces that I just love. In a way, you're both artists."

She left it to the two women to get further acquainted while she concentrated on driving through Tacoma and then Seattle. After a while, Bridey leaned forward to ask, "What's the plan for today? I bet Seth you'd have printed agendas for us to follow."

Giving her friend a guilty look in the rearview mirror, Abby nodded. "Yeah, I do, but that's mostly so that I don't miss touching base with any of the artists I'm supposed to talk to. We should still have plenty of time to take in the sights at each of the two fairs we're visiting today. Are you looking for anything in particular?"

"I'd love to find a cute lamp for the baby's room. Maybe some clothes for her, too."

As soon as Abby heard the pronoun Bridey used, she whooped, "So it's a girl?"

Bridey beamed with pride. "Yeah, she is. We'd planned to keep it secret, but Seth let it slip to his family a couple of days ago. Once we told my family, we figured we should just let everyone know."

Dayna twisted around to look back at Bridey. "I take it that this is your first?"

"Yeah, it is. And to be honest, I'm just as wound up about it as Seth is. We've had so much fun picking out baby furniture. My husband is an artist, so he's done some spectacular wood carvings for her room. He's also painting a mural of a woodland scene that will take up an entire wall. It's just lovely."

Abby smiled. "I can't wait to see it."

Then she asked Dayna, "Is there anything in particular you need to do this weekend or are you just browsing?"

"Tomorrow afternoon I plan to check in with my business partner at some point. It's Wendy's weekend to cover the booth that we share, and I want to see how things are going. Sales on my pottery have been falling, and I'm not sure why. If that trend continues, we both might need to start working every weekend again so we can cover more events."

Abby frowned. "I thought you cut back on your appearances at the fairs to concentrate on the classes you've been teaching and because it would give you more time at the wheel."

Her friend looked pretty frustrated. "That was the plan, and it worked pretty well when we first started doing it. I don't know what's changed, which is why I need to talk to Wendy."

Dayna drew a deep breath and let it out. "Sorry, I didn't mean to unload on the two of you. We're supposed to be having a good time, not whining about my problems. Are you shopping for anything in particular, Abby?"

"I might do some early browsing for Christmas presents."

"If you think of something specific, I can probably aim you in the right direction. I know a lot of the various vendors, not just the ones who do pottery."

"Thanks, I appreciate it. To keep on schedule, we can spend about three hours checking the place out. I would also suggest we grab lunch before heading on to the next stop."

Bridey lit up. "Just as long as we save time for dessert. I might regret it when I have to weigh in at my next doctor visit, but I plan to have an elephant ear with my lunch. I've been craving one ever since Abby invited me on this expedition."

Dayna laughed. "What's not to love about fried dough covered in cinnamon and sugar? How about you, Abby? What's your guilty pleasure?"

Drawing a deep breath, Abby let it out with a big smile on her face. "The sugary perfection known as the funnel cake. I probably shouldn't, but I won't be able to resist."

Bridey wasn't having it. "Hey, no guilt allowed. This should be a weekend where we can indulge ourselves. It's not like any of us do this sort of thing all the time."

Abby met Bridey's gaze in the rearview mirror again and grinned. "It's a deal. I'll take care of business as soon as we get there. After that, nothing but fun with no guilt."

With that settled, she drove the last few miles to the fair.

* * *

At their first destination, Abby and Bridey wandered past the booths together while Dayna stopped to visit with some artist friends. Bridey quickly found the perfect lamp for the baby's room while Abby picked up some small gifts for her mother and the ladies from the quilting guild. She also wanted to get something for Tripp, her tenant and almost boyfriend. After passing by several booths, she stopped to study some custom-made knives in a glass-fronted display case. While she admired the craftsmanship, she finally decided they just weren't what she was looking for. Hoping she'd have better luck at one of the other fairs, she hustled to catch up with Bridey, who was just paying for several little outfits at a nearby booth.

While the clerk bagged the baby clothes, Bridey sighed. "I don't know about you, but I think I'd better take a break if I'm going to last through the show tonight."

Abby held out her hands. "Why don't I take your bags and stash them in the car? While I do that, you can go stake out a table in the food court and rest. I have two more people to touch base with, and then we can have lunch. I'll text Dayna to let her know the plan."

"Sounds good. I'll get a cold drink and wait for you two to catch up."

The trip to the car and back didn't take long. When she returned to the fair, Abby studied the map that laid out where all the various vendors were located. Luckily, the two she still needed to speak to were located near each other. When she reached the first one, she browsed the artwork on display while the woman seated behind the table in the back finished ringing up the only customer in the tent.

Abby assumed she was looking at Bonnie Simon, a watercolor artist who specialized in painting flowers of all kinds. Abby was no expert, but the woman had a delicate touch with the details and a fine eye for colors. The flowers appeared so real that it wouldn't surprise her to catch the scents of roses and lilacs. She really admired a pair of the smaller paintings that would be perfect on her bedroom wall.

"Hi, are you looking for something in particular?"

Abby turned to smile at the woman. "I'm actually here to talk to you for another reason, but I'll definitely be taking two of your paintings with me when I go. They're lovely."

Her comment clearly pleased the other woman. As they shook hands, the woman said, "Please call me Bonnie. How can I help you?"

"I'm Abby McCree, a member of the city council in Snowberry Creek. You're scheduled to be part of our arts and crafts fair next week, and I'm here to thank you personally for agreeing to come. I also wanted to see if there's anything we can do to make sure everything goes as smoothly as possibly for you."

Bonnie gave it some thought. "Not that I can think of, although it would be nice to choose who I'm next to at the fair. It might come as a bit of a shock, but you know how people talk about artists being temperamental? Well, it's true in some cases."

Her smile faltered a bit as she paused to look

around, as if making sure no one else was listening. "Luckily, they're in the minority. Besides, there's no way to let all of us cherry-pick who we're parked next to. You'd never get the fair up and running."

She was right about that not being practical, so Abby settled for saying, "I'll cross my fingers that you end up next to someone you like."

Bonnie grinned. "Thanks, I appreciate the thought. But now that I think about it, there is one thing that might make things go smoothly. A fair I was at last week was an hour late opening up because they were short on the help needed to get things set up. Most of us have the process down pat, but we can always use some extra muscle to help fetch and carry."

That made sense. "I know our committee reached out to the local veterans group. A lot of them have volunteered to help with the setup and teardown."

Abby held out her business card from the council. "This has my number on it if you think of anything else."

She spent the next few minutes studying the artwork Bonnie had on display. It was a difficult decision, but she finally settled on a pair for the wall above her bed. "I think I'll take the two of old roses. I inherited an old Victorian house a while back from my aunt, and both the roses and those rhododendrons look like they came straight from her garden."

Bonnie took the two paintings back to the table to wrap them in cardboard and brown paper to protect them. "Sounds like your aunt had a green thumb."

"She did. I'm doing my best to take care of everything, but it's definitely been a steep learning curve." Abby picked up her paintings. "I look forward to seeing you next weekend."

"Thanks for stopping by, and I hope you enjoy the paintings."

Abby's last stop didn't take long. The artist in question was doing a brisk business selling his stained-glass art and could only spare a minute. Abby gave him her card and promised to check in with him at some point during the fair in Snowberry Creek.

With her duties done, she followed the tempting scent of barbecue wafting in the air to the food court. She'd worked up quite an appetite, and there definitely was a pulled pork sandwich in her immediate future. It would feel good to catch her breath before the three of them headed down the highway to their next stop.

Chapter 2

The second fair offered a breathtaking view of Bellingham Bay to the west and glimpses of the Cascade Mountains to the east. At times, they could also see the summit of Mount Baker, one of the snowcapped volcanoes located along the I-5 corridor in Washington. So lovely. Abby hoped to make quick work of meeting with the remaining three vendors on her list while Dayna and Bridey browsed the fair. With luck, she'd be able to pick up a few more gifts, especially one for Tripp.

As they approached the park entrance, it became obvious that something was bothering Dayna. She'd grown quieter ever since lunch. Clearly something had taken the shine off the day for her. When they waited while Bridey used the restroom, Abby asked, "Is everything all right?"

Dayna stood staring off into the distance, her expression somber. Finally, she blinked and turned to face Abby. "I talked to a couple of my potter friends at the last fair, and what I heard is disturbing. It seems they all are quite happy with how their sales are going. In fact, they said this has been their best season in years."

That didn't make sense. "Then why are your sales down?"

"Good question. One I intend to ask Wendy when I see her tomorrow. I didn't want to press anyone too hard for details for fear of setting off alarms. Most of the people I talked to are also friends of Wendy's, and I'd rather not give her a heads-up that I'm not happy with how things are going."

Dayna sighed. "And maybe it's just bad luck that we didn't do well at a couple of fairs. Still, one woman acted a bit odd, kind of like she knew more than she was willing to share. But then again, maybe I'm just being overly suspicious."

Abby gave her a quick hug. "I'm sorry. I know what it's like to start doubting your business partner."

That much was true. In Abby's case, the problem was compounded by the fact that her partner had also been her now ex-husband, who'd been cheating on two fronts. In the end, Chad had bought out her half of their business as part of the divorce settlement. Thanks to that windfall and her unexpected inheritance from Aunt Sybil, Abby didn't need to be in any big hurry to start another career. Dayna didn't have that luxury.

Her friend hugged her back. "I'll be fine, one way or the other. For now, I'm going to shove all the worry into a box and enjoy the rest of the day."

"Sounds like a plan."

Abby could only hope that it would be that easy

for her friend to shed her concerns for a little while. When Bridey rejoined them, she pointed to where a couple of volunteers were handing out maps of the fair. They each took one and then stood back out of the flow of foot traffic to get their bearings. Abby took a few seconds to study their choices before asking, "Okay, ladies, where do we start? Right, left, or straight ahead?"

Bridey pointed to the right. "It looks like there's a wooden-toy booth that way. I'd like to check it out."

The decision made, they merged back into the crowd making its way through the fair. While Bridey and Dayna checked out the toy booth, Abby wandered on down the way to where another wood-carver had his wares on display. She coasted to a stop in front of a chess set.

While not full-sized, it wasn't as small as some of the other travel sets she'd seen. It was beautifully made in natural wood tones. The chess pieces themselves were simple in their styling, but truly lovely. She liked how the case was hinged and opened flat to form the game board, and the inside was cushioned to protect the pieces when the case was being carried.

Tripp would love it.

He and some of his friends from the veterans group liked to hang around after their meetings to play chess. Right now he had an old plastic set he stored in a cardboard box held together with camo-colored duct tape. She could already picture Tripp and Gage Logan, the local police chief and fellow veteran, studying the board as they tried to out-maneuver each other.

The man behind the counter stopped in front of her. "Can I help you?"

She glanced at the vendor's name tag as she smiled at him. "Maybe, Mr. Hostler. This chess set would be a perfect gift for a friend, but I almost hesitate to ask how much it costs."

He winked at her. "Well, let's just say he'd have to be a pretty good friend to deserve a gift like this one."

She'd been afraid of that. If it wasn't just so absolutely perfect, she would've thanked him and walked away. Instead, she gave him a considering look. "Are we talking having to eat ramen for dinner for a few weeks or are we talking second mortgage territory?"

That had him laughing and shaking his head. "No, it's not that bad. This set is normally two hundred fifty dollars. But because I like your sense of humor, I'll let it go for two twenty-five."

Time to play hardball. "Come on now, I'm funnier than that. How about two hundred dollars instead? And did I mention the man I'm buying it for is a decorated veteran?"

He narrowed his eyes in suspicion. "Seriously?"

She met his gaze head on. "Yep, twenty years in the Special Forces. I wouldn't lie about that."

"Lady, you do drive a hard bargain, but I can respect that." He held out his hand. "You have a deal."

Abby whipped out her credit card before he could change his mind. When he handed her the receipt and the bag containing the chess set, he smiled again. "Thank your friend for his service for me."

"I will."

Happy with her purchase, there was one question left unanswered. Would she be able to wait until Christmas to give Tripp his present? Somehow, she doubted it, but that was a problem for later. Right now, it was time to check the last few vendors off her list.

Two hours later, Abby followed her friends through the front door of the hotel. "If you'll watch my things, I'll go get us checked in."

Bridey immediately sat down on a nearby couch with a sigh of relief. Abby didn't blame her. She suspected they were all really looking forward to getting a massage. Thankfully, there was no line at the check-in counter, so the clerk made quick work of completing their registration and handed over three card keys. "Your suite is on the top floor in the west wing. It has one bedroom with a king-sized bed and a second with two queens."

"Thank you, that's perfect."

He looked past her to where Dayna and Bridey waited. "Would you and your friends like help with your luggage?"

They didn't have all that much and under ordinary circumstances Abby would have handled it herself. However, this was all about splurging a bit and enjoying a few luxuries. Besides, Bridey wasn't the only one feeling a little tired. "We'd appreciate it, thanks."

He waved to get the attention of one of the bell-hops standing over by the concierge's desk. "Heath, would you please help these ladies with their bags?"

The bellhop grabbed a cart and hustled over to where Abby had rejoined her friends and passed out the room keys. Once Heath had everything situated, he led them over to the bank of elevators along the back wall of the lobby. As they filed into the elevator, Bridey grinned at Abby. "I don't know if I've thanked you for inviting me along on this adventure, but I really appreciate it."

She placed her hands on her baby bump. "It might be years before I get to do something like this again."

It was hard not to envy her friend's excitement over her pregnancy, but Bridey and Seth deserved every bit of happiness they'd found together. Giving Bridey a quick hug, she said, "Then we'll make tonight one to remember!"

Then she offered each of her friends a high-five. "The first round of drinks is on me, even though it has to be sparkling grape juice for you, Bridey."

Bridey rolled her eyes. "Fine, I accept my assigned role. I'll watch as the two of you get sloppy drunk and then pour you into bed. At least I won't be the one with a massive headache tomorrow while we make the rounds at the fairs."

Pinning Abby with a superior look, Bridey put her hand on her chest with a dramatic sigh. "I just hope I don't have to tell the mayor how you showed up all hungover when you're supposed to be representing the fine city of Snowberry Creek."

Acting very much put-upon, Abby gave Bridey a mock glare. "Fine, I'll behave . . . well, mostly, anyway."

Dayna pouted. "And here I was hoping we'd all

have a few too many and end up at an all-night tattoo parlor. Seriously, it's been way too many years since I've done that."

Bridey looked intrigued. "Really? What kind of tattoo did you get? Can we see it?"

Dayna nodded in the direction of their helpful bellboy. "It's a flower, but things could get a bit awkward if I showed it to you right now."

Luckily, the elevator came to a stop before the conversation could continue. Heath looked as if he was struggling to hold back a laugh. Abby grinned and doubled his tip as he departed their suite.

Contrary to Bridey's playful predictions, Abby had felt great on Sunday morning as they made the rounds at the first fair on their list. The previous evening had been the perfect blend of relaxing and entertaining. After dinner, they killed time until the show began in the casino, playing the slots and a few hands of blackjack. Happily, Lady Luck was with them, and all three walked away with more money than they'd started with. Admittedly, their combined winnings would barely cover the cost of lunch at the fair. Still, a good time was had by all.

They'd just arrived at the final stop on their trip. The day was quite a bit warmer than the previous one, so they stopped at a fresh lemonade stand located just inside the entrance. While they waited in line, Abby studied their surroundings, taking note of what kind of booths were located so near the front of the fair. It was probably too late for the Snowberry Creek committee to make any changes, but she thought they might find the information useful for the next year. Rather than relying solely on memory, she snapped several pictures with her phone. She also stuck the map in her purse with the ones she'd picked up at their previous stops.

With that done, she considered what should come next. "There are only two people I need to check in with at this fair. One is called Madam G. Evidently she's a psychic who reads palms and stuff like that. The other is one of the main headliners at the Snowberry Creek fair, so I might need to spend a little extra time with him. Still, I'd like to see as much of this fair as I can before we head back home."

Bridey took a long drink of her lemonade before answering. "It shouldn't take long to make the rounds if we keep moving, but we can always stop if one of us spots something interesting. Do we want to eat lunch before we get started or just stop when we get hungry?"

Abby gave it some thought. "I'd just as soon wait until later if that's okay. I'm not all that hungry yet. Besides, once I talk to Josiah Garth and Madam G, I'll be done with my official duties and can relax."

As they walked down the aisle, Bridey asked, "So, what kind of artist is Josiah Garth?"

"He works with wrought iron. I've seen a few of his pieces online, and they're quite striking." She studied the map again and then looked around to orient herself to where they were. "His booth is down to the left at one of the major intersections where he'll get the most traffic. It looks like his booth also takes up a lot more space than any of the others around it."

"That sounds like something Josiah would insist on. To be fair, though, some of his pieces are pretty sizeable, so he probably does need the extra space." Dayna leaned in closer to glance at the map in Abby's hand. "Besides, his name is always a big draw. Most fairs are willing to give him whatever he asks for just to keep him happy. Sometimes he asks for a lot."

That didn't sound good. After checking to make sure no one was paying any attention to their conversation, Abby whispered, "Is he a prima donna?"

"I've heard he can be, but I've never had any problem with Josiah. There's also a definite upside to working any event he's part of because of the crowd he draws."

Dayna patted Abby on the shoulder. "My advice is to tread carefully and charm the heck out of him. But, hey, no pressure."

"Very funny."

"Seriously, you'll do fine. Like I said, I've never had any trouble with him. I can't say the same for Wendy, though. She made the mistake of asking the management at one fair to control his line. Evidently, it was long enough to block access to several other booths, hers included. Josiah didn't take the complaint well at all."

Did the Snowberry Creek fair committee know about Josiah's reputation? Abby knew they'd worked long and hard to convince the man to attend their fair even though it didn't offer either the size or established reputation offered by most of the other venues he was used to attending.

When they were about to turn onto the main aisle toward Josiah's booth, Abby spotted a sign identifying a large, red-striped tent just ahead as Madam G's Parlor. The woman must have been open for business because a pair of giggling teenagers were just leaving. There was no telling what the psychic had told them, but both girls looked decidedly happy with what they'd heard. Abby didn't actually believe in psychics, but it appeared the woman knew how to please her customers.

She paused to point toward Madam G's tent. "She's the one other person I still need to talk to. Do you guys want to come with in me?"

Dayna held up her hands and backed away. "Nope, I'm good, but I look forward to hearing all about the reading she does for you."

Like that was going to happen. "I'm not looking for a reading. I'm here to represent Snowberry Creek and the art fair committee. As soon as I give her my business card, it's on to my next stop."

"Good luck with that." Dayna's grin was a tad wicked. "From what I hear, the woman takes her work a little too seriously, which is why I'm not setting foot inside her tent."

"Okay, how about you, Bridey? Are you going to abandon me, too?"

Bridey didn't hesitate. "Yep, but I'll wait here and send you all kinds of long distance moral support."

Feeling mildly betrayed on two fronts, Abby ignored their grins. "All right, cowards, wait here and hold my drink. This shouldn't take long."

She hoped. Bracing herself, she marched resolutely toward her target. But when she reached the entrance, she hesitated. It almost felt as if she should somehow request permission to enter, but there was no bell to ring or door to knock on. Before she could decide how to proceed, a woman's voice called out, "Please, come on in."

She had only a vague idea of what a psychic should look like, but Abby had to admit that Madam G didn't fit that image at all. She was an attractive woman most likely somewhere in her late fifties. Her silvery blond hair was cut in a short bob, her makeup had been done with a deft hand, and that navy pantsuit would have looked at home in the executive boardroom at most companies. It was possible the woman was a client, but there was no one else in the tent, and Abby had just come through the only doorway.

"Madam G?"

The woman offered Abby an amused look. "Let me guess. You were expecting someone wearing a garish caftan and a turban?"

Her good-natured grin had Abby admitting the truth. "Yeah, I guess I was. I've never met a psychic before, and I jumped to the wrong conclusion. I apologize."

"Don't worry about it. It's a common misconception." Madam G waved her hand toward the chair that sat across the small table from where she was seated. "Shall we get started?"

"Oh, no, I'm not here for a reading." Abby whipped out one of her business cards and dropped it on the table in front of Madam G as if that alone would protect her from any unwanted predictions about her future. "I'm Abby McCree, and I'm here on behalf of the Snowberry Creek city council and the committee for our upcoming fair. We wanted to touch base ahead of the event to thank you again for agreeing to come and to see if you have any special concerns or requests we should know about."

The woman studied the card as she traced Abby's name with a well-manicured fingertip. "Nice to meet you, Ms. McCree, and I appreciate your stopping by, but I can't think of any special requests right off the top of my head."

"Well, it will be our first fair, and we want to make sure it's a success for everyone involved."

Setting the card aside, Madam G once again motioned toward the chair. "I should still do a reading for you. Free of charge, of course."

"Oh, that's very kind of you, but my friends are waiting for me."

"I'm sorry, but I really must insist. Touching your card has stirred my gift. Please be seated."

It was the last thing Abby wanted to do, but she also didn't want to offend the woman by refusing her offer. She reluctantly settled into the chair. "What do you need me to do?"

Madam G held out her hands. "I just need to take a quick peek at both of your palms."

After setting her purse on the floor by her chair, Abby held out her hands. Madam G cradled them in her own as she leaned forward to study them. What truths did the woman think she'd see etched in the lines that crisscrossed Abby's palms? Something had her nodding as if her suspicions had just been confirmed.

"The new life you began not long ago suits you much better than the previous one. You've made new connections that will impact your life from this point on. Some are friends, but one will become more than that."

Madam G paused long enough to lift her gaze to meet Abby's directly as she smiled. "I'm quite pleased for you, my dear. You've made some difficult choices, even painful ones, but they were obviously the right ones for you."

Wow, that assessment definitely hit a little too close to home. Granted, Madam G hadn't been all that specific about the changes she mentioned, but still. Abby didn't know what kind of response was necessary, so she settled for simply saying, "Thank you."

But when she tried to withdraw her hands, Madam G tightened her grip on them. "I'm sorry, Ms. McCree, but there's more to be learned here."

Trying not to grimace, Abby had no choice but to wait for the woman to continue. "There will be two men in your immediate future. Neither will bring you harm, but they definitely arrive with a profound aura of darkness surrounding them. Their path should not be yours, but you will feel a powerful pull to follow. I can't see where it will lead you, but once you start . . . if you start . . . you must follow it to the end."

At that dark pronouncement, she released Abby's hands. After blinking several times, she smiled. "I hope that helps. Thanks for stopping by, and I look forward to seeing you again next weekend."

Abby knew a dismissal when she heard one. "Until then."

On the way out, she had to sidestep another group of teenagers heading in to see Madam G. Hopefully she'd have a cheerier message for them than the gloom and doom she'd offered Abby at the end of her spiel. She hustled across to where her friends stood waiting for her. Bridey held out the lemonade she'd been holding for her. "You don't look happy. Is everything okay?"

"I'm fine. I just needed a second to adjust to the bright sunshine after the dim interior inside the tent."

Dayna gave her a thoughtful look. "She gave you a reading, didn't she?"

"Yeah, she did. Mostly she said that any changes I'd made in my life recently were the right ones. I can see why it would be easy to think she really had some special insight into people's lives with comments like that. Most people have changed something in their life, even if it's switching to decaf coffee."

"I'm betting that's not all she told you, though."

This wasn't the right place to dissect the rest of Madam G's reading. "It was more of the same . . . you know, vague and open to interpretation."

Not to mention scaring her more than a little. "We'd better get moving if we want to get back home by dinnertime."

Rather than dwelling on the two men with dark auras in her future, she took a long sip of her lemonade and let it wash away the last vestiges of discomfort from Madam G's pronouncements.

Chapter 3

Turning the corner, Abby quickly spotted where Josiah Garth had set up shop. There was a table along the front that had a pair of signs labeled PAY HERE and INFORMATION.

Abby slowed to a stop, unsure what to do. This visit might take longer than she'd expected. "If you guys want to go on ahead, I'll catch up after I check in with Mr. Garth. Considering the crowd, it looks a bit doubtful that he'll have any time for me right now."

"I'm pretty much shopped out, so don't worry about me." Bridey pointed down the way toward an empty bench under a couple of shade trees. "I'll go sit over there and people watch until you come get me."

Once again, Dayna's good mood disappeared. "It's time I talk to Wendy. There's no reason for the two of you to get caught up in my mess, so I'll go do that now. The good news is that our booth is located right around the corner from Josiah. Hopefully, we're doing a brisk business, and I've been worried for nothing."

"Good luck, Dayna."

Her friend glanced back over her shoulder as she walked away. "Thanks, I may need it. At least I won't have to keep wondering what's been going on."

Abby waved one last time and got in line. As she waited, she really hoped whatever Dayna learned from Wendy wouldn't put an end to the two women's friendship. From what Dayna had told her, they'd been close for years.

Regardless of how things turned out, at least she would finally get her questions answered. Living with doubt was never easy. Abby had always regretted not confronting her husband sooner. Maybe she and Chad might've saved their marriage if only she'd spoken up when she first suspected something was wrong. But that was water under the bridge, and there was no changing the past.

Meanwhile, she shuffled forward another step as the person at the front of the line walked away. The table was arranged so that the cashier was seated at the far end while the line snaked along in front of the table. That gave potential customers a chance to browse through three-ring binders containing pictures of Josiah's work. The first notebook Abby looked through contained pictures of wrought iron gates, which ranged from simple designs to ornate works of art. The next notebook focused on amazing decorations for the yard as well as the house, but it was the final one that she found riveting. His furniture designs were nothing short of stunning.

It was all Abby could do not to toss her credit card to the woman seated at the table and order one of everything until her card maxed out. When the last person in front of her left, Abby carefully set aside the notebook and the temptation it represented.

The young woman smiled. "Did you have a question?"

Abby gave the notebook one more longing look before turning her attention back to the matter at hand. Pulling out one of her business cards, she offered it to the woman and introduced herself. "I represent the city council in Snowberry Creek. Mr. Garth is scheduled to be at our fair next weekend. If possible, I'd like to touch base to see if there's anything we can do to make sure everything goes smoothly for him. We're all thrilled that he agreed to come."

"Nice to meet you. I'm Jenny Garth, Josiah's niece as well as his assistant. Let me tell him you're here."

Then she glanced back over her shoulder to where Josiah stood listening to another man. Josiah looked artsy-craftsy in worn jeans and a loose-fitting chambray shirt with the sleeves rolled up. His gray-streaked hair brushed his collar and looked as if he'd recently run his fingers through it a few times. In contrast, his companion was incredibly overdressed for a small town fair. His navy suit was obviously expensive, and his silver hair was perfectly styled. Distinguished looking, he was the kind of handsome that probably would draw feminine attention wherever he went.

However, right now his face was flushed red in

anger as he struggled to keep his voice pitched low enough to keep their discussion private. Abby couldn't hear more than the occasional word, but the tension in his body language spoke pretty clearly. By way of contrast, Josiah looked just as angry, but his temper was running freezing cold rather than hot.

Finally, the man threw his hands up in the air and snarled, "Don't threaten me, Josiah, or you'll hear from my attorney."

He started to walk away, but Josiah grabbed his arm and derailed his charge toward the exit. Whatever he said next only added fuel to the fire, because the look the other man gave Josiah had him backpedaling out of reach with his hands held up in surrender. After a brief silence, their discussion picked up where it had left off, with both men looking only slightly more in control.

Wincing a bit, Jenny looked back to Abby. "Sorry, but this isn't a good time right now. Could you maybe come back later? The fair officially ends at five today, but we'll be here at least an hour or two beyond that, packing up."

What choice did Abby have? She hadn't planned to stay that long at the fair, but it looked as if she might have to if she really wanted to speak to Josiah directly. She pointed to her business card. "I'll try, but in case I can't, would you please tell Mr. Garth he can reach me at that number if he has any concerns or special requests?"

Jenny looked relieved that Abby was being reasonable about the situation. From what Dayna had told her about Josiah, he probably wasn't an easy man to deal with, even for his niece. Jenny's smile brightened up again. "I'll be glad to. Just in case, here's one of Josiah's cards and one of mine as well."

After tucking them in her purse, Abby looked around. For the moment, there was no one in line behind her. Rather than rush off, she didn't immediately step away from the table. "I'm sure you hear this all the time, but his work is truly amazing."

As she spoke, she nodded toward a row of garden stakes on the other side of the booth. Her favorites were topped with ornate finials that formed a twisted basket surrounding a brightly colored glass ball. The stakes themselves spiraled down to a point at the bottom, so they could be easily inserted in the ground. Jenny looked pleased by Abby's compliment. "I'm glad you like them. I'm also Uncle Josiah's apprentice, and I helped make those."

Abby couldn't blame her for taking pride in her work. "I'd like to buy that blue one on the end, the green one next to it, and the red one on the other end of the row."

Jenny went to fetch them. "Are these the three you wanted?"

"Yes, and they're truly lovely."

Jenny made quick work of wrapping them up and processing the payment. Abby slipped her credit card back in her wallet. "Thanks again for your help. And if I don't see you later today, I'll be sure to catch up with you next weekend in Snowberry Creek."

"I'll look forward to it."

Abby picked up her package and headed down

the aisle to where Bridey waited. There was no sign of Dayna, so Abby sent her a quick text to tell her that she and Bridey were ready to grab some lunch and would order something for her at the same time. It was a bit worrisome when her friend hadn't answered by the time they sat down to eat. Of course, it could be a good thing that Dayna's discussion with Wendy was running so long. Maybe it meant they were working things out.

Sadly, she feared that might not be the case.

Bridey confirmed Abby's suspicions a few seconds later. "Uh-oh, here comes Dayna, and she looks pretty upset."

Abby stood up and waved to get Dayna's attention, who headed toward their table. After she sat down, Abby offered her the food and drink she'd bought for her. "I got you a chicken sandwich and potato salad. We also got cream cheese brownies for dessert."

Dayna's smile looked forced. "Thanks, I wasn't looking forward to standing in line right now."

When she made no move to even pick up her fork, Abby reached over to put her hand on Dayna's arm. "Is everything okay?"

By that point, her friend's eyes glistened with tears. "I found out why I haven't been making as much money as I expected. Evidently when Wendy works, she puts very few of my pieces on display. If today is any example, even those were in the back where they could barely be seen. Everything else is hers."

Bridey slammed her palms down on the table, startling both Abby and Dayna. "What is wrong with that woman? If she's not happy with the current arrangement, she should've been adult enough to say so."

Dayna sniffled a bit and blew her nose on a napkin. "She's clearly mad, but she didn't want to tell me what has her so upset. She gave me some lame excuse about not wanting to air our dirty laundry in public."

By that point, Dayna's hands were clenched in white-knuckled fists. "When I pushed her on it, she finally said that I was so busy hanging around with the movers and shakers at the galleries where I've had showings that I thought I was too good to help old friends. When I pointed out that I had introduced her to several of the gallery owners, she accused me of bad-mouthing her to them since none of them offered to display her work. That's not true, but she didn't want to hear it. So I packed up what little of my work that she'd bothered to bring with her and set the box back out of her way. I told her I would pick it up it before I leave the fair."

Abby patted her on the shoulder, knowing it was not much of a comfort. At least it kept Dayna talking. "Anyway, I had already started to walk away when Wendy suddenly announced loud enough for people in the general area to hear that my talent was not up to her standards. Something about people taking one look at the quality of my work and just walking on by the booth. She won't risk tanking her own career by letting me ride on her coattails."

Bridey frowned big-time. "That's awful. Can you file a complaint with the fair officials?"

Dayna shook her head. "There's nothing they

can do. Besides, it could potentially backlash and cause me problems when I try to book this fair next season."

Impressed by Dayna's clearheaded thinking, Abby said so. "I'm not sure I would've handled being insulted as well as you did. How did you manage to stay so calm?"

"I didn't." Dayna took a long sip of her lemonade and calmly set the glass back down on the table. "On the way out, I bumped into a table and one of her hideous teapots fell off and broke. It was an accident. Well, mostly anyway. Wendy was gearing up to throw a major hissy fit, but just then several customers came in. Her eyes shot daggers at me as I dropped enough money on the counter to cover the cost and walked out."

Abby had a powerful urge to give Wendy a piece of her mind, but that would likely just make things worse for Dayna in the long run. "Where have you been all the rest of the time?"

"I needed to walk off my temper, so I did a couple of laps around the outside of the fair. I wanted to take a hammer to every piece of pottery that had Wendy's signature on it. That wouldn't solve anything."

Bridey was frowning big-time. "Aren't you worried about what she'll do to the stuff you packed up?"

Dayna just shrugged. "I really don't care. It's better to cut my losses and move on. We'll still have to figure out how to divide up the remaining fairs we've already booked. It's too late for each of us to get separate booths."

Gosh, what a mess. Dayna was doing her best to be pragmatic, but Abby knew she had to be torn up by such an awful betrayal. Wendy's actions hadn't just ruined their friendship; Dayna's income would also take an unexpected hit.

She gave Dayna a quick hug. "Well, at least you're already scheduled to work at the Snowberry Creek fair next weekend. Let me know if I can help."

"Thanks, I might take you up on that." Dayna drew a ragged breath and finally picked up her sandwich. "Moving on. How did it go with Josiah?"

"Actually, I didn't get to speak with him. He was tied up talking to someone when I got there, so I spoke to his niece instead. She seems really nice."

Dayna's expression brightened up a bit. "From everything I've heard, she's an accomplished metal-worker in her own right."

"She said she was both her uncle's assistant and his apprentice." Abby unwrapped the three garden stakes she'd bought. "She actually helped make these. I thought they would look good in the rose garden in front of the house."

Bridey picked up the red one and held it up so that the glass ball caught the sunlight. "This is lovely. Were there more of these left?"

Abby nodded. "Yes, and there were several other designs to choose from. I've got to say that after looking at the prices on his furniture and wrought iron gates, I'm surprised that he still does small things like this. Talk about sticker shock. Some pieces go for well into the thousands."

Dayna didn't look at all surprised. "Josiah does a better job than some artists at selling his large ticket items, but a lot of people simply can't afford to spend that kind of money. Smaller items like these sell well at fairs and provide good advertising for his more expensive designs."

Abby carefully rewrapped the yard stakes and set them aside. "His niece suggested I swing by again to see if Josiah was available to talk. I'm not sure that's absolutely necessary."

After picking up her sandwich, she said, "Let's finish eating and then make one last pass by Josiah's booth. If he's still too busy to talk, I say we call it a day unless there's something else either of you want to look at."

Bridey pointed to a nearby food truck. "The baby has me craving some ice cream to go along with my brownie. Otherwise, I'm pretty much shopped out. How about you, Dayna?"

"Sounds good to me. A double scoop of mocha ice cream would help end the day on a high note."

Abby knew she was friends with these two people for good reason. "Ice cream it is. And while we're in the vicinity of Wendy's booth, we can pick up your box and take it to the car before she has a chance to trash anything."

For a brief second, Dayna's expression turned bleak again. "That ship has probably already sailed, but I guess it's worth a try. Regardless, I'm over it."

She really wasn't, but Abby accepted the small lie. At least Dayna was acting more like her usual cheerful self by the time they reached the ice cream truck. There was nothing like a double scoop of something cold and creamy to fix what ails you.

* * *

When the ice cream and brownies were nothing but pleasant memories, the three of them wandered back in the direction of Josiah's booth. Dayna and Bridey were chatting away about a television series they were both addicted to when Abby turned the final corner and got a clear look at his booth. Frowning, she slowed to a stop. "Well, that's odd."

Bridey moved up to stand beside her. "What's odd?"

"Josiah's niece-slash-assistant specifically told me that they would still be here packing up for at least an hour past closing time." Abby pointed down the way. "But look—the flaps on his booth are all down and tied shut."

The vendors on either side of Josiah's booth were all still open and doing a brisk business, so it wasn't as if the entire fair decided to shut down early. Had something happened that forced Josiah to close down unexpectedly? Bridey leaned forward a bit and frowned. "It looks like there's a note attached to the flap. Could be they just decided to grab a late lunch or something."

They continued forward until they got within reading distance of the handwritten note that simply said SOLD OUT. That was weird. "Huh, if that's true, they must have had quite a run on sales right after I left."

Also looking skeptical, Dayna offered a different explanation. "Maybe he just wanted to leave early. Regardless, the fair organizers won't be happy about it. Of course, if he actually did sell out, there's not much they could say."

Just in case he or Jenny did come back, Abby

scribbled a quick note on the back of one of her business cards saying she'd stopped by again and stuck it under the edge of the tape holding the makeshift sign in place. At least now she could call it a day in good conscience. The committee back in Snowberry Creek would be glad to know that she'd made contact with everyone on her list. She'd also had a great time hanging out with Dayna and Bridey, but it was time to head back home to Zeke. While her furry roommate loved hanging out with his buddy Tripp, the big dog would be relieved to have her back where she belonged.

"Let's retrieve your box, Dayna, and head out."

Her friend wrinkled her nose. "I'll go by myself. There's no reason to expose the two of you to Wendy's snark."

"Are you sure?"

Dayna stood up straighter, shoulders back, as if bracing herself for trouble. "Yeah, I won't be long. I'll meet you at the car."

Abby didn't like the idea of completely abandoning Dayna to face Wendy alone. Instead, she pointed at a coffee stand a short distance away. "I want something cold to drink on the way home. Bridey and I will wait for you there."

Dayna glanced back over her shoulder and smiled. "Make mine an iced mocha."

"Will do."

Abby had just finished paying for their order when Dayna rejoined them. It was impossible to miss the fact that she wasn't carrying a box.

Abby handed Dayna her drink. "No luck?"

"Thanks for this." Then, after taking a long sip, Dayna said, "Like Josiah, Wendy has gone missing in action, and I didn't want her to catch me rooting around in the booth. She hadn't brought many of my pieces anyway, so it's no great loss."

The sharp edge in Dayna's voice said that probably wasn't exactly true, but once again Abby didn't call her on it. The three of them fell into companionable silence as they sipped their drinks on the way back to the car. She didn't know about the other two, but she was looking forward to a hot shower, a cold glass of wine, and some quality time with Zeke.

And if Tripp played his cards right, he might just get a snazzy new chess set.

Chapter 4

By the time Abby got home, she was more than ready to stop moving for a while. All three of them agreed the weekend had been an unqualified success. Well, except for Dayna's problems. The only other disappointment was that it was clear that Tripp wasn't at home. His pickup was missing, and the lights were off in the small mother-in-law house he rented from her. The only question was if he'd taken Zeke with him when he left.

The second she unlocked the back door she knew Zeke was also gone. He always came running to greet her before heading outside to do a quick patrol of the yard. Upon his return, he would allow her to give him a hug and a bit of a scratch behind the ears before demanding a treat.

This time only silence greeted her. Maybe it was because she was tired, but it was pretty depressing to come home to an empty house. She'd also made up her mind to give Tripp his chess set at the same time she let Zeke test out one of the new toys she'd bought for him. Logic said she could still do all of that whenever they returned, but she couldn't help but be a bit disappointed. Granted, she hadn't given Tripp a specific time to expect her back, but still.

By the time she'd made two more trips out to the car to bring in her suitcase and the last of the items she'd purchased over the weekend, she'd talked herself into a better mood. It wasn't Tripp's fault she was tired, and he'd been nice enough to watch Zeke for her while she was gone.

She was still upstairs stashing the gifts that wouldn't be needed until Christmas when she heard the back door open. That was followed by a deep voice calling her name and a loud woof from her missing roommate. She shoved the last gift up on the shelf in the guest room before stepping out into the hall to call out, "I'll be right down!"

Both Tripp and Zeke stood waiting for her at the bottom of the steps. She was gifted with a slurping kiss from one and a rib-crunching hug from the other. Now this was more like the home-coming she'd been hoping for.

Tripp released his hold on her and stepped back to afford Abby easier access to Zeke. "So how did your adventure go? I'm telling you right now I'll be disappointed if the three of you didn't do at least one thing you're too embarrassed to tell me about. And to be clear, I've been imagining all kinds of wickedness."

That had her laughing. "Just how much trouble do you think we could have gotten into when Bridey couldn't even drink?"

"Well, that is disappointing." He paused to give Zeke a considering look. "It also means I probably shouldn't tell you that Zeke took advantage of your absence to hang out with disreputable characters at the local watering hole. Your biker buddy Gil and his brother claimed him as their good-luck charm when they faced off against me and Gage playing pool. Considering they beat us four games out of five, he had some serious mojo going on for them."

He reached down to ruffle Zeke's fur. "The doofus pigged out on bar grub and managed to help himself to some beer before we could stop him. Luckily, one of us stayed sober enough to drive us back home."

As always, Abby wasn't sure how much Zeke actually understood when he listened to them talk, but he clearly knew he was the topic of conversation. He sat at attention, his tongue lolling out in a big doggy grin. He definitely was proud of himself, but she couldn't hold him responsible for his misadventures. No, the blame for that lay right at Tripp's size-thirteen feet.

She did her best to feign disapproval. "Luckily for you, he doesn't look like he's suffering any ill effects from his big night on the town. I'm even glad you two had such a good time. I wouldn't have wanted him sitting around feeling all sad from missing me too much."

Tripp shook his head in disgust. "Actually, that's why we ended up going to the bar. The big dope kept moping around, heaving big sighs and whining as he tried to get back into your house every time I took him out to patrol. It made it impossible to do anything productive. When Gage said he needed a pool partner, I figured the bar would be a good distraction for both of us."

She tore her attention away from Tripp long enough to pat Zeke on the head. "I'm sorry for abandoning you to the questionable company of this guy and his pool-hustling buddies."

Zeke gave her hand another lick to show that all was forgiven. Then Tripp stepped between them, standing so close that she had to tip her head back at an uncomfortable angle just to see his face. "He's not the only one who missed you. How are you going to make it up to me?"

So many enticing ideas popped into her head. "Well, what would it take to make you happy?"

Because even if the chess set might do the job, somehow the way Tripp was staring down at her made her think he might have something else in mind. He took another small step toward her, his hands coming to rest on her shoulders. His mouth curled up in a teasing smile as he leaned in close. She wasn't sure where this was headed as her pulse kicked into a higher gear. Neither of them had been in a big hurry to define their relationship, but it hovered somewhere between "good friend" and "something more," depending on the day and the circumstances.

Right now, this felt like one of those "something more" moments. Bracing herself for the impact of one of his hit-and-run kisses, she let her eyes drift closed. But instead of kissing her, he softly whispered, "What would make me really happy is getting whatever present you bought for me at the fair."

She jerked free of his grasp and glared at him. "Very funny. What makes you think I bought you anything at all?"

He grinned and retreated a step. "Sorry, but I couldn't resist. Besides, we both know you wouldn't have spent all that time looking at cool stuff and not bought presents for both of us."

"Even if I did, only one of you deserves to get whatever I might have bought." She jabbed him in the chest with her finger, "And I'm pretty sure it isn't you."

With that, she sidestepped past him and started toward the kitchen. "Come on, Zeke, let's get you some treats and then you can see what I brought you."

Tripp must have belatedly realized that his teasing had fallen flat, because he hustled down the hall right behind her. He caught her arm and used her momentum to swing her right back around to face him. "Abs, I'm sorry. I didn't mean to upset you."

"Fine."

Although it wasn't, and he clearly knew it. "For the record, Zeke wasn't the only one who missed you. I kept wishing I was the one hanging out at the fairs and the casino with you instead of your friends. The truth is that I'm the one who called Gage and invited him to play pool, not the other way around."

This time, he did give her the kiss she'd been hoping for, taking his time and doing it right. As apologies went, it was a dandy. After another quick hug, she led their small parade the rest of the way to the kitchen. Zeke parked himself right in front of the counter where she kept his treat jar, his tail doing a slow sweep back and forth across the floor in anticipation. She pulled out several of the organic cookies that she baked for him on a regular basis.

"Here you go, boy."

While he happily devoured the first couple, she went back down the hall to where she'd stashed Zeke's new toys along with Tripp's chess set. It wasn't until she returned to the kitchen that she noticed the bag sitting by the kitchen sink. Her mood brightened even more when she saw the logo was from the local diner in town.

Tripp looked pretty pleased with himself. "I figured you would appreciate not having to cook tonight, so I picked up two of Frannie's fried chicken dinners along with two pieces of pie for dessert. That's where we were when you got home."

This time, she was the one who instigated the hug along with a quick kiss on his cheek. "And that right there is why you're not going to have to wait until Christmas to get what I bought for you at the fair."

First, she gave Zeke another treat and then offered him the big ball made from twisted rope that she'd gotten for him. He made quick work of the cookie and then settled down on his bed in the corner with his new chew toy. By that point, Tripp had taken his usual seat at the kitchen table. Eyeing the happy dog, he shook his head. "That should keep the fur ball happy for a long time."

Abby joined Tripp at the table. "The booth

where I bought it specialized in all kinds of great chew toys for dogs. It's a local company, so I can always buy more later."

She hadn't missed the fact that Tripp's gaze kept wandering back to the other bag she'd brought out of the closet. Rather than make him sit in suspense any longer, she pushed it across the table toward him. "Like I said, originally this was supposed to be your Christmas present. However, I knew the second I bought it I couldn't make you wait that long. I hope you like it."

He tugged the bag a bit closer to his side of the table and then rested his hand on top of it. "Do I deserve this?"

She shot him an impish grin. "Probably not, but I bought it for you anyway. Quit stalling and just open it. If you don't like it, you can always regift it to one of your buddies. I'm sure someone will find a use for it."

By that point, she wasn't sure which of them was more nervous as he finally reached into the bag and gingerly removed the chess set. He stared at it for several seconds before making another move. Finally, after setting it on the table, he gently trailed his fingertips across the wooden surface. "Abby, the inlay work on this is amazing."

As he spoke, he flipped the latch and slowly opened the case until it lay flat. Gently lifting out first the black queen and then the white one, he held them up for closer inspection. The look of absolute wonder in his dark eyes was all the thanks she would ever need.

"You like it."

He shook his head as he set down the queens

and reached for a king and one of the bishops. "No, I don't. I *love* it."

When he had removed all the pieces from their individual spots, he turned the chess board over and set them in place. "Now I'm sure I don't deserve this. It must have cost a fortune."

She wouldn't lie to him about that, but she pointed out, "The man I bought it from gave me a discount when I told him you were a decorated soldier. He said to thank you for your service."

Tripp smiled and nodded. She knew from experience that those occasional acknowledgments of the sacrifices made by those who served in the military really meant a lot to him. "Wait until the guys at the veterans group see this. It's a huge step up from the cheap plastic set we've been using. There'll be some serious chess set envy going on. I'll also have to get a package of sanitizing wipes so they can clean their grubby mitts before they touch it."

That seemed a bit extreme, but it wouldn't surprise her if he meant it. "You could always call Gage and invite him over. I'm betting there's enough of Frannie's chicken in that bag for all three of us."

"I would, but he and his daughter had something going on tonight. Maybe I'll drop by the police station tomorrow for a quick game on his lunch break. We can always hide out in one of the cells so no one will know if the game runs long."

Gage was Snowberry Creek's chief of police. Since the police station was in the same building as the mayor's office, Tripp was probably right that Gage shouldn't play chess at work. However, there were plenty of times that Gage put in way more hours than he ever got paid for. He deserved to steal a few back once in a while when things were quiet. The man was good at his job, and the town was lucky to have him.

Back in the day, Gage had spent time in the military police before joining the Special Forces and then as a homicide detective in Seattle before taking the job in Snowberry Creek. Fortunately, the town didn't have all that much serious crime. But when something bad happened, Gage usually headed up the investigations himself since he had far more experience dealing with murder cases than any of his deputies.

Abby should know. She'd been drawn into several of his recent cases since moving to Snowberry Creek. But all of that was firmly in the past, and she had absolutely no desire to ever get involved in a police investigation again. Even so, the memories sent a quick shiver through her, which she did her best to ignore.

If Tripp was surprised when she abruptly stood up, he didn't say anything despite the puzzled look he gave her. She pasted a bright smile on her face, hoping to ward off any questions. The man was incredibly protective and even a mention of her past misadventures was sure to spoil his mood.

"I don't know about you two, but I'm hungry. How about I warm up our dinners now?"

"Sure thing. Give me a minute to pack this up, and I'll set the table and feed Zeke." As he carefully put the chess pieces back into the case, he gave the dog a stern warning. "To be clear, the chicken is only for the two-legged members in this crowd. You get kibble."

Zeke responded with a smug look that clearly disagreed with Tripp's assessment of the current situation. He knew from long experience that each of them would slip him the odd bite of chicken and even a few green beans for good measure. The only part of the meal that was strictly off-limits for him was the dessert. No one in their right mind would share Frannie's pie with anyone else, especially if Tripp had bought coconut cream, Abby's favorite.

It didn't take long to get their dinner on the table and Zeke's in his bowl. It really hit the spot. Afterward, they took their dessert out onto the back porch and settled in to watch the sun go down, the perfect end to a great weekend.

And as much as she'd enjoyed her time away with Bridey and Dayna, it felt good to be home.

Monday morning came way too soon, so the cloudy weather and intermittent rain showers fit Abby's mood perfectly. She really wanted to sleep in, but sadly she had places to be and things to do. It wasn't the first time she'd envied Zeke and his freedom to choose his own sleep schedule. Even if he got up when she did, he was often back to napping as soon as he finished breakfast.

But not this time. "Come on, dog. Let's get your walk out of the way before I need to be at the mayor's office. After that, I have to drop by to see Pastor Jack to talk to him about what I learned at the fairs this weekend."

That was just the start of her busy day, but Zeke wasn't the least bit interested in her itinerary.

Sadly, if it didn't involve his morning walk or his treat jar, he really didn't care. She didn't blame him. It wasn't as if she was looking forward to back-to-back meetings herself. She snapped Zeke's leash to his harness and let him lead the charge out of the house. At least the rain had stopped. But judging by the sky, it was only a temporary reprieve.

Tripp was just coming out of his house, no doubt heading off for his morning classes at the local university. He tossed his backpack into the front seat of his pickup before walking across the yard to meet them. As usual, he stopped to give Zeke a thorough scratching. His quick reflexes didn't save him from disaster when Zeke suddenly jumped up and put his muddy paws on Tripp's shirt and then let loose with one of his enormous snorts. The impact sent both man and dog down to the soggy ground in a tangled mess.

Abby laughed as Tripp picked himself up and tried to brush the mud off his jeans. He glared down at the unrepentant dog. "Thanks, dog. Now I have to change clothes, which means I'm going to be late."

Abby tugged hard on Zeke's leash to keep him from trying to restart the wrestling match. "Sorry about that. We'll get out of your way to avoid any further fashion mishaps. Are we still on for pizza and watching the ballgame tonight?"

By that point, Tripp had retreated to a safe distance from Zeke. "Yep. I'll be back early enough this afternoon to get my studying done before the first pitch. I'll order the pizza."

"But you bought dinner last night."

He waved off her concern. "We're not keeping score. I'll see you then."

Tripp ducked back in his house while she and Zeke headed down the driveway. She studied the sky as they reached the sidewalk and turned left toward the national forest where they both loved to walk. "We might stay dry if we hurry."

Zeke was busy sniffing the neighbor's bushes to see if any of the other dogs who frequented the area had been by recently. Abby had no idea what kind of intel Zeke gathered from his inspections, but she'd always imagined that trees, shrubs, and fire hydrants did double duty as canine message boards.

They made the loop through the forest in good time and were almost back to the house when a familiar car slowed to turn into her driveway. She wasn't expecting to see Gage Logan today, but maybe he and Tripp had set up a time to take the new chess set for a spin. On second thought, that didn't make sense considering Tripp had just left for class.

When a second car pulled up and parked in front of her house, she froze for a second. It was one thing for Gage to stop by without calling first. He was a close friend with a certain fondness for sharing a cup of coffee over a plate of freshly baked cookies at her kitchen table. No, it was the man getting out of the other car who set her pulse to racing.

Most of the time, she liked Ben Earle nearly as much as she liked Gage, but having a homicide detective show up without warning was rarely a good thing. Even if she'd been willing to give the two men the benefit of the doubt, the grim expression on Ben's face, combined with the regret on Gage's, pretty much negated that possibility. She coasted to a stop just shy of where the two men stood waiting.

Normally, Zeke would've done his best to tow her over to Gage, anxious to greet yet another one of his favorite people. Clearly sensitive to her current mood, he whined softly and maintained his position next to her, leaning in hard against her leg. She took comfort from his solid presence as she waited for one of the two men to tell her what was going on.

"Hi, guys, what's up?"

After exchanging a quick glance with Ben, Gage mustered up an encouraging smile. "Abby, maybe we should take this discussion inside. If you'd like to invite Tripp to join us, that would be fine."

His offer to call in moral support only made it clearer that the situation was going to get far worse before it got better. "He's at school."

If she stood a chance of making it inside without Gage and Ben catching her, she might have made a run for the safety of the house. But with both of them now standing between her and the front porch, that wasn't going to happen.

Mustering up a scrap of courage, she asked, "How bad is it?"

She'd directed the question to Gage, but it was Ben who answered, his handsome face set in grim lines. "Do you want to tell me why I found not one, but two of your business cards at a crime scene?"

Her brain couldn't process the question, much

less come up with a coherent answer. She stood there staring at the two cops, wishing like crazy this was just a bad dream. Sadly, it wasn't. Suddenly, she was flashing back to Madam G spouting all that nonsense about two men surrounded by darkness.

Still trying to get her head around the woman's uncanny description of Ben and Gage, the only response she could come up with was, "You're kidding, right?"

"I wish he was, Abby." Gage started toward her, no doubt hoping to get her moving in the right direction. "Let's go inside and talk. I'll even make the coffee."

There was no way around the situation; she could only try to get through it as best she could. Shoulders back and head held high, she took a step forward and then another. Just as she reached Gage, Mother Nature decided to do her part in making the already bad day worse. The sky opened up and the rain came down in buckets, drenching all four of them before they could reach the porch.

Soaked to the bone and terrified, she was shaking hard enough to drop her keys. Gage patiently picked them up and unlocked the door for her. After handing them back, he took Zeke's leash from her. "Why don't you go upstairs and put on some dry clothes? I'll grab towels from the downstairs bathroom for Ben, Zeke, and me. By the time you get back downstairs, I'll have a fresh pot of coffee brewing and maybe some cookies for us to share. The sugar hit will do us all some good."

She wanted to argue that it was her job to play gracious hostess when guests came calling. That's what her late aunt had taught her, but right now they all knew she wasn't up to it. Instead, she trudged up the stairs, all the while wishing like heck she didn't have to come back down anytime soon.

Chapter 5

It was easy to change clothes. Fixing anything else—not so much. Her image in the mirror over the bathroom sink was nothing to brag about considering her complexion was washed out and her hazel eyes dull and lifeless. Too bad. She didn't have the energy or desire to deal with makeup, not for two men intent on messing up her day with their stupid dark auras.

After brushing her hair back into a ponytail, she started back down the stairs. That's when it occurred to her that Ben hadn't actually mentioned the nature of the crime that had brought him to her door. But considering he was a homicide detective, logic said that something really bad had happened at one of the fairs she'd been to over the weekend.

Looking back, there had only been a handful of times when she'd given out more than one of her business cards at a single stop, usually when more than one artist displayed their work in the same booth. She stopped halfway down the stairs to think back over the past two days. She started a mental list of every instance she could think of, but it made no sense to stand there stewing over the situation. The men waiting in her kitchen already had answers to all of the questions spinning nonstop through her head. Sighing, she continued down the steps.

Gage had made good on his promise to have the coffee ready and waiting. He'd also raided the freezer to heap a plate high with some of the peanut butter cookies she'd baked a few days back. They probably hadn't had enough time to thaw, but apparently neither of her uninvited guests cared. Ben finished off the one in his hand and reached for another while Gage filled a mug with coffee and slid it across the table to her.

Wrapping her hands around the mug, she soaked in its warmth as she watched Zeke. He'd positioned himself between the two lawmen while quietly eyeing the three treats stacked in the center of the table just out of his reach. When Ben noticed the dog's ever hopeful look, he immediately gave him one of the cookies. Abby arched an eyebrow as she studied the three of them. "So, gentlemen, how many treats has Zeke conned you into giving him?"

No one made eye contact, but Gage did his best to look innocent. "Let's just say not as many as he wishes we had, but more than we probably should have. That dog has turned mooching to an art form."

She smiled for the first time since they'd arrived. "Nice to know that some things never change."

After sipping her coffee, she reached for one of the peanut butter cookies, more to have something to do than because she was actually hungry. Both men seemed to take that as a signal that she was ready to get down to business. Under other circumstances, she would have found it amusing when first Gage and then Ben pulled nearly identical spiral notebooks out of their shirt pockets and opened them to a new page. It wasn't the first time she'd wondered if those notebooks were part of standard police gear everywhere.

Next, both men noted the date at the top of the page and then checked their watches for the time and wrote that down as well. As they did, she glanced at the clock on the stove and stifled a groan. How on earth could she have forgotten that she was due at city hall in a matter of minutes? She also had another scheduled stop after that, but it was unlikely she'd be in the right frame of mind to rush off to meet up with anyone after the three of them were finished talking.

"Guys, I know you want dive right into whatever you want to talk to me about, but I was supposed to meet with Connie Pohler. I should let her know I need to reschedule. I can send a text, so it won't take but a minute. I won't mention why I can't make it, just that something unavoidable came up."

Without waiting for them to respond, she sent a quick message to Connie, the mayor's assistant, asking if they could reschedule. With her usual efficiency, Connie responded with the new date and time before Abby had finished typing the message to Pastor Jack at the church. After sending his text, she muted the phone and set it aside. There would be plenty of time to deal with all of that after Gage and Ben were gone.

"Sorry about that." Turning to Ben, she said, "You mentioned something about my business cards."

Ben nodded. "Before we get to the specifics about that, give me a rundown about what you did over the weekend. Gage knew something about your plans, but I'd rather hear it directly from you."

"How detailed do you want me to get?"

He shrugged. "I never know what will turn out to be important."

Ben still hadn't told her exactly what had happened, but she wasn't in a hurry to find out. Assuming he'd get around to telling her eventually, she took a deep breath and launched right into her explanation. "As the newest member of the city council, I was assigned to be the liaison between the rest of the council and the committee in charge of Snowberry Creek's art fair. That entailed me visiting several different events over the weekend to touch base with various vendors who are scheduled to attend our fair this coming weekend."

To give him time to catch up with his note-taking, she ate her cookie and then called Zeke to her side of the table. Running her fingers through his fur, she picked up where she'd left off, explaining that she'd invited her friends to join her for the weekend. "Early Saturday morning, I picked up Dayna and Bridey, and we drove straight to the first fair."

"Once you were there, did you stick together the whole time?"

She gave the matter some thought, but it was

hard to remember after hitting four fairs in two days. Finally, she shook her head. "No, not the entire time. Bridey was looking for some things for her baby. I was mainly there to talk to the artists, but I also wanted to do some shopping of my own. My friend Dayna is a potter, and she stopped to visit with several friends who were working at the fairs. The three of us met up again for lunch before leaving for our second stop."

He made several notes before looking up to meet her gaze again. "Then what?"

She was getting increasingly more uncomfortable with this whole discussion, but she had no choice but to continue. "We went on to the second fair and did pretty much the same thing. We were together part of the time, but not always. After making the rounds there, we stayed the night at that new hotel and casino they built east of I-5 up north. Do you need to know how we spent our time there?"

Ben kept writing as he answered, "The more details you can give me the better."

Why? His lack of explanation was starting to frustrate her. If something bad had happened at one of the fairs, how would knowing how she and her friends had spent their evening help with his investigation? Knowing Ben, he wouldn't be all that forthcoming even if she started peppering him with a few questions of her own. Fine. If he wanted details, she'd give him details.

"We checked in at the front desk. Well, actually, I checked us in while Bridey and Dayna waited on a leather couch in the lobby. It was a lovely caramel color. The desk clerk gave me exactly three keys to the room, and a bellhop named Heath helped us with our luggage. The four of us took the elevator to the top floor of the west wing, where I had booked us a two-bedroom suite. The room was done in seafoam green, cream, and navy blue. I didn't much care for the artwork on the walls, but that's just me. Bridey and I shared the room with two queen beds while Dayna took the other one, which had a king. There were two bathrooms and a small balcony that overlooked the fountain in front of the hotel. And did I mention it had a small kitchenette, too? Not that we did any cooking. That would have defeated the whole purpose of a weekend getaway, don't you think?"

Gage quickly stifled a grin when Ben glanced up from his notebook long enough to frown at her. "Abby, I realize you are understandably not happy to be doing this, but you also know I don't have any choice but to ask you these questions. Please keep the décor details to a minimum and just give me the basic facts."

"Sorry, Ben. I get snarky when I'm upset." Without waiting for him to comment, she picked up where she'd left off. "After unloading our luggage, our next stop was the spa in the hotel. We all had appointments for massages and other stuff. When we were done there, we went back to the room just long enough to change clothes before going to dinner at the casino next door. We also had tickets to a show there. The three of us played the slots and blackjack until it was time for the show to start."

"Did you go anywhere after that?"

"No, just back to the suite. It had been a long

day, and we needed to make an early start Sunday morning."

Ben flipped to yet another page in his notebook. "Okay, tell me about Sunday."

"We had breakfast at the hotel before heading to the first fair. We made the rounds, stopping to browse along the way. I spoke with several more of the people on my list. The three of us might not have spent every minute together, but we also didn't stay there all that long. It was a much smaller event than the others, and we wanted to move on to the fourth fair as soon as possible."

"What happened when you got to that one?"

"The plan was to split up and then rendezvous for a late lunch before heading back home. I needed to take care of the last bit of my committee business. Bridey had some more shopping to do, and Dayna planned to meet up with a friend. The two of them share a booth selling their pottery, working alternate weekends working at the fairs."

"So how long were the three of you separated?"

"To be honest, I don't know exactly. Bridey and I actually ended up staying together pretty much the whole time. While I met with the last vendor on my list, Bridey waited on a bench a short distance away. Dayna left to meet with her friend."

"Tell me about the vendor you met with."

Interesting. Something had definitely changed, because this was the first time Ben had asked for details about any of the people she'd been sent to visit. He'd definitely gone on point, a hunter with his prey actually now in sight. Ben was no threat to her, but that didn't make it any easier to face off against him when he was in full-on cop mode. "His name is Josiah Garth, a well-known artist who works with wrought iron. I'd never heard of him before I became involved in the fair plans, but I do know the committee was thrilled that he agreed to come to our fair."

"What did you and Mr. Garth talk about?"

Abby sat back in her chair, struggling to remain calm as she was beginning to suspect where this conversation was now headed. "Actually, he was busy talking with someone else when I got there. I only spoke with his niece, Jenny Garth, who is also his apprentice. She suggested I come back if I really needed to talk to him. Otherwise, she promised to give him my business card and tell him I had stopped by."

Considering Ben's intense interest in this particular interaction, she decided to go into as much detail as she could. "As I waited to talk with Jenny, I glanced through the notebooks that contained pictures of Josiah's more custom work, which is truly stunning. Despite the price tags, it was really tempting to order something for myself. In the end, I bought three of his decorative yard stakes for my yard. After that, Bridey and I headed for the food court, and I texted Dayna to let her know where we'd be."

"Did Ms. Fisk respond immediately?"

His use of Dayna's last name startled her. She was pretty sure she'd never mentioned it, so he'd already known it beforehand. Was there a reason for that or was she overthinking things? Again, now wasn't the time to ask. "No, she didn't."

"And did that strike you as odd?"

"Not at all. She knew we'd wait until she was

done talking to her friend. To save time, I bought her lunch as well as my own since the lines were getting pretty long. We'd just sat down when Dayna arrived."

If Ben wanted to know the nature of Dayna's conversation with Wendy, he could ask them directly. Abby already felt as if she were talking behind her friends' backs. Plunging ahead with the story, she said, "After we finished eating, I told them why I needed to swing back by Josiah's booth. However, it was closed."

"Was the fair about to shut down?"

"No, it was supposed to be open for another couple of hours. In fact, Jenny mentioned that they would be there past closing time to pack up."

"Could they have simply stepped away for a few minutes?"

"Maybe, but there was a handwritten sign posted that claimed they'd sold out." She frowned. "I found that surprising. When I'd been there, they still had a lot of stuff for sale. Unless someone bought them out, I can't imagine how they would have sold that many items in such a short time. Anyway, just in case they did return, I wrote a note on another of my cards and stuck it under the edge of the tape holding up their sign."

She was about out of energy, but at least she was also at the end of her tale. As she paused to catch her breath, Gage topped off everyone's coffee. Abby smiled and headed for the finish line. "I drove both of them back to their houses and then came home. Tripp and Zeke were gone when I got here, so no one saw when I actually arrived. They came back not long afterward, though. Tripp had picked up dinner at Frannie's so neither of us had to cook last night."

Gage grinned at her. "And I'm betting he also sprung for pie."

"Of course. He likes Frannie's pie as much as I do. Besides, he knew he was going to have to confess that the two of you corrupted Zeke by taking him to the bar to play pool while I was gone. Seriously, Gage, who would give this innocent boy pub grub and then let him wash it down with beer?"

She patted Zeke on his wrinkled forehead. "Don't worry, Zeke. It's not your fault. They were supposed to be the adults in the room."

Gage didn't look the least bit guilty about what had happened. "I wasn't the one who brought Zeke to the bar, and it was Gary who left his beer within Zeke's reach. We managed to grab it before he got more than a slurp or two. I bought one of the hamburgers that dog scarfed down, but you can't complain about that. If you've got problems with how he spent his evening, take it up with Tripp."

"I tried, but that man is sneaky. He knew how much forgiveness a piece of Frannie's coconut cream pie would buy him."

Ben cleared his throat to bring their attention back to him. "While I'd love to hear more about Zeke's misadventures, can we move on?"

Just that quickly, the mood shifted from light to dark. Her part of the discussion might be over, but obviously Ben had something left to say. Whatever it was couldn't be good, but that wasn't news. She'd been dreading this moment from the second he'd gotten out of his car.

No more dancing around the issue. She looked him straight in the eye and simply asked, "Who died?"

Although by that point, there was only one logical answer to that question.

Crossing his arms across his chest, he confirmed her suspicions. "Your instincts were right on the money, Abby. Josiah Garth didn't run out of things to sell at the fair. He was murdered, most likely just about the time you and Bridey sat down to eat."

Chapter 6

The bleak expression reflected in Ben's eyes was a familiar one to Abby. It was how cops looked when they were dealing with the aftermath of yet another murder.

"How did it happen?" She couldn't help but ask even though she wasn't at all sure she wanted to know.

"There's a lot I don't know, like who shut down his booth or if that had anything to do with his death." He tapped his pen on the table, a nervous habit when he was trying to make sense of a situation. "It seems to have been a murder of opportunity, especially considering he was killed with one of those yard stakes you mentioned. It would take someone pretty determined to drive one of them all the way through his chest like that."

Gage snapped, "Darn it, Ben! She didn't need to hear that."

Her stomach lurched at the imagery that put in

her head. Now she'd never be able to display the ones she'd bought without thinking of one of them stuck through a man's body.

Ben closed his eyes and pinched the bridge of his nose. "Gage is right, Abby. I should know better. Sorry."

At least now she knew why he'd sought her out as part of his investigation. "I wrote the time on the back of the second card I left for Mr. Garth. That's how you knew not just that I'd been there, but when."

"Yeah. We found the first card on the table at the front of the booth. The second was actually on the ground just inside the tent rather than stuck to the sign. Maybe it fell when someone lifted the flap as they entered or left the booth."

He finished off his coffee. "At least finding your cards has helped narrow the time frame for us. We know he was alive and well while you were talking to his niece, and that he most likely died between that time and when you came back to leave your card the second time."

"But, Ben, I have no idea if anyone was in the booth when the three of us stopped by the second time. I didn't hear anyone talking or moving around inside, so it could have happened anytime after I left the first time or even the second."

"That's true, and as far as I've been able to find out, no one knew anything about Garth closing down early. He also hadn't sold out of stock. Having said that, someone complained to the management about Josiah's booth being closed. Evidently he'd scheduled an appointment to talk to Garth about a big order for some custom furniture. Considering the guy drove up from Portland just for that purpose, he wasn't happy to find that the booth had shut down early."

He paused to glance back through his notebook again. "You were there at three thirty, and the guy from the fair committee called nine-one-one at three forty-seven. It appears the irate customer had already been by the booth and was off looking for someone in charge when you came by and left your card."

Even as upset as she was, she could do the math in her head, and it added up to the murder happening within a pretty narrow time frame. "So, you're right. He died after I left the first time and most likely before I came back."

Ben nodded. "Yes. I'm figuring half an hour for you and Bridey to get to the food court and get your meals, and adding in a few more minutes until Ms. Fisk rejoined you. Since you were anxious to finish up your business at the fair and head home, you probably didn't linger over your lunch."

"And you would be wrong about that. We decided to get ice cream to go with our brownies, so that meant standing in another line before we ate dessert."

Gage grinned and shook his head. "And you always accuse Tripp of having a sweet tooth."

She gave him a haughty look. "Everyone knows fair food calories don't count. That's the rule."

"Yeah, right." He picked up the last peanut butter cookie from the plate and took a bite. "If that's true, then I think that same rule should apply to food eaten in the line of duty."

That had even Ben rolling his eyes. "I want to be there when you try selling that idea to your daughter."

"Me too," Abby said, laughing. Gage's teenage daughter watched her father's diet like a hawk. Having lost her mother to cancer at an early age had made Sydney determined to take good care of her remaining parent. To give the man credit, Gage did his best to comply with Syd's demands. That didn't keep him from occasionally splurging on baked goods when he visited Tripp and Abby. He was also known to fall off the wagon when he ventured into Bridey's coffee shop.

"You two have no idea how hard it is to live up to Syd's standards. Sometimes I can't wait until she leaves for college even if most of the time I hate the entire idea of her being gone."

Shaking his head, he set the rest of his cookie down. "Are we about wrapped up here, Ben?"

"Not quite." He flipped back through his notes. "You said Josiah was talking to someone else when you stopped by the first time. Any idea who that might have been or what they were talking about?"

"I didn't know him, and Jenny never said who he was. I'm guessing he and Josiah knew each other since Jenny didn't act surprised to see him. He appeared to be somewhere in his early fifties, a shade over six feet tall, silver-gray hair, and expensively dressed. There was a lot of tension between them. I couldn't hear what Josiah said, but the man yelled Josiah would be hearing from his attorney."

By that point, Ben was scribbling notes like crazy.

Once he got caught up, he asked, "What happened then?"

"The other guy started to walk away, but Josiah grabbed his arm to keep him from leaving. They went back to talking, but too quietly to be overheard. Besides, I was concentrating on what Jenny was telling me."

"Was the man still there when you were ready to leave?"

Abby closed her eyes and tried to replay the scene in her head. "I think so, but I wasn't really paying any attention. Jenny was helping me pick out . . ." She hesitated, not wanting to think about those yard stakes she'd bought. "I paid for my purchases and left."

Ben was acting as if all of this was news to him. Hadn't Jenny told him about her uncle's argument? Surely she would have known the police would be interested in hearing about that. "I'm surprised Jenny didn't tell you all about this. She saw them, too."

"Actually, we're still looking for Ms. Garth. We don't know when she left the fair other than it was after you saw her."

Was Josiah's niece actually a suspect? It certainly didn't look good for her to have disappeared at around the same time her uncle was killed.

"She gave me her business card when I was picking out the yard art I bought. I don't know if it would have any information that you don't already have, but I can get it for you."

"I would appreciate it."

She hustled down the hall to where she'd left

the folder that held all her paperwork on the dining room table. She'd stapled an envelope inside the folder to hold all of the business cards she'd collected at the various fairs.

Back in the kitchen, she shuffled through the cards until she found Jenny's. She'd also given Abby one of Josiah's cards, so it was easy to compare the contact information on them. The business addresses were the same, but the e-mail addresses and phone numbers were different. She pushed them across the table toward Ben. "I would appreciate it if you would photocopy those when you get a chance and send me a copy."

"Will do." He tucked them in his pocket and then pointed at her folder. "Any chance you have a list of all the people you met with?"

She pulled out the agenda she'd taken to the fair. It contained all of her handwritten notes, so she was reluctant to let it out of her sight. "I haven't had a chance to update my spreadsheet since I got home. I'll do that today and send you a copy if it would help."

Although she had no idea why it would. Ben's case centered around Josiah Garth. Most of the people she'd talked to had been nowhere near the man on the day he was killed. Ben scanned the names on her list and then flipped through the rest of the cards before returning them to her. "I would appreciate a copy of the list since you've noted the times you met with each person. That will help validate the timeline for Josiah's death."

"I'll send it to you later today."

Abby stuck the papers back in her folder. Feeling more relaxed than she had since the two men had shown up, she gave Zeke the last treat as she waited for Ben to make a move toward leaving.

That lasted all of about thirty seconds. Once again Ben had his game face back firmly in place. "I do have one other line of inquiry I need your help with, Abby."

"And what's that?"

"You mentioned your friend Ms. Fisk left you and Bridey, to go meet with her friend. I believe the other woman is actually her business partner— an unhappy one, from what I've heard."

Well, rats. How much did he already know? Rather than assume he was aware of the argument between Dayna and Wendy, she did her best to tap dance around the problems the two were having. "That's right. Dayna wanted to check in with Wendy to see how things were going. They alternate weekends selling both of their wares. That way it isn't necessary for both of them to attend every fair. It also means they don't often get to see each other."

"And this friend's booth was situated just around the corner from Josiah's."

Okay, the man definitely knew more than she'd hoped. "I think so. I never went near it myself."

Ben sat back in his chair and stared at her, his disappointment in her answer all too obvious. "So you don't know anything about the very public fight the two women had?"

It was time to fess up. Any attempt on her part to avoid answering him could only make things worse for Dayna, not to mention Abby herself.

"Dayna was upset when she joined us for lunch. Like I said, when Dayna works at their joint booth, Wendy has the weekend off. The same was true in reverse. Dayna said lately her personal sales have fallen off dramatically on the weekends when Wendy works."

"And?" Ben prodded when Abby stopped talking.

"And Dayna wanted to see what was going on. It turns out that Wendy had only a handful of Dayna's items on display, and those were located at the very back of the booth where they were almost out of sight." She so didn't want to continue, but she knew Ben wouldn't give her any choice. "For the record, I personally didn't witness any of this. I only know what Dayna told me, but I believe her. Right in front of a bunch of customers, Wendy announced she didn't display it because the quality of Dayna's pottery wasn't up to her standards."

Anger for her friend had Abby's temper flaring. "Which was an out-and-out lie. Dayna is a talented artist whose career has recently taken off. Several galleries now feature her work on a regular basis. Apparently the same can't be said for Wendy, so I have to think she's being spiteful out of jealousy."

"Even if Dayna is the one being wronged here, why did she deliberately break one of Wendy's pieces?"

Well, that certainly didn't help Dayna's case. "Dayna admitted that something broke when she bumped into one of the displays, but she said it was an accident. I'm not sure, but I think it happened when she was packing up her pottery since

Wendy wasn't making any real effort to sell it. Regardless, Dayna paid for the broken teapot and walked away."

"Did she see Wendy again after that?"

"Not that I know of. Why?"

"Josiah's booth isn't the only one that closed early. Ms. Larabie packed up and left shortly after her altercation with Ms. Fisk. We wanted to talk to her to see if she'd noticed anything that might help with our investigation. That's when the other vendors told us about the fight between Dayna and Wendy. She's not been home that we can tell, and she's not answering her phone. We find it curious that two women have gone missing around the time a man was murdered."

This time he closed his notebook and actually put it back in his shirt pocket. "It's always possible their disappearance has nothing to do with Josiah's death. However, we'll keep searching until we get answers."

"I do know Dayna didn't retrieve the pottery that she'd boxed up. She said Wendy's booth was closed, and she didn't want to go in unaccompanied. It wasn't worth the risk of getting into another argument with Wendy or giving the woman a chance to accuse her of anything."

"But you only have Ms. Fisk's word for that."

Abby might normally like Ben, but this wasn't the first time the two of them had crossed swords over her defense of someone she cared about. "Her word is good enough for me, Ben."

And on that note, she had something else to say on the subject. "If you have any more questions about my weekend and my friends, you come to me. I was there on official business. Bridey and Dayna were just along for the ride. I probably can't stop you from talking to Dayna, but I want your word that you won't bother Bridey with this nonsense."

"A murder is hardly nonsense."

Ben's tone was pure ice, but she refused to be intimidated. "I never said it was, Detective Earle. You know full well I was referring to your questions about Dayna's personal business. Her problems with her ex–business partner had nothing to do with Mr. Garth's death. That aside, Bridey only met Dayna two days ago, which would hardly make her an expert on her life or character. She's pregnant and doesn't need to be upset needlessly."

She jabbed a finger at him to emphasize one last point. "I'll also be calling her husband to give him a heads-up on the situation."

Ben clearly didn't appreciate the threat. "That's not necessary or wise."

"Sorry, but I think it is. I don't know how you treat your friends, but I protect mine."

Deciding she'd had enough of the entire situation, she lurched to her feet. "I'm not a suspect, and I've cooperated all I'm going to. I'll send you the list as I promised, but it's time for you to leave. Like right now."

A movement outside the kitchen window renewed her determination to put this disaster behind her. Tripp was back. No doubt he'd had to park out on the street since Gage's car blocked the driveway. Knowing him, he'd be heading this way any second to find out what was going on. But if she got to him first, he would offer a safe harbor for her and Zeke.

"One more thing. While I was at the fair yesterday, one of the vendors I met with was a psychic. When Madam G insisted on reading my palm, she warned me that two men would bring darkness to my doorstep." Abby gave each man a hard look before continuing. "She said I shouldn't follow whatever path these two mystery men were headed down. I'm thinking that was some pretty sound advice.

"You can see yourselves out." Standing up, she pointed toward the hall that led back toward the front door. "Gage, I apologize to *you* if I'm being rude. Please lock the front door on your way out."

Then she marched to the back door and called Zeke to her side. "Come on, boy. Let's get out of here."

Ben called after her, but she slammed the door shut and kept walking. No doubt he'd be back to badger her again at some point. But for now, she'd had enough.

Chapter 7

That Zeke remained glued to Abby's side as they cut across the yard spoke to how rotten Abby's mood was. Normally, he would've bounded ahead of her the second he realized where they were headed. She appreciated the dog's emotional support even if it only lasted until Tripp stepped out onto his front porch.

"I was just about to head your way to see what's going on. I recognized Gage's car, but wasn't sure who owned the one out on the street. Did something happen?"

When she didn't immediately answer other than to jerk her head in a nod, he started toward her, picking up speed the closer he got. She walked straight into his powerful arms. Her eyes burned with the urge to cry, but she did her best to hold back on the waterworks. It took a few seconds to bring her emotions back under control enough to talk.

"The man I bought those yard stakes from was

murdered right after I met with his niece at his booth yesterday. Ben Earle is handling the case and needed to take my statement about the entire weekend." She offered him a small smile. "Don't worry. I'm not a suspect, or even much of a witness for that matter."

Tripp's temper always ran hot whenever someone upset Abby, and this time was no exception. "Of course not, and I'll be having a long talk with that idiot Ben about dragging you into it."

He would, too. Tripp was fiercely protective of the people he cared about, and she was pretty much at the top of that list. For a few seconds, she savored the image of Tripp teaching Ben some manners. However, Tripp had ended up in one of Gage's jail cells once already when he tried to protect a homeless veteran suspected of killing a local farmer. As the detective in charge of the case, Ben Earle hadn't much appreciated Tripp's determined efforts to prevent him from tracking down his main suspect.

"I might be mad at Ben, but he's just doing his job. Besides, I'm not sure Gage would appreciate having to toss you back in the slammer."

"She's right about that."

Abby about jumped out of her skin. How long had Gage been standing there? She lifted her head to peer around Tripp. "I thought you'd left. I'm pretty sure I told you to."

"I did." His mouth quirked up in a small grin. "But I came back."

"Obviously. The question is why?"

Tripp answered this time. "Gage is actually here to ooh and aah over my fancy new chess set. Since he's off duty this afternoon, we were going to squeeze in a couple of games. While I was at it, I invited him to hang around for dinner and to watch the baseball game with us. I didn't figure you'd mind if he joined us."

Then he stopped to look at the expression on her face and then at Gage's. "But maybe I'm wrong about that."

Gage took off his hat and ran his fingers through his salt-and-pepper hair. "Just say the word, Abby, and I'll leave. This has been a rough morning for you, and you've probably had your fill of cops for the day."

She might be still ticked off at Ben, but Gage had only been there to support her. He'd also offered his own rough comfort with hot coffee and cookies. She stepped back to face the police chief more directly. "Thanks for being there for me, Gage, and you're welcome to join us tonight."

"If you're sure." He studied her for several seconds. "Ben's usually more tactful. It's not really an excuse, but I doubt he's had more than an hour or two of sleep since he got called to the fair yesterday."

She did her best to let go of her anger. "It's not entirely his fault. I swore I'd never get involved in another murder case, and having my name coming up in another one knocked me a bit sideways. I probably would have been okay if he hadn't kept harping on Dayna's problems with Wendy. I may have overreacted"—not that she really thought so—"but I can't stand the thought of someone else getting dragged into this mess for no good reason."

"Ben knows that, too."

If so, then why hadn't he bothered to apologize? But that was a discussion for another day. Now that her temper was back under control, she still had council business to take care of. "You two go enjoy your game. I've rescheduled one meeting this morning, but I'm hoping I can at least get in to see Pastor Jack. If I leave for a while, can Zeke hang out with the two of you?"

The dog sat at her feet while she scratched behind his ears. "He'll be happier with you than being left alone. In fact, if you'd rather play at my kitchen table, you can help yourselves to whatever you can scrounge in the fridge for lunch and dessert."

She offered Gage a teasing grin. "You already found my stash of peanut butter cookies."

Tripp frowned at her. "You never told me you'd baked peanut butter cookies."

Pointing at Gage, she said, "I never told him either. He just helped himself."

Gage immediately defended raiding her freezer. "I thought you might need something to go with the coffee I made for you. You were pretty shaken after Ben told you why we were here. A hit of sugar was bound to help, and there wasn't time for a run to Bridey's shop for peach muffins."

Tripp didn't buy that excuse for a second. "That explains why *she* needed cookies. That doesn't justify you and Ben helping yourselves, too. I'm pretty sure she baked them to go with the ice cream I planned to bring along with the pizza tonight."

Gage studied Tripp with more than a little suspicion. "Abby, at any point in time did Tripp mention bringing ice cream tonight?"

If their antics were aimed at cheering her up, it was working. "Nope, not a word."

Tripp rolled his eyes. "Of course I didn't. It was going to be a surprise."

Gage smirked. "Then she couldn't have baked the cookies to go with ice cream she knew nothing about, could she?"

By that point, she couldn't help but laugh. "He's got you there, Tripp. And just so you know, I'd appreciate something besides vanilla this time. A day like this one calls for some serious chocolate."

Shuddering, Tripp reluctantly agreed. "There will still be vanilla, because everyone knows it's the best. However, considering the extenuating circumstances, I'll throw in a pint of chocolate, too. Maybe even some hot fudge topping as a special treat."

"Make it a half gallon, because I like chocolate, too." Gage reached for his wallet. "I'll even pay for it to make sure you get the good stuff."

Tripp stuffed the money in his jeans pocket. "Now that that's decided, I'll go fetch the chess set."

Feeling far better than she had before leaving the house, she looped her arm through Gage's. "Come on. I'll fix a fresh pot of coffee. You guys can have the kitchen, and I'll make my calls from the dining room."

Tripp turned back toward his place. "See you in a bit."

Zeke chose to stay with Tripp when Abby and Gage started for her back porch. As they walked, she could tell Gage had something he wanted to say but wasn't sure if he should. Because of their friendship, the least she could do was listen to whatever it was. "Go ahead and spit it out, Gage. I promise to behave. I do try to limit myself to one tantrum a day."

He immediately slung his arm around her shoulders and gave her a quick squeeze. "You had every reason to be upset this morning. Ordinarily I would've given you advance warning, but Ben was already headed your way. I hoped things would go smoother if I came with him. It didn't exactly work out that way, and I'm sorry."

She struggled with how to respond, but finally settled for just laying it on the line. "There's no easy way to break the news that I've somehow stumbled into yet another murder case. I don't know why this stuff keeps happening to me, but I really wish it would stop. Even if I'm involved in only a really minor way this time, it's still tough. That's why I don't want Ben going anywhere near Bridey. She barely knows Dayna, and she had no interactions with anyone related to Josiah Garth's death or either of the two missing women."

"Ben said to tell you that if he does end up having to talk to Bridey at some point, he promises to go easy on her. He's well aware that all she can really do is corroborate part of your story."

"Fine, but I'm still going to warn Seth. If you think I'm protective of Bridey, you should see him. Seriously, he actually made her bring the baby monitor they bought for the baby's room on our trip in case she slept in a different room than me. You know, so I could keep an eye on her all night long. We took it out of the box and put in the batteries, in case he checked, but then we just put it back in her suitcase without ever turning it on."

Then she bit her lip and winced. "Oops, I wasn't supposed to tell anyone that part. You won't snitch on us, will you?"

His eyes widened in mock horror. "And risk the wrath of the woman who runs the only coffee shop in town? Do you really think I'm that much of an idiot?"

She offered him an impish grin. "Maybe I should take the Fifth on that particular question."

Gage came to an abrupt halt on the bottom step of her back porch. "You know, Ms. McCree, I've never believed Tripp when he insists that you have a mean streak. Looks like he was right all along."

"Sorry, lawman, but I calls them as I sees them."

Then she unlocked the back door and headed inside.

Luck was with Abby, because Jack Haliday did have time to see her. The pastor was one of her favorite people in Snowberry Creek. She'd gotten to know him when they'd worked together on a fundraiser for the veterans group that he'd founded. Having been in the military himself, he had started the group in order to help the veterans in the area. She had a lot of respect for everything the group had accomplished. Not only did they support each other, but they were the first to volunteer whenever there was work to be done.

This time, Jack and his fellow veterans had offered to help out at the art fair, mostly to provide the physical labor needed to get everything set up. He'd also helped design the general layout of the fair, so she was supposed to give him any feedback she'd collected over the weekend from the vendors who would be attending.

That wouldn't take long since no one had made any special requests. The only serious glitch anyone had mentioned was the delay in opening one of the fairs because they hadn't recruited enough people to help with the setup. Otherwise, she had the maps from the four fairs to give him, and she'd saved the pictures she'd taken to a flash drive for him.

Jack's secretary was nowhere in sight when Abby arrived. She knocked on his door just hard enough to be heard in case he was on the phone or with someone. Before she could sit down to wait, his door opened and the man himself stepped out. "Abby, welcome! Come on in and have a seat."

Jack motioned her toward the love seat and pair of leather chairs situated in the back corner of his office. Once she was settled, she handed him the tin of cookies she'd brought him.

He lifted the lid and gave a happy sigh. "My favorite—oatmeal, blueberry, and walnut. Do you have time for me to make a pot of tea for us? I have a nice Darjeeling that will go perfectly with these. I also have an herbal blend that a lot of people find quite soothing."

She should really get back to the house, but it wouldn't hurt to spend a little extra time with Pastor Jack. "I could really use some of the herbal."

When her voice cracked just a bit, he immediately set the tin down on the end table between the chairs. As always, his world-weary eyes saw too much. "Something's happened."

She offered him a shaky smile. "It's definitely been one of those days. A cup of tea with you will go a long way toward improving my outlook on life."

Instead of immediately pressing for details, he patted her on the shoulder on his way to raise the blinds on the window behind the love seat. "I'll be right back. While I'm gone, relax and enjoy the view. It always helps me smooth out the bumps when things get a bit rough."

He waited until she nodded before heading out the door. She closed her eyes for several seconds before checking out the view Pastor Jack had mentioned. The window faced the small wooded area at the back of the church property. The flower bed that ran along the front edge of the trees had been planted with a vivid mix of perennials. The overall effect was far from orderly, but she rather liked the colorful chaos. There was also a stone bench tucked in one corner, the perfect spot to enjoy a sunny day.

"I can't tell you how many sermons I've written sitting on that bench."

She smiled up at Jack. "I can see why. It's beautiful. Who planted all of that?"

Jack looked pleased at her compliment. "Actually, I did. I find digging in the dirt relaxing."

"Well, you did a great job."

"Thank you."

He set two cups of tea and a couple of napkins down on the table before sitting in the chair next to hers. A comfortable silence settled between them. By the time she'd finished half of her tea and one of the cookies, she felt a little better even if she wasn't quite ready to pour out her woes to the patient man seated next to her.

As an opening gambit, she pulled out the maps and the flash drive. "I picked up copies of the maps from each of the fairs I attended this weekend. I know it's too late to make any major changes, and I'm not sure there's any right or wrong way to do things."

He paged through the maps. "These are great. I'll pass them on to whoever heads up next year's fair."

Next, she handed him the flash drive. "I took a few pictures at each event as well, figuring sometimes it's easier to visualize things with a photo than with a line drawing."

"I'm sure they'll be appreciated."

The silence was back again. Jack didn't appear to be in any great hurry, content to let her take the lead. Gathering up her scattered thoughts took a little time. Finally, she gave up and just started talking. "I love Snowberry Creek and the life I've built here. It's been good for me in a lot of ways. While I might complain about all the committees and events I get volunteered to help with, I've also made a lot of good friends that way. It's also helped me feel as if I'm part of something bigger, something more important than growing a company's quarterly earnings."

Jack's smile didn't quite reach his eyes. "I get that, Abby. I'm proud of the time I spent in the service of my country. It may seem contradictory to some folks, but my experience in combat is what led me to become a pastor. Here in Snowberry Creek, I've found a home and a renewed purpose in knowing that I can help people in so many ways."

He sipped his tea, maybe to give her time to process what he'd just said before continuing. "But that doesn't mean it's always easy or that bad things don't happen to make me question some of the choices I've made. I think that's true for all of us. It's just part of life."

It was nice to hear that she wasn't the only one who sometimes wondered if she'd somehow gone totally off the rails when it came to the life she'd envisioned for herself. "You know that I've been drawn into multiple murder cases. That never happened before I came here." She turned to face him more directly. "It's happening again."

Pastor Jack handed her a box of tissues. It wasn't until then that she realized that the view out the window had become quite blurry. Blotting away the tears, she sighed. "Sorry, Jack. I didn't mean to unload all this on you. I'm sure you have church matters you should be dealing with right now."

"I always have time for my friends, Abby. Now tell me what's going on. Nothing you say will go any further than this room."

When still she hesitated, he gave her an encouraging nod. "Sometimes just talking with a friend about whatever is bothering you brings its own clarity. You'll find I'm a good listener."

And he was. For sure, her spirit felt much lighter walking out of Pastor Jack's office than when she'd walked in.

Chapter 8

Tuesday morning had started off with an early call from Dayna to say Ben Earle had indeed paid her a visit. From the way Dayna kept babbling about what he'd had to say, it was obvious the discussion had been a bit contentious. It didn't help that Wendy was ignoring not just Ben's calls, but Dayna's as well. Dayna wanted to retrieve the last of her work that Wendy had at her studio and was understandably reluctant to show up at the woman's house with no warning.

Rather than try to soothe her friend's worries over the phone, Abby had suggested that they meet for coffee at Bridey's shop after Abby's rescheduled meeting with Connie Pohler in the mayor's office.

Luckily, it hadn't taken all that long to give Connie a brief rundown on the weekend's events. Abby had sent her a copy of the spreadsheet with all the vendor information ahead of time to give

Connie a chance to read it over prior to their meeting. Thankfully, Connie had already been aware of Josiah Garth's untimely death over the weekend.

Connie confirmed the chairman of the fair committee had also been informed and was currently working to deal with the situation. The news had definitely thrown a big wrench into the works for the fair committee. They'd been depending on Josiah Garth's reputation to draw a larger crowd than a first-time small-town fair could expect.

It wasn't Abby's problem—or her fault, even if somehow it felt that way. When Connie's phone rang, Abby used it as an excuse to leave, waving on her way out. She stopped out in the lobby long enough to text Dayna that she was on her way to Something's Brewing, which was just a short walk down Main Street from city hall.

Upon arriving at the shop, she paused inside the door to look around. There was no sign of Dayna, but there was one rather unexpected figure seated at a table in the back. While it wasn't unusual for Gage Logan to pick up a shot of caffeine on his way to the office, Abby had only rarely seen him actually sit down to drink it during working hours.

Gage immediately waved and motioned for her to join him. She signaled that she was going to order first. At least that would give her enough time to come up with an explanation for why she couldn't sit with him. It wasn't as if he didn't know all about what had happened over the weekend and that Dayna's name had come up in Ben's investigation. It was also understandable that the two of them might have a lot to talk about, most of which Dayna wouldn't feel comfortable discussing in front of the local police chief.

The barista on duty already had Abby's usual drink started before she reached the counter, so the only question was which of Bridey's decadent bakery creations Abby would choose this time. After scanning the selections, the decision turned out to be a no-brainer. Her personal mantra was that when in doubt, always go with the gooey butter cake, a coffee cake that had evidently originated in St. Louis. She pointed to the top shelf in the glass counter. "I'll take four pieces of that. Three are for here, the other to-go."

Tripp would never forgive her if she failed to bring him a piece. When her order was ready, she picked up the small tray and headed for Gage's table. She set a piece of the cake down in front of him, but he didn't look nearly as grateful as he should have. In fact, he pushed the plate over to her side of the table. "Sorry, Abby, but I'm trying to be good, especially considering I overdosed on pizza, ice cream, and cookies last night."

"Too bad, Gage. Having your covetous gaze watching every bite I eat would take the high shine off my own eating pleasure."

Sighing as if much put-upon, he pulled the plate back to his side of the table. "Fine, you evil woman. You've guilted me into it. But if Syd finds out, I'm aiming her in your direction."

She wasn't that easily intimidated. "Go right ahead, lawman, but then I'll tell her about the peanut butter cookies you helped yourself to yesterday. How would Syd react to learning that you went rooting around in someone else's freezer without permission?"

She was pretty sure he muttered "mean streak" under his breath as he picked up his fork.

When she didn't immediately dig into hers, he frowned. "Why aren't you eating yours?"

"Because I'm meeting Dayna. She should be arriving any minute now, and we'll move to a different table." She winced just a bit and lowered her voice. "She might not feel comfortable talking in front of you, even though it's not your case. I'm sorry."

He shrugged and went back to eating. "Don't be. Lots of people aren't comfortable around me, even those whose names haven't popped up in the course of a murder investigation. Comes with the territory."

Okay, that made her mad. "The idiots should know better. We're lucky to have someone of your caliber heading up the department. Name some names, mister, and I'll give them an earful about their stupid attitudes."

His eyes twinkled at the way she'd leapt to his defense. "Down, tiger. Like I said, it comes with the territory. Friends like you and Tripp go a long way toward making up for those who fail to appreciate my charm."

She still didn't like it but figured he was fully capable of defending himself against all comers. Before she could say so, the bell over the door chimed, announcing the arrival of another customer. A quick look over her shoulder confirmed that it was Dayna. "Well, my friend is here."

Before she could stand up, Gage stopped her.

"Actually, I'd like to meet her if you wouldn't mind introducing us. I won't hang around, though. I'm due at the office in a few minutes."

"Getting a late start today?"

"I've been coming in later one day a week. That way my hours overlap with the second shift, and I can touch base with the evening crew on a regular basis. I also come in early one day a week to check in with the officers who work nights."

Another reason he made such an effective chief of police. "I'll give her a heads-up and let her know I already bought her a piece of gooey perfection. We'll be right back."

Making good on his promise, Gage quickly finished both his coffee and the treat she'd bought him. He stood as she and Dayna approached the table. Abby made the introductions. "Dayna Fisk, this is my friend, Gage."

After a brief glance at his badge, Dayna held out her hand. "Chief Logan, it's nice to finally meet you. Abby has mentioned you often."

"I'm sure she has." His wry grin made it clear he wasn't about to ask the nature of those comments. Meanwhile, he gave Dayna's hand a quick shake and motioned to the chair on the other side of the table. "Please, sit down."

Gage waited until both Abby and Dayna were seated to speak again, this time with his game face on full display. "As I told Abby, I need to leave, but I want to say something about what's going on. I was with Abby when Detective Earle spoke to her yesterday, and I'm guessing he also showed up on your doorstep last night or early this morning."

He waited for Dayna's nod in confirmation before continuing. "Abby has dealt with Ben before and knows that he's good at his job. He works for the county, not Snowberry Creek, but I would have him on my roster anytime. Having said that, dealing with situations like this isn't easy for anyone involved. Even though it's not my case, I will do my best to run interference with Ben if either of you need me to."

With that unexpected offer, he tossed one of his business cards down on the table in front of Dayna. "If you need me for any reason, don't hesitate to call. That number is good twenty-four seven."

Picking up his empty dishes, he stood. "Enjoy the gooey butter cake, Ms. Fisk, but a word of caution. Don't believe Abby if she tries to convince you that Bridey has some magical way of making all of those delicious calories disappear."

"Thanks for the advice, Chief Logan." Dayna shook her head sadly. "She and Bridey gave me that same story about the calories and fat content in elephant ears, funnel cakes, and cream cheese brownies as long as we ate them at a fair. The waistband in my favorite jeans tells a different story."

He was still laughing as he headed for the exit, stopping to deposit his empty plate and cup in a nearby bin on his way out. Dayna waited until the door closed behind him to comment. "I don't have a lot of experience dealing with the police other than the odd speeding ticket over the years, so I'm no expert. Would I be wrong if I said that was weird?"

Abby had found Gage's offer to be a bit puzzling, too. "Kind of, but I do have a lot of respect for Gage. So does Tripp. I would take the man at his word even though it's not clear how much influence he has over how Ben Earle handles the investigation."

"But wasn't he with Detective Earle when he talked to you about our weekend?"

"Yeah, he was. Ben knows Gage and I are friends, so I'm guessing he gave him a call when my name came up in his investigation. Again. "

Sighing, she added, "I actually first met Ben when Tripp was a witness in a case he was handling. The poor guy found out the hard way that I can be a bit difficult to deal with when a friend of mine ends up in his crosshairs. The truth is that I actually like Ben most of the time."

Dayna relaxed just a little. "Good to know. Needless to say, I found the whole experience to be pretty darn scary."

Abby could sympathize. "I know. For now, enjoy your coffee and don't let that cake go to waste. We'll talk afterward."

Sadly, a good cup of coffee and an even better piece of gooey butter cake took a regrettably short amount of time to consume. It was tempting to order another round of drinks to further postpone what was sure to be a tough discussion. That would be cowardly, and right now Dayna needed Abby to be strong for her, not the scaredy-cat she really was despite her best intentions.

Setting aside her empty cup, Abby dredged up a reassuring smile as she met Dayna's worried gaze head on. "So, Ben Earle paid you a visit."

Dayna took great pains to fold her paper napkin

neatly before answering. "He did. I've never had a cop show up on my doorstep before and hope I never do again. Talking to Detective Earle in my own living room wasn't pleasant, but I guess it was better than him hauling me back to some interrogation room at his headquarters. That would have been even more scary."

Seeing her friend so badly shaken had Abby's temper stirring to life. "Did he try to bully you? Because if he did, the good detective and I will be having words."

"I wouldn't describe it in those terms. More like he was relentless, as if no detail was too small and the reasoning behind anything I did was of critical importance to his investigation." Dayna went from smoothing out her napkin to tearing it into neat little shreds. "He did tell me that my version of the events over the weekend aligned in general with what you'd told him. Of course, I knew more about some things simply because you weren't with me. You know, like when I talked to Wendy."

Why was he so focused on Dayna's actions when it was Abby who'd spoken to Jenny? "But he described you as a witness? Not a person of interest."

After thinking about it for a few seconds, Dayna shook her head. "Not directly, anyway. He said that we'd witnessed some of the same things. I'm afraid that's not quite the same as him saying I was just a witness in his investigation."

No, it wasn't, but it was also possible Abby was reading too much into it. "Was there any one point in your story that he seemed fixated on?"

"He started by asking if I'd seen Jenny Garth at all since she's gone missing, too. I told him I'd only seen her at Josiah's booth when you were about to stop to talk to her. After that, he asked where I was between the time I broke Wendy's teapot and I joined you and Bridey for lunch. He wanted to know if I stopped to talk to anyone or knew of someone who could verify that I was doing laps outside the perimeter of the fair."

That didn't bode well. What did he think Dayna had been up to besides walking off her anger? And what did her being mad at Wendy have to do with the murder he was investigating? At best, Dayna had only a tenuous connection with Josiah Garth and his niece. That's only because they worked the same summer fair circuit. So did lots of other people.

"I take it Ben still hasn't located Wendy?"

"No, he hasn't. He asked me if I knew anyone she might have gone to stay with. Her family lives back East, but I gave him the names of some of the other artists she's friends with. I've tried calling her myself a few more times with no luck. Of course, it would come as no surprise if she was just ducking my calls. I'm thinking about driving by her house to see if she's actually home. Even if she isn't, I have a key to her workshop and could just let myself in to pack up my stuff."

"I wouldn't do that, especially if there's a chance the police are watching the place." Abby meant that. She could personally testify that the police didn't much appreciate civilians getting anywhere near their investigations, no matter how good their intentions were. "Did he say anything else?"

"Not much, but I somehow got the distinct impression that this could be only the opening salvo. I fully expect to find him back on my doorstep if he doesn't find Wendy soon." Dayna shuddered. "Or maybe especially if he does, depending on the circumstances. Maybe he thinks something bad happened to both Jenny and Wendy."

What an awful idea, but Abby's own thoughts had wandered in that direction, too. It was all so puzzling. "He said no one at the fair had any idea about why Wendy left early. You would think someone at one of the other booths would've asked her what was going on when she suddenly gathered up her stuff and took off."

Dayna looked a bit disgusted. "Yeah, you would. The vendors might not all be the best of buddies, but we usually try to look out for each other. The good detective did point out that he'd heard about us having words from several people working at nearby booths. It's probably better that he didn't tell me which ones. If I don't know who snitched, I can pretend I still like everybody."

Time to switch directions. "Did Ben say if he had any leads on Jenny Garth?"

"No, he didn't. It's really weird that two women disappeared at nearly the same time, especially from such a public place. Unlike Jenny, Wendy took all her stuff. Doesn't that make it seem like she left of her own accord?"

Abby agreed with her assessment. "Yeah, it seems unlikely that anyone else would've taken the time to have her pack up all her stuff if they were forcing her to leave. I'm sure there'll be a logical explanation for her sudden departure once Ben finally tracks her down."

Dayna was looking more shaky by the minute. "Are you thinking whoever killed Josiah also did something to Jenny? You know, because she witnessed what happened to Josiah."

"Not necessarily." It was possible, but it didn't make sense under the circumstances. "If she was there when it happened, why not leave her body with Josiah's? And if they kidnapped her or something like that, how did they get her out of the fair without being seen?"

Dayna bit her lower lip as she thought. "I can't imagine."

Abby had one idea. "A lot of the booths put down big rugs when they set up their displays. I suppose it's possible someone could have wrapped up her up in one. You see that done in books and movies all the time."

Surprisingly, that brought a small smile to Dayna's face. "Lady, you really need to lay off reading all those murder mysteries."

Dayna had a point. Maybe that's what left Abby predisposed to pondering the possibilities in the real cases that Gage and Ben investigated. "You're probably right. But even if the perp could get their hands on a big enough rug at the fair, it would be a huge risk. Surely someone would've noticed something weird going on."

Before Dayna could respond, two to-go cups of coffee slammed down on the table, startling Abby into letting out a loud yelp. Her face burned in embarrassment as she tried to figure out how on earth she had missed Bridey's approach. Her friend smirked as she pulled out a chair and sat down.

"So, girlfriends, what are you two talking about that has you so jumpy?"

Abby didn't want to be the one to tell Bridey that the three of them had come within spitting distance of one murder scene as well as a pair of possible kidnappings. She'd already made good on her threat to give Seth a much appreciated heads-up in case Ben did decide his investigation couldn't possibly be complete without him hassling a pregnant woman for no good reason.

Still fumbling for a reply that wouldn't immediately lead the discussion in a dangerous direction, she reached for the coffee. "Thanks for this. Your radar must be working today, because I was about to go order a second round."

After taking a sip of the steamy hot goodness, she carefully set it back down. "So, did Seth like everything you bought over the weekend?"

"He did. He also told me that you called to warn him that I might be hearing from the police about our exploits. Any reason you didn't tell me yourself?"

Busted. "I thought there was no reason to upset you unnecessarily if it turned out that Detective Earle didn't need you to corroborate anything. I just wanted to make sure Seth was forewarned."

Bridey sat back in her chair with a heavy sigh. "You meant well, but I'll tell you the same thing I told Seth. I'm not helpless or fragile. Don't use my pregnancy as an excuse to keep me out of the loop."

Sadly, the woman was right. "Point taken, and it won't happen again. But how did you find out? I can't imagine Seth would have said anything if he wasn't forced into it."

"You know him well, but unexpected circumstances sort of forced him into confessing how you and he had conspired against me."

Abby cringed, but at least Bridey's wicked grin suggested her friend wasn't really all that mad. "What happened?"

"You're aware that Seth helps me set up before the shop opens. What you might not know, though, is that Ben Earle is often one of the first customers through the door."

She chuckled as she leaned back with her hand on her baby bump. "The poor guy was just here to get his coffee and a box of muffins to go. As soon as Seth saw him walk in, he went all alpha male and charged out of the kitchen to shove himself between me and Ben. I think he shouted something like 'Get away from my wife. She doesn't know anything about anything. Take your order and go. No charge.'"

Okay, that was kind of funny. "How did Ben react?"

"Actually, he was a good sport about it. He quietly assured Seth that he'd just come in for the coffee and muffins. He had no reason to talk to me about the 'anything' Seth was referring to. Then he caught my eye and told me if I had questions that Seth wouldn't or couldn't answer, I should talk to you."

Some days having good intentions didn't pay off, so Abby did the only logical thing. She told Bridey everything.

Chapter 9

Wednesday turned out to be a good news/bad news kind of day, with more emphasis on the bad. Sometimes it just didn't pay to answer the phone. At least Gage had called with one bit of good news. Ben Earle had finally tracked down Jenny Garth. She was physically fine but understandably shaken to learn of her uncle's death. At least that accounted for one of the two missing women. Abby crossed her fingers that Wendy would turn up soon.

She appreciated Gage had let her know that much, but it was incredibly frustrating to have so many unanswered questions spinning through her head like a hamster on a wheel. She couldn't ask Ben, and Gage would've already told her if he'd wanted her to know more.

That left asking Jenny directly, and Abby had no excuse to reach out to her. One brief conversation at the fair didn't exactly make them friends. At least not of the caliber that would justify Abby showing up on Jenny's doorstep with a casserole and a whole lot of questions. That would be sailing right through friendly concern right into big-time rude territory. She'd just have to settle for being relieved Josiah's niece was safe and sound.

Good news served up with an order of frustration on the side.

The next call had come from Pastor Jack on behalf of the fair committee. Abby's presence was requested at the emergency meeting scheduled for two o'clock that afternoon. Evidently they were still dealing with the fallout from having lost their star attraction. For one thing, all of their advertising had included the promise that Josiah would be front and center at the fair. They had to decide if another of their vendors had the clout to fill that primo spot.

Technically, Abby would only be at the meeting so she could share the updated information with the rest of the city council. But past experience had taught her that she'd walk out of that meeting with an assignment that would mostly likely keep her up to all hours and scrambling to get it finished. Oh, she could politely but firmly refuse to take on whatever task they tried to saddle her with after pointing out she wasn't part of the actual committee.

Like that would ever work.

The real problem was that several of the people on the committee were close friends, starting with Pastor Jack. It would take someone possessed of stronger resolve than she had to tell that man no. She considered it his superpower. Everyone in town knew he would never refuse anyone who reached out to him for help. So, yeah, she was on the hook for who knew how much slave labor over the next few days.

As bad as that was, it still wasn't the most concerning bit of news she'd received in the short time since she'd poured her first cup of coffee. She usually took her caffeine black, but a morning like this one definitely warranted a dollop of heavy cream and a heaping spoonful of sugar—maybe even two.

Sighing, she racked her brain trying to figure out what to do about the third call that had come right on the heels of Pastor Jack's. That one had been from Dayna. Evidently, she'd still been unable to touch base with Wendy about picking up her pottery. Ordinarily, the delay in getting her stuff back wouldn't be a major setback.

However, a local gallery had called to see if Dayna had more of a certain kind of vase available. They were hand thrown, varying only slightly in shape. The upside was that a wealthy customer wanted twenty of them for gifts at a special event. The downside was that she needed them by the weekend. Dayna had twelve in her workshop, but she couldn't make the rest within the required time frame. However, she'd given Wendy about the same number to sell two weeks ago. If they hadn't sold, Dayna stood to make a tidy profit on the sale, but only if she could get her hands on them in time.

She'd checked in with several mutual friends again, but no one had spoken to Wendy. That left her no option but to let herself in to Wendy's workshop to pick up her stuff. Once again, Abby did her best to talk her out of going while Wendy was still missing in action. By the time they finally hung up, Dayna had managed to convince Abby to accompany her to Wendy's at some point if the woman didn't turn up soon. It was smart of Dayna to not go alone, but it was just plain dumb for the two of them to sneak into the workshop, key or no key.

Dayna was normally pretty pragmatic, but at that moment all she could think about was this golden opportunity to get her work in front of a whole new audience. The wealthy woman was chairing a large charity event and planned to include the vases in the gift baskets for some of the largest donors to the cause.

Despite all of that, Abby needed to convince Dayna that losing the sale might be the best thing in the long run, under the current circumstances. Before she could come up with a strategic plan, her phone rang yet again. Seriously? Weren't three calls in less than an hour enough for any one person? The phone was over on the counter, so she couldn't check the caller ID without getting up. Right now she didn't have the energy. Rather than answering, she waited to see if whoever was calling would leave a message.

When the phone went silent mid-ring, she breathed a sigh of relief. Zeke had been dozing in his bed, but he lifted his head to see what was going on. "It's okay, big guy. If the person on the other end of the line couldn't be bothered to leave a message, the call couldn't be all that important."

He woofed softly, conveying his agreement before resuming his nap. Sadly, her relief was short-lived, because the darn phone started ringing again. Resigning herself to her fate, she took her cup over to the counter to top it off while she answered the call. One glance at the screen had her rethinking her decision. Of course, if she didn't take the call, she'd probably end up with an uninvited—and unwanted—guest on her doorstep in short order.

Bracing herself for more bad news, she answered. "Hi, Ben. What can I do for you?"

"Sorry to bother you, Abby, but we need to talk."

His tone said he really meant what he said on both counts. He had something to say or maybe to ask, and he felt bad about it. Of course, that meant whatever he had to tell her was probably only going to make her already rotten morning even worse. "Do I need to come to you or should I put on a fresh pot of coffee?"

He didn't hesitate. "Coffee would be great. Also, would you like me to ask if Gage could meet me there?"

The situation was getting worse by the minute if a homicide detective thought she might need the chief of police to run interference. "No, that's okay, but I have to be at a meeting of the fair committee at two o'clock. I'll be home until then."

"Actually, I can be there in about ten minutes."

He sounded tired, no doubt from the long hours he would have been putting in dealing with this latest case. "That's fine, but one question, Ben."

"And that is?"

"Muffins, cookies, or apple pie? I have all three."

"Surprise me." His accompanying chuckle came through loud and clear.

He and Gage both found her nearly uncontrollable urge to offer refreshments to anyone who crossed her threshold endlessly entertaining. She liked that she'd helped brighten what had to be yet another in a long line of dark days spent in the course of his job. They might sometimes end up on opposite sides of his investigations, but that didn't change the fact that she respected Ben's determination to learn the truth.

Meanwhile, she made good on her promise to have fresh coffee and a sweet treat waiting for him. He was a friend, after all. Sadly, if his investigation eventually led him back to Dayna's door, that might just change.

When Ben finally arrived, she took one look at him and ordered him to have a seat at the table. Ben made a habit of dressing well, with his shirts crisp, his tie perfectly aligned, and his shoes polished to a glossy shine. Not this time. She'd also guess he was a week or more late for a haircut. "You look as if you haven't eaten in a week."

He dropped into his usual chair. "Feels like that sometimes."

"Before we get started, let me make you a sandwich and heat up a bowl of soup to go with it. Once you've finished those, I'll warm up a jumbo piece of the apple pie."

"Bless you, woman. I was going to stop at Frannie's diner after this, but I'd just as soon not have to deal with the crowd."

Before gathering the sandwich makings, she got out three of Zeke's favorite pumpkin cookies and set them down in front of Ben. "Dole those out to him as you pet him. You know they say spending time with a dog is good for the soul."

Petting Zeke really did work some doggie magic because Ben looked more like himself by the time she set his soup and sandwich on the table. She sat in the chair across from him and watched him tuck right into the makeshift meal.

"Would you like another sandwich or more soup?"

He carried the empty plate and bowl over to the sink. "No, that was plenty, or will be after the piece of pie you promised."

"You got it."

A few minutes later, he swallowed the last bite and eyed the rest of the pie on the counter for several seconds before slowly shaking his head. "I'd consider asking for seconds on the pie, but I'll leave the rest for Tripp. I don't have time to go to the gym to burn off this many calories, and I figure it never pays to get between him and his favorite dessert."

"You've got that right, Ben. That man has a serious sweet tooth." Not that she had room to talk. She sat back in her chair and asked, "So what's up?"

"Before we get to that, Gage and I are curious about something you said the other morning." The twinkle in his eyes told her that at least they were more amused than concerned about her comments.

"And that would be?"

"That a psychic felt compelled to warn you about us."

Her cheeks flushed pink. "Oh, that."

"Yeah, that. Do you make a habit of that kind of thing? Because neither of us thought you were the type to take a fairground psychic's mumbo jumbo all that seriously."

He was enjoying this a little too much, not that she blamed him. "I don't. Not usually, anyway."

"So why this time?"

The teasing note in his voice was gone, so he might actually be serious about this new line of inquiry. Interesting.

"Madam G was on my list of vendors to talk to on my grand tour last weekend. And you and Gage are right. It's not my kind of thing, and I had no intention to have a reading done. I even tried to get Dayna and Bridey to enter the tent with me, but they both refused."

At the mention of Dayna's name, Ben sat up a bit straighter. "Did they say why?"

She gave a snort of disgust. "Dayna said Madam G wouldn't let anyone escape without a reading, whether or not they even wanted one. Who knows? Maybe she cornered Dayna at some point in the past. She didn't say, and Bridey preferred to wait outside."

Ben offered Zeke another cookie before speaking again. "So what was it like? Did Madam G have incense burning, a huge crystal ball, and spooky music?"

Okay, that was funny, especially since it was the exact same image Abby had expected at the time. "Actually, her outfit was more corporate chic. She also does tarot card readings, but she insisted on looking at my palms. I tried to refuse and told her I was there on behalf of the Snowberry Creek fair, not for a reading. That worked about as well as it does when someone tries to tell Connie Pohler no."

Ben shuddered, having no doubt crossed paths with the mayor's assistant at some point in the past. The woman had a talent for convincing even the most reluctant citizen in Snowberry Creek to volunteer for some committee or project. The amazing thing was, that same citizen would some-how walk away feeling as if taking on the huge time suck had been their idea in the first place.

"Anyway, Madam G studied my hands for a few seconds and then cautioned me that in my imme-diate future I would encounter two men surrounded by a dark aura. She claimed their path shouldn't be mine, but that I'd feel the pull to follow them anyway. She didn't know where the path would lead, but if I did start down it, I needed to con-tinue all the way to the end."

This time his chuckle sounded a little forced. "No wonder you weren't happy when we showed up uninvited at your house."

There was no reason to confirm it. She'd al-ready made her opinion on that subject perfectly clear. "On a brighter note, she also 'saw' that I'd recently begun a new life that suits me better than my old one, so I've got that going for me."

"Good to know that she's not just a purveyor of gloom and doom. I do feel bad about imposing my dark aura on you."

She would've laughed, but it was easy to see that Ben meant exactly what he'd said. "Don't worry about it. I might get upset when I brush up against one of your cases, but I still consider us friends."

"That's also good to know." Once again he eyed the pie on the counter. "I'd miss hanging out here and getting to pig out on homemade soup and pie."

"It's always nice to know my cooking skills are appreciated." To further lighten the mood, Abby added, "Besides, after I thought about it later, Madam G might not have been talking about the two of you at all. It could've been Tripp and Zeke having to confess to their misdeeds, playing pool and dining on bar food and beer while I was gone."

That had Ben smiling again as he checked the time. "We should get back to business. You ready?"

When she nodded, he reached for a folder that he'd laid to one side when he first sat down. "Gage told you that we located Jenny Garth."

As he spoke, he pulled out his usual spiral notebook. "That's what I wanted to talk to you about."

Interesting that he'd come to her about Jenny Garth. Had Josiah's niece told him something that made him question Abby's statement about their brief encounter at the fair? "I'm not sure I can tell you any more than what I already have. I only saw her the one time, and we haven't been in contact since."

"I know." He pulled a photo out of the folder and slid it across the table. "I was wondering if you could confirm this is the gentleman you saw with Josiah when you were talking to Ms. Garth."

She studied the photo for a few seconds before

answering, even though she'd recognized the face immediately. "That's him."

Ben jotted down a brief note and then looked up. "How can you be sure if you only saw him the one time?"

"Even if I hadn't seen him with Josiah, he would've stuck out in my memory because he was way too overdressed for the fair." She tapped her fingertip on the photo. "Different suit, but otherwise this is exactly what he looked like. Seriously, Ben, who wears a tailor-made suit and a silk tie to wander around a park looking at pottery and eating funnel cakes? Not that I actually saw him eat anything, but you know what I mean."

She handed the picture back to Ben. "Who is he?"

"His name is Damon Wray, and he's an art gallery owner from Seattle. From what I can tell, Mr. Wray likes to feature up-and-coming local artists in his gallery and then acts as their agent on the pieces that sell. Judging from his website, he handles paintings, sculpture, pottery, blown glass, and most interestingly at this particular moment, wrought iron."

"So he and Josiah Garth had a business relationship."

"Yes. Jenny Garth said that Mr. Wray displayed Mr. Garth's more high-end pieces in his gallery. That exposure has netted Garth a lot of lucrative contracts for his work over the years. She wasn't sure how long they'd been working together, but she knew it had been at least ten years. That's when she started helping out in her uncle's workshop."

Abby blinked. Jenny hadn't looked old enough

to have been working that long. "Really? How old is she? I would have guessed no more than in her early twenties."

"Good guess. She's twenty-two. Evidently her parents both worked, so she hung out and did her homework at her uncle's workshop after school until they picked her up. He eventually paid her a little money for sweeping the floors and doing some filing. Over time, she got interested in what he was doing and talked him into taking her on as an apprentice."

That was right on target with what Jenny had told Abby. "She mentioned that to me. Evidently she helped make the garden stakes I bought."

He nodded. "That's probably why she asked about what would happen to the pieces that were already finished."

"What did you tell her?"

"That as far as I knew, it would all be considered part of his estate and would be dealt with by the terms laid out in his will or his trust if he had one. That's not exactly my purview, so I suggested she check with his attorney."

Abby was willing to bet that Ben would be really interested to learn what provisions Josiah Garth had made for the distribution of his estate. Sadly, money was always right at the top of the list for possible motives when it came to murder. She hoped that Jenny would at least be allowed to market the items she'd personally made. Losing her uncle and her job in one fell swoop had to have knocked the young woman's life sideways.

Ben clicked his pen a couple of times. "We've gone over this before, but I'd like you to tell me again about the interaction you witnessed between Josiah and Mr. Wray at the fair. No detail is too small. Even your gut feelings might prove helpful."

Abby let the events play out in her head like a movie. "Bridey was getting tired, so she decided to wait for me on a bench farther down the aisle instead of coming with me. I stood in line in order to talk to Jenny. While I waited, I glanced through the notebooks on the table that contained pictures of Josiah's work. One was all wrought iron gates and fencing. Another had furniture, and the third featured a lot of his smaller pieces . . . mostly decorations for the house or the yard."

Ben frowned as he met her gaze. "Like the yard stake that was, um, found at the crime scene."

"Yes." At least he'd tried to put it more tactfully than he had in their previous discussion. Still, she shivered at the reminder that Josiah Garth had been skewered with one of his own wrought iron stakes.

Rather than dwell on that image, she moved on. "At that point I was concentrating on the notebooks and waiting my turn to talk to Jenny. It wasn't until I introduced myself and told her why I wanted to speak with Josiah that we both looked around to see where he was."

She borrowed Ben's notebook and pen to sketch the layout of Josiah's booth. "The table was located here on the aisle where shoppers passed by. It was set up so customers could browse the notebooks as they waited to ask questions or check out. Behind the table, there was an open area where people could wander around and look at the items that were on display."

She paused to point at her drawing. "His booth was at least twice the size of the ones on either side. The other shoppers were at the far end while Josiah and Mr. Wray were closer to where Jenny and I were talking. The fair was crowded and noisy, so it wasn't possible hear every word the two men said. Their body language seemed pretty clear, though. There was an awful lot of tension between them. Josiah might have controlled his temper better than Mr. Wray, but it was still there. Like I said before, I clearly heard Mr. Wray tell Josiah that he'd be hearing from his attorney."

"Tell me again how Josiah responded to that threat."

"He caught Mr. Wray by the arm to stop him from walking away. I don't know what Mr. Wray said at that point, but Josiah backed off and held his hands up like he was assuring the other man he would keep his hands to himself. I'm only guessing about that, of course. That's when Jenny said that her uncle was busy and suggested I come back later if I really needed to talk to him personally. I gave her my card to give to her uncle, paid for my purchases, and left."

"And you never saw any of them again after that?"

"Nope. The booth was already closed by the time I went back. I left the second business card to let them know I had come by, but that was all. We left the fair not long after that."

Ben nodded as if I had just confirmed something for him. "Thanks, Abby. I appreciate your patience in going over all of this again for me."

"Did Jenny say why they closed down early? Or where she has been all this time?"

By that point, Ben flipped the cover closed on his notepad and tucked it away. No doubt it contained the answers to so many of her questions. Too bad there was no way he'd ever let Abby get her grubby mitts on it. Based on their past interactions, the man only doled out information on a need-to-know basis. Sadly, she didn't have the credentials that warranted much in the way of sharing.

Ben's mouth curved up in a small smile. The jerk knew full well that curiosity was killing her right now. Then to her surprise he actually answered her question and then some. "Jenny claims that after some heated discussion, Josiah had allowed her to leave early, even though they were scheduled to be at the fair for several more hours. Evidently she works every weekend during the fair season, so Jenny generally gets her days off during the week. This particular week, she had plans to spend time at a cabin Josiah owns up in the Cascades. She wanted to reach the cabin before dark. Evidently, it's in a pretty remote area."

"And she was going all by herself?"

"So she says. We're still trying to confirm that, but I'm leaning toward that being true. The purpose of the trip had more to do with work than pleasure. She's been taking art classes to learn more about design and other related stuff. The summer quarter is about to end, and she needed some quiet time to finish her class projects. Apparently there's a small workshop attached to the cabin, where she could avoid interruptions. She claims to have turned off her phone for the same reason. I saw the finished pieces, although there's no way to verify she put the final touches on them over the past few days."

Abby mulled over the implications of Jenny's explanation. "It sounds like her uncle may have unknowingly saved her life by letting her leave early."

Ben shook his head. "That's quite a leap. Even if someone held a grudge against Josiah, that doesn't mean it would have extended to Jenny as well."

"True." Another thought popped into her head. "Did anyone at the fair hear her arguing with Josiah?"

Because some busybodies had definitely snitched on Dayna's encounter with Wendy. It would seem that they would have also picked up on flaring tempers in Josiah's booth. However, Ben's desire to share had evidently run its course.

"Thanks again for feeding me, Abby. I really appreciate it."

"Anytime, Ben."

She followed him to the front door. He'd just stepped out on the porch when one last question popped out of her mouth with no warning. "Any luck tracking down Wendy Larabie?"

"Not yet. No one seems to have any idea what happened to her."

"Regardless, there's no reason to think her disappearance has anything to do with Josiah's death or her argument with Dayna."

Just that quickly she was looking at Ben Earle, homicide detective—not the friendly guy who had just chowed down at her kitchen table. "Abby, I'm going to offer you some advice that you're not going to like."

"Which is?"

"Don't ask questions when the answers will only upset you."

Then he walked away, leaving her staring at his back. She hated that his advice was right on the money. He may not have actually answered her specific question, but he'd told her enough to know things weren't looking good for her friend—and that was the very definition of upsetting.

Chapter 10

After closing the door, Abby briefly considered taking Zeke for a relaxing walk, but a glance at the Seth Thomas clock on the mantel had her rejecting that idea. There was only a little more than an hour left before she had to be at the church for the fair committee meeting.

She could use some fresh air, and pulling a few weeds might help burn off the anxiety left from Ben's parting comment. "Come on, Zeke, let's go hang out in the backyard."

He woofed his approval and bolted for the back door. She slipped on the sneakers she reserved for messy jobs and filled a water bottle to take outside with her. After all, pulling weeds while doing some big-time worrying about her friend was bound to be thirsty work. She also filled a bowl for Zeke and set it out on the porch in case he got overheated while dozing in the sun.

To give the dog credit, he would likely patrol

the perimeter of the yard for rogue squirrels and other vermin. Lately, the local rabbit population had become particularly brazen with their incursions. It was unlikely Zeke could actually catch one, but the mastiff-mix was pretty darned determined to eradicate them from his personal territory. It was as if their long ears and fluffy tails offended him on some level.

He immediately set off on his usual route, nose to the ground and sniffing hard. Only a few steps into his journey, he paused long enough to bark as he looked back in her direction. Clearly those pesky bunnies had been back. "Thanks for the warning. I'll let you know if I spot any on the prowl."

Satisfied she had his back, Zeke continued on his mission. At least his bunny-hunter antics went a little way toward improving her mood. Meanwhile, she looked around the backyard to see which flower bed required attention. Sadly, from where she stood, there wasn't a single weed that needed pulling, no doubt thanks to Tripp's efforts. He'd originally leased the mother-in-law house on the back of the property from her late aunt. Sybil always rented it to a college student at a reduced rate in exchange for doing chores that she needed help with

Abby had known about the arrangement when she inherited the place, but she'd expected the current resident in the one-bedroom house to be another student in their late teens or early twenties. She'd been pleasantly surprised to find out that this time Sybil had rented it to a twenty-year veteran of the Special Forces who stood two inches over six feet and had the prettiest caramel brown eyes Abby had ever seen.

Tripp had retired from the army in his late thirties to enroll in a nearby college to finish his degree. One of the standing jokes between them was his stubborn refusal to tell her what degree he was working toward. His truck was gone, so no doubt he was at school studying advanced basket weaving or maybe how to teach kindergartners how to color within the lines.

It was hard to tell what future career that man had envisioned for himself.

For now, she would ponder the possibilities, the more ridiculous the better, while she deadheaded the rosebushes.

An hour later, her mood much improved, she made a quick stop at Something's Brewing for a large salted caramel coffee. When she walked into the church basement, several of the committee members were already seated at the long table in the middle of the room. Jack smiled and motioned for her to take the seat next to his. He eyed the cup in her hand. "You do realize we always provide free coffee and tea."

She wrinkled her nose. "I know, but you don't top it off with salted caramel. I needed the fancy stuff this afternoon."

He leaned in closer, his teasing smile morphing into one of concern. "Another bad day?"

"Nothing I can't handle."

Probably, anyway.

He patted her on the shoulder. "Let me know if I can do anything to help."

"I will."

Bless the man, just knowing she had him in her corner meant a lot. However, her personal problems weren't the reason they were all here today. She really wasn't looking forward to whatever emergency project she was likely to get stuck with, but at least it would give her something else to think about while it lasted.

She whispered, "Any idea how badly the loss of Josiah Garth's presence is going to affect the fair?"

Jack shrugged. "There's no way to know, but the mayor and the committee chair are pretty concerned. We all want the fair to be a success."

Hopefully, the loss of a single vendor, even a major one, wouldn't prove to be catastrophic. But it was anyone's guess what the long-term effects would be considering this was the inaugural year for the fair.

At that moment, Bruce Redding walked in and headed right for the chair at the head of the table. He set down a stack of folders, but remained standing. "Okay, ladies and gentlemen. If you want coffee and whatever goodies Jack has set out for us, get them now. And to be a bit blunt, take a potty break if you need one. Once we start, I plan to plow right through the agenda. We have work to do and little time to get it done."

There was an immediate mad dash toward the coffee urn and a box of pastries from Bridey's shop. Others headed down the hall to where the restrooms were located. At least everyone took Bruce at his word and hustled. Abby didn't know the man well, but she was friends with his daughter Callie Jenkins. Her husband, Nick, was another member of the veterans group, along with two more guys he'd served with. Abby and Tripp had enjoyed several outings with the three men and their wives.

She really loved all of the new friendships she'd made since moving to Snowberry Creek. Back when she and Chad had lived in a condo in the city, they'd barely even known what their neighbors looked like. For sure, they'd never been close friends with any of them. The two of them had been too focused on growing their business to have time for anything else. Besides, if you didn't know your neighbors, you didn't need to worry about what was going on in their lives. That kept things simple, and both she and Chad had thought they were happy with the life they were living.

As it turned out, that hadn't been true for either of them.

Even so, she was pretty sure neither of them had ever had any desire to move to a small town. It was the painful changes in her life caused first by her divorce and then the death of her aunt that had forced Abby out of her comfort zone. Now she had an ever expanding group of friends who ran the gamut from her biker buddy Gil to the elderly ladies of the quilting guild. Instead of complicating her life, each and every one of them had enriched it. They would come running if she needed help, and she would do the same for them.

That also went for old friends like Dayna. Somehow, someway, Abby would find a way to help solve her current predicament. But if all else failed, she would give in and accompany Dayna to pick up her vases if Wendy didn't turn up soon.

"If you'd open your folders, we can get started."

Bruce Redding's announcement dragged her attention back to the matter at hand. Scanning the agenda, she was surprised to see her name was bullet number one on the page. When she sent Bruce a questioning look, he smiled at her. "Don't worry, Abby. I'm not going to ask you to make a speech or to take over running the fair for us."

He offered her a sly smile and added, "Not this year, anyway."

Everyone laughed as she swiped her hand across her forehead and said, "Whew! Good to know."

"I do want to thank you again for your efforts to touch base with a good number of our vendors over the past weekend. Can you share anything you might have learned?"

"The people I talked to were actually pretty excited to have a new venue where they could display their wares. It's a bonus that we're still an easy drive for people from Olympia north to Seattle and beyond."

"Did they have any suggestions or special requests?"

"The one thing several suggested was to have plenty of extra people around to help with setting up and to fetch and carry. Recently, one fair ran into problems because they had underestimated the number of helping hands to have on deck. That delayed the opening of the fair by a couple of hours. For obvious reasons, neither the vendors nor the customers were happy about that."

She turned to Pastor Jack. "I made sure to tell anyone who mentioned the problem that our fabulous veterans group had volunteered to help with exactly that. I can't tell you how many folks asked me to extend their thanks for volunteering and to all of you for your continuing service to our country."

Jack positively beamed with pleasure. "I'll share that message with everyone at our next meeting."

"I also collected business cards from a bunch of artists that I met who aren't scheduled to be here this year but who might be interested in including our fair in their schedule next year. I've already passed the names along to Connie in the mayor's office, but I also put their contact information into a database. If anyone wants a copy, just e-mail me."

Bruce jotted something down and then smiled at her. "Thanks for doing that, Abby. Connie will likely make sure a copy gets into the notebook she's set up for next year's committee. But just in case, I will also attach a copy to my final report. No use in anyone having to start over from ground zero."

Bruce paused to scan his notes. "Moving on. Thanks to the unfortunate events of this past weekend, we've needed to rearrange a few booths at our fair. As a result, we've updated the map to reflect those changes. Pastor Jack has offered to let us use the church's copy machine to run off the new one. I need someone to volunteer to do that and get them boxed up."

After two people agreed to take on that chore, Bruce continued down his list. "We also need to redo the flyers we're mailing out to everyone in town. They have to be at the post office first thing in the morning if we want people to get them before the weekend."

Abby knew most of the people at the table had jobs and family commitments to deal with. Her personal schedule allowed her more flexibility, not to mention they all had a bunch of other stuff that needed to get done with the fair only days away. Knowing she'd probably regret it, she raised her hand. "Can you tell me what getting the flyers ready to go would involve?"

She was already regretting asking the question when Pastor Jack whispered "Sucker!" under his breath. Bracing herself for the worst, she waited for Bruce to answer.

"The changes have already been made in the design, and the copy shop in town will be printing the new version and the mailing labels on an emergency basis."

Well, at least she wasn't going to have to stand in front of a copy machine for hours and hours. Bruce went on talking. "Once everything is printed, we'll deliver it to the volunteer's house. The flyers have to be folded, sealed with stickers, and then the mailing labels applied."

So nothing hard, just time-consuming. With luck, she could draft Tripp into helping. Better yet, maybe she could drum up some teenagers to help. Abby had no problem paying them for their time. Heck, she'd even throw in pizza to fuel their efforts, as a bonus.

"Okay, I'll do it." Glancing around the table, she

added, "If anyone knows some kids who'd like to earn a few extra bucks, give me their name and number."

At that point, Pastor Jack gave her a soft nudge. "How about the youth group here at the church? We have a program where they can earn their way to church camp in the summer by logging volunteer hours. Any cash donation you'd like to make would go into the fund."

"Perfect. Let me know how many pizzas and how much pop to order. It will be my treat."

Bruce made a show of checking that huge chore off the list. After thanking her and Jack for taking it on, he made quick work of the rest of the agenda. People immediately started packing up, but Bruce held up his hand to regain their attention. "I have one more announcement to make. I wasn't able to confirm the details until right before I arrived, so there was no time to amend the agenda. I apologize for that."

He waited for everyone to settle back down before continuing. "As you all know, we've had to choose a different vendor as our headliner this weekend. With such short notice, it wasn't possible to find someone else of Josiah Garth's caliber to fill that spot. However, one of the vendors who was already scheduled to come has offered to step in. Madam G, the psychic we invited, is going to set up her tent in the center of the fair, right where Mr. Garth's was going to be. Besides giving readings, she's also offered to hold a private séance on Saturday evening. There will be a limited number of tickets sold, which will be pretty pricey. She's offered to donate all of the proceeds to the town in

Josiah Garth's name. Evidently the two of them were longtime friends, and she wants to honor his memory."

Wow, just wow. That was generous of Madam G. She wouldn't have been Abby's first choice to headline the fair, but it probably made sense to pick someone who wasn't in direct competition with the remaining artists scheduled to appear. She had to wonder if Ben Earle had caught wind of the decision to feature the psychic and that's why he'd asked Abby about her. Not that it mattered. She didn't need to be worrying about Madam G and her tales of black auras and good connections in Abby's life, with all that she already had on her plate. She'd been dreading taking on another project, even one that was so short-term. But as she packed up to leave the meeting, she was surprised to find herself looking forward to the evening. Riding herd on a bunch of teenagers was bound to be both high energy and exhausting. By the time they got everything done, she should be too tired to do anything but crawl into bed and sleep once she got home.

Tomorrow would be soon enough to worry about Dayna.

Chapter 11

Thursday morning started off with a call from the fair committee chairman to announce another meeting. Abby had been outside with Zeke and Tripp when Bruce had called, so all Abby got was a bare-bones message with no details about what had happened now. Too bad she didn't have a legitimate reason to skip out on this one. Being tired probably wasn't a good enough excuse, even if it had been committee business that had kept her up until one in the morning putting address stickers on the last few flyers for the fair.

Her young assistants had worked hard and accomplished a lot in the time they'd been there, but their parents had understandably wanted them back home at a decent hour. By nine thirty, her remaining work crew had consisted of just her, Pastor Jack, and Tripp. She'd kicked both of them out around twelve and then finished boxing up the flyers by herself. They'd both protested, but Tripp had morning classes and Pastor Jack no doubt had pressing duties at the church. At least Tripp had insisted on dropping the flyers off at the post office for her on his way to the college.

After helping him load the boxes into the bed of his truck at what felt like the crack of dawn, her plan had been to drag herself back to bed to grab another hour or two of sleep. She hadn't even gotten as far as her bedroom door when Zeke started raising a ruckus downstairs. That was quickly followed by the doorbell ringing. What now? Leaning against the wall, she considered her options. It was so darn tempting to ignore the summons and hope the person would go away. Crossing her fingers, she stayed right where she was for several seconds, just in case it was a delivery person ringing the bell to let her know that a package had arrived. The only problem with that possibility was that she hadn't ordered anything recently.

The bell tolled a second time, leaving her no option but to surrender to the inevitable and trudge back down the steps. At least Zeke stopped barking as soon as he heard her coming. She paused on the bottom step and tried to gauge what his body language said about whoever had come calling. It wasn't anyone he knew, that much was for sure. If it had been Gage, Dayna, or even one of the ladies from the quilting guild, his tail would've been wagging like crazy as he waited for her to let their guest in. On the other hand, if he'd perceived the visitor to be a threat, he'd be poised for action, his chest rumbling with a deep growl. Instead, he sat quietly, intently staring at the door as if withholding immediate judgment on the stranger on the other side.

Interesting.

She latched on to his collar and gave it a sharp tug. "Okay, boy, you need to move back a bit so I can open the door."

The dog reluctantly retreated a few steps, giving her just enough room to see out the narrow window next to the door as she unlocked the dead bolt. A good look at the woman standing on the porch only left her more confused. What on earth was Madam G doing there, and how had she found out where Abby lived? More importantly, why had she bothered to seek her out in the first place?

Only one way to find out. She opened the door just far enough to slip out onto the porch while blocking Zeke's efforts to follow her. "Madam G, what an unexpected surprise."

The woman was dressed in another tailored suit, this time a silver-gray pinstripe partnered with a black silk shell. Despite her well-groomed hair and makeup, somehow she looked a little less well put-together than she had when they'd first met at the fair.

"Ms. McCree, I'm sorry to disturb you." After no doubt taking quick note of Abby's barely combed hair, faded sweatshirt and holey jeans, she added, "And I probably should have called first. If this is a bad time, I could come back later."

Forcing a smile she certainly didn't mean, Abby shook her head. "No, that's all right. Forgive my appearance, but I was up late last night working on a special mailing for the fair committee. A friend offered to take the flyers to the post office this morning, so I had to be up bright and early to help load them in his truck."

And why was she apologizing for how she was dressed while rattling on about stuff that was none of Madam G's business? Like the woman said, she should have called first. Besides, if the woman really was a psychic, shouldn't she have already known that it wasn't a good time to drop by? Abby managed to keep the snark to herself. For the sake of the fair committee, she shouldn't be rude, no matter how crabby she was feeling right now. "Would you like to come in? I was about to make myself a cup of tea."

"I would love a cup if you're sure it wouldn't be too much of an imposition."

It was tempting to admit it was an imposition, especially since she had an important meeting to get ready for. But as always, Abby found herself channeling her late aunt's old-school manners and therefore lied. "It's not an imposition at all."

Before opening the door, though, she ought to forewarn her unwanted guest about her furry companion. Thankfully, Zeke took to most people and had good manners. But at nearly a hundred pounds, he could be pretty intimidating to people who weren't comfortable around dogs.

"I'll need to introduce you to my furry roommate. Zeke's a mastiff mix. His size can be a bit startling when you first meet him. I promise he's a gentle giant."

For the first time, Madam G's smile looked more genuine. "I actually adore dogs, and I'd love to meet him."

Abby took her at her word and opened the door. Zeke sometimes showed amazing sensitivity when it came to meeting people. Instead of greeting their guest, he remained seated and let Madam G approach him instead. She held out her hand for him to sniff as she gushed over him. "Oh, you're a handsome one, aren't you?"

He preened at her praise as he gave her hand a big slurp with his tongue and then eyed her purse as he wagged his tail. The older woman laughed. "And a big flirt, too. I'm sorry, boy, but I don't carry treats around in my purse."

Abby motioned down the hallway. "If you'll follow me, you can sit at the kitchen table while I put the kettle on."

Then she gave Zeke a hard look. "And if you mind your manners, I might even dredge up a couple of treats for you."

There were a few words that Zeke clearly understood, and "treats" was at the top of the list. He woofed happily as he trotted toward the kitchen, leaving her to escort their guest. Madam G took a seat at the table while Abby got out the promised treats for Zeke. With him taken care of, she brewed the tea and sliced some nut bread for the two humans in the room. It didn't take long to get everything ready and then join the psychic at the table.

"You shouldn't have gone to all this trouble, but I do appreciate it. I skipped breakfast this morning." Madam G stirred some sugar into her tea and then added a bit of cream. "I'm afraid I haven't been myself since learning about Josiah's death. He and I, well, let's just say we were quite close friends for over twenty years. He was an amazing man, and his death has thrown me for a loop."

Something in her voice had Abby thinking that the artist and the psychic had been something considerably more than mere friends. There was no telling how Josiah had felt about Madam G, but it was clear the woman had harbored some pretty strong feelings for the man. "I'm sorry for your loss, Madam G."

The woman offered Abby a small smile. "Oh, I should have introduced myself sooner. Madam G is just my stage name. I'd love it if you called me Greta."

"Only if you'll call me Abby." Without giving the woman a chance to respond, Abby finished what she'd been about to say. "I actually never had the chance to meet Mr. Garth, but I did talk to his niece Jenny briefly. I do know he was an amazing artist, and I'm sure his death has hit a lot of people hard."

Greta's eyes glittered with a hint of tears. "It has. I can't imagine what kind of monster would have killed Josiah. No one will feel safe until the murderer is behind bars." She took a small sip of her tea. "And that is what I wanted to talk to you about. I've made several calls to the detective in charge of the case to offer my help in finding the killer, but he refuses to take me seriously."

She sniffed as she dabbed at her eyes with the paper napkin Abby had set out for her. "I need to help. I owe that much to Josiah. The problem is that my tent was located some distance away from Josiah's. Even if I hadn't been busy with my own clients, I couldn't have seen anything from inside my tent, and I was too far from his location to have heard anything."

Given that information, was the woman actually surprised by Ben's reaction? Abby could just imagine how his co-workers and superiors would react to him relying on a fairgrounds psychic to help solve his case for him. It was always possible she might be able to offer some serious insight into the man's life and personal relationships. But there was no way the by-the-book detective wanted to know what the woman's tarot cards and crystal ball had to say about the murder.

Abby struggled to come up with something to say that wouldn't be insulting. "I'm sure Detective Earle would appreciate any pertinent information you might have about the events leading up to Mr. Garth's death."

Greta's frustration was clear to see. "That's just it. No one seems to have heard or seen anything. His niece deserted him and left Josiah there by himself. If she'd been there like she should've been, he would still be alive today."

What did she think Jenny could've done to protect Josiah? The artist had been bigger and considerably more muscular than his niece. If he hadn't been able to ward off a vicious attack, it was doubtful that having Jenny there would have changed the course of events.

After all, the killer hadn't hesitated to commit cold-blooded murder in the midst of a busy fair with only the questionable protection of a canvas tent to shut out the rest of the world. That seemed incredibly reckless, yet the perpetrator had managed to pull it off and walk away with no one the wiser. Someone that coldly calculating wouldn't have risked leaving a potential witness alive to raise the alarm. Abby's gut feeling was that if Jenny Garth had been with Josiah when he was attacked, she would've died as well.

"I'm not sure what Jenny could've done to protect her uncle. It's doubtful the killer would have let her escape to call for help or anything. Personally, I'm glad she wasn't there to witness what happened or possibly have been harmed herself."

Her shoulders slumping in defeat, Greta finally nodded. "You're right, of course. I would never want Jenny to come to any harm. I just get can't past how Josiah died, alone and in pain."

Abby got that, but so far nothing in their conversation had explained why any of this had led Greta to her door this morning. "Was there something you needed me to relay to the fair committee? I can put you in direct touch with the chairman if that would help."

Greta waved off her offer. "I've already talked to Mr. Redding several times."

Well, duh. After all, Bruce had already announced the committee's decision to move Madam G's tent to the location that had originally been designated for Josiah. Then there was the matter of the séance on Saturday evening.

"I'm sorry. I knew that. The committee really appreciates your willingness to go the extra mile by holding a séance. I'm sure it will be a huge success."

Abby's compliment had Greta sitting up straighter, her expression showing a renewed purpose. "It should be. As to why I'm here rather than talking to Mr. Redding, I've heard from several people that you are friends with not just Detective Earle but also the chief of police here in Snowberry Creek. It also sounds as if you've had quite a bit of experience dealing with murder investigations."

She paused as if waiting for confirmation. Who had Greta been talking to about Abby? Whoever it was, she wished they'd kept their mouths shut and their noses out of her private business. The last thing she wanted was for people to spread rumors about her being some kind of amateur sleuth. She couldn't very well deny having been drawn into several police investigations, but she'd also vowed to never do so again. Yet here she was, being dragged step-by-step down that path Madam G herself had warned her about.

"Both the Snowberry police department and the county sheriff's office have strict policies against private citizens getting involved in any active case."

That much was true. Both Ben and Gage had made that perfectly clear to her on multiple occasions. "I've learned to stay out of their business. Believe me when I say they don't take it at all well when someone else questions one of their witnesses or tries to do any investigating on their own. I certainly wouldn't go anywhere near the crime scene."

Greta didn't seem inclined to take Abby's advice to heart. She leaned forward, her mouth turned up in a determined smile. "I'm sure all of that is true, but I don't have any intentions of talking to witnesses. Besides, from what I can tell, there weren't any. As far as the crime scene goes, I went back by the park where the fair was held. Everything is gone, so there's nothing to see. I'm assuming they had someone pack up Josiah's booth after the police finished their forensics investigation. Maybe Jenny did it."

Okay, all of that sounded good, but the woman was definitely up to something. Against her better judgment, Abby needed to know what it was, if for no other reason than to give Ben Earle a heads-up, anonymously if possible. Meanwhile, Greta was rummaging through her purse looking for who knows what. With a look of triumph, she pulled out several large strips of paper and set them on the table.

"I would like you to be my personal guests at the séance on Saturday night." She pushed the papers closer to Abby's side of the table. "I sense your reluctance, but you have no choice."

"And why is that?"

"Because you failed to heed my warning to avoid the course the two men with dark auras would be following. Now that you've taken the first few steps, you must continue on to the end. The path to the truth leads right through my séance."

Really? Could the woman be any more melodramatic? Was she really upset by Josiah's death or was she using it just to further her own notoriety as a psychic? Suddenly it occurred to Abby that those two things might actually be two sides of the same coin.

"What exactly are you hoping to accomplish at the séance?"

Madam G's answering smile turned coldly cal-

culating. "Why, I would think that would be obvious. That detective might not like me talking to
any witnesses, but he can't possibly object to me
talking to the victim himself."

Stammering like a fool, Abby blurted, "But
he's . . . Mr. Garth isn't . . . he can't . . . you know,
talk. He's dead."

Greta picked up her purse and stood. "He
might not talk to the police, but Josiah will talk to
me. And when he does, he'll tell me who killed
him. I knew Josiah better than anyone, and he
won't rest in peace until justice is done. I mean to
see that happens."

She pointed at the tickets on the table. "You need
to be there. The others are for the two policemen
and your friend Dayna. The fifth one is in case you
want to bring a date."

Then without explaining what purpose Abby's
presence would serve, Madam G picked up her
purse, stalked back down the hall and out the front
door.

Chapter 12

Abby wasn't sure how long she sat there staring at the tickets, her mind numb. When Zeke nudged her, the small connection was enough to get her brain back to firing on at least a few cylinders again. After replaying Madam G's announcement in her head several times, she came to the unavoidable conclusion that she couldn't keep this particular bombshell to herself.

Stroking Zeke's soft fur, she pondered who to call first. Tripp would be a good place to start, so she texted him to see how soon he would be home. With that done, it was a coin toss whether to call Ben or Gage next. Feeling a bit cowardly, she settled on reaching out to Gage in the hope he'd run interference with Ben for her.

Gage answered on the second ring. "What's up, Abby?"

"It's important I talk to Ben about something that just happened. It's about his case, but it concerns both of you."

After a brief silence, Gage asked, "Are you okay?"

Bless him for being more worried about her than he was about Ben's investigation. "I'm fine. Well, mostly anyway. I just need to tell you something neither of you will be happy about."

"Okay, I'll give him a call and text you when I know something. How about Tripp? Will he be there, too?"

"I texted him, but he might be in class. I'll let him know what's going on when I hear back from him."

After hanging up, she sighed. "Zeke, sometimes it really doesn't pay to get out of bed. I'm in no shape to face an unhappy Ben Earle right now. Maybe a shower will help."

It didn't.

She barely had time to dry her hair and slap on a little makeup before her doorbell started ringing again. Based on the information Gage had texted her, he and Ben were bringing lunch for all of them. Still, it was a little early for him and Ben to be there already. No matter. The sooner they got there, the sooner she could dump this big mess on them. However, the person standing on her porch wasn't any of the three men she was expecting. "Dayna, come in."

When her friend remained frozen right where she was, Abby joined her out on the porch. "What's wrong?"

Because something was, that was for sure. It had to be big-time serious considering how pale she was and the way her hands were shaking. Dayna's eyes were dull when she finally met Abby's gaze. "No one can find her, and people keep asking me what's going on. Why would they assume I'd know any more than they do? One person even hinted that I'd done something to her. I have reason to be mad at her, but we used to be friends."

She looked pretty forlorn by that point. "Abby, I'm afraid something bad has happened."

Clearly worry over Wendy's continuing absence had Dayna reeling. As dazed as she was acting, Abby was amazed that her friend had managed to drive there without running amok. In fact, Dayna's car was parked with the nearside front tire up on the grass in front of Abby's house, and the front bumper was stuck several inches into the rhododendron in the corner flower bed. Abby wasn't worried about any damage to the landscaping. It would recover in no time. Right now she wasn't so sure Dayna would.

"Come inside."

She injected enough authority into her voice to make it a command rather than a suggestion. When that didn't spur Dayna into action, Abby took her by the hand and all but dragged her inside. The living room was closer, but she bypassed that in favor of the kitchen. Even if she hadn't been expecting Gage and company any minute, she would've done the same thing. Dayna needed something bracing to warm her through. The only question was if a big mug of chamomile tea would be enough to do the job or if she should lace it with some brandy, like Tripp had done for Abby in the past. In fact, both she and her mother had benefited from its medicinal properties on several occasions.

"Sit." She pushed her friend toward the nearest chair. "Stay."

That Dayna didn't protest being ordered around with the same commands Abby normally reserved for Zeke spoke to how frazzled she was. That confirmed the need for Tripp's special brew. After putting on the kettle to boil, Abby got the brandy out of the cabinet and the tea out of the canister.

A soft knock at the back door announced the arrival of another guest. Zeke woofed as Tripp let himself in. He stopped to pet the dog. "Good morning, Abby. Dayna."

Smart man that he was, he immediately added the presence of the brandy on the counter to the total lack of response from Dayna and came up with the right answer. He sidled closer to Abby and whispered, "What's wrong?"

She glanced at her friend. "She's upset that Wendy is still missing, and she hasn't been able to sleep. I'm hoping a cup of your special tea might help with that."

While she finished preparing the magic brew for Dayna, Tripp put on a pot of coffee. "I think I just heard a car pull up out front. It's probably Gage, but he texted to say Ben Earle will be right behind him."

He jerked his head in Dayna's direction, still keeping his voice low. "Are they expecting extra company?"

"Not that I know of." Abby shot a worried look in Dayna's direction, who continued to stare off into space. Did she even know where she was at this point?

"They might not be happy about it."

She'd thought of that, too. "What was I supposed to do? Ask her to come back later?"

Dayna finally spoke up. "Don't worry. I'll leave."

Abby wasn't about to let her walk out the door in the condition she was in. "That's not necessary. Besides, I've just fixed this special tea for you."

Dayna wrapped her hands around the mug as soon as Abby set it on the table. "That feels good. I'm not sure why I'm so cold, but I just can't seem to get warm."

After taking a sip, she looked puzzled. "I'm not sure I've ever had this particular blend before."

Tripp grinned. "I bet you haven't. You'll find it particularly soothing to the point of making you really drowsy."

Dayna immediately took another sip. "That would be nice. I couldn't sleep at all last night . . . or the night before, for that matter. With everything that's going on, I can't seem to shut my brain off enough to relax."

Okay, that might just solve the problem of what to do about Dayna not being invited to attend the upcoming meeting with Gage and Ben. As if that thought had conjured them up, both men were suddenly peering in the back door window. Tripp must have decided it was his job to play host this morning. He opened the door and waved them in. "Hi, guys. I don't know if you've ever met Abby's friend Dayna."

Ben instantly went all stone-faced. "Yes, we've met."

Gage didn't hide his surprise at having an unexpected addition to their gathering. "We actually crossed paths at Something's Brewing a couple of days ago."

By that point, Dayna looked a bit scared as she struggled to stand up. "You're obviously busy, Abby. I should go. I'll call you later."

Abby blocked her way. "Sorry, that's not happening. You're so tired that you can't see straight. Let me pour you another cup of tea, and then we'll head upstairs to the guest room. After you finish the tea, you can stretch out and rest for a while."

That Dayna didn't argue was a relief. Abby topped off the tea but left room for more of the special ingredient. Gage's eyebrows shot up in surprise, probably at the amount of brandy Abby had just dumped into the mug, but at least he didn't say anything.

"Tripp, show them where things are. I'll be back down in a few minutes."

He knew where she kept everything, so the three men should be able to deal with putting lunch together without her help. She herded her friend down the hall and up the staircase. She'd been concerned Dayna would insist on leaving, but she seemed willing enough to accept Abby's offer of hospitality for now.

Dayna hovered in the doorway while Abby turned down the bed. "Come on in and get comfortable. Would you like to borrow some pajamas to sleep in?"

Dayna shook her head. "No, I won't be here that long. Sorry I'm interfering with your plans. I didn't think to call to see if you were alone or if you were having friends over."

Abby hated the hint of betrayal in her friend's bloodshot eyes. "We're just having lunch, while I talk to Ben and Gage about something. It has to do with my role as liaison between the city council and the fair committee."

That wasn't stretching the truth too much. Abby barely stifled a big yawn. "Sorry, I'm operating on about five hours of sleep myself. By the way, I have another committee meeting this afternoon. If you wake up and find me gone, that's where I'll be. Hang out here until I get back. Maybe we can grab dinner somewhere tonight."

At that point, Dayna sat down on the edge of the bed and toed off her shoes. When she was done, Abby pointed to where she'd set the tea on the bedside table. "Finish that before you lie down. The bathroom's right next door. If you need anything, stand at the top of the steps and holler, and I'll come running."

"Thanks, Abby. You're the best."

Right now, she really doubted that, but she smiled back at Dayna as she closed the door. She'd done everything she could for her friend for now. With any luck, the combination of chamomile and brandy would put Dayna down for the count. She really wished she could fix a cup for herself. Regrettably, between this meeting and the one after that with the fair committee, there wasn't a nap anywhere in her own future.

Her other guests had been busy bees during the time she'd been gone. The table was set for four, complete with silverware, napkins, and steaming mugs of coffee.

Gage was just sitting down. "Is Dayna all right?"

It was nice of him to ask, but Abby couldn't resist giving Ben a quick glance to gauge his reaction to Dayna's presence. When he didn't respond, she didn't press the matter. "Evidently she didn't get much rest last night, but the tea should help her relax enough to sleep. I have a fair committee meeting at the church after this, so it might be a while before I have a chance to talk to her again."

She took her seat. "So what's for lunch?'

Tripp finished unloading the bags that Gage had carried in. He stacked what smelled like pulled pork sandwiches on a platter and got out spoons to serve up the side dishes he'd already set on the table. It looked like there was potato salad, some macaroni and cheese, and slaw. Yum, it all looked delicious.

She reached for the potato salad. "Boy, this all looks great. I take it you got it at Owen Quinn's barbecue joint."

Ben feigned shock. "You think we couldn't have cooked all of this ourselves?"

"I figure you could. I'm just doubting you actually did."

That had Gage laughing. "We're busted, Ben. There's no fooling this woman."

She pointed across the kitchen. "Especially when there's a couple of Owen's carryout bags sitting on the counter."

After setting the sandwiches on the table, Tripp said, "You guys go ahead and get started. I'll be with you in a minute. I want to cut the pie while I'm up."

As Gage passed Abby the slaw, she smiled. "Thanks for doing this. Today started off extra early. I had to hit the road running, and things haven't slowed down at all. I apologize if I'm acting a bit frazzled."

The jerks snickered and made no attempt to deny the truth of that statement. "Be careful. I'm also crabbier than usual, thanks to being up to all hours working on a last-minute project for the fair committee. They're scrambling to deal with losing their headliner, and I got roped into helping."

"Like that surprises anyone." Tripp finished dishing up the pie and joined them at the table. "That bunch knew they had you signed, sealed, and delivered the second you walked into that meeting yesterday. The only thing I don't understand was how I also ended up sticking labels on hundreds of flyers, too. At least Pastor Jack's kids were earning their way to camp."

She rolled her eyes. "You got fed free pizza, didn't you? That should count for something."

He held up his hand and wiggled his fingers. "A couple of slices of pepperoni pizza doesn't make up for a whole bunch of paper cuts. Those suckers sting."

Really? That's what had him upset? "Gage, are you sure Tripp was really in the Special Forces? Because I can't imagine one of those guys would whine about a paper cut."

"Yes, he was, and he has the medals to prove it." Gage then pointed a finger in Tripp's direction. "And you should know better than to antagonize

Abby when she's operating on little or no sleep.
I've faced heavily armed enemies who were less
scary. At least wait until she's got more caffeine in
her system."

She folded her arms across her chest and glared
at each of them in turn. "Great, now you're ganging up on me."

"Sorry, Abs."

Not that Tripp looked the least bit apologetic.
Neither did Gage for that matter. Ben had managed to stay out of the discussion and instead concentrated on eating. Deciding he had the right
idea, she ignored Gage and Tripp until she finished her sandwich. She still hadn't told Ben and
Gage why she'd invited them over. Knowing how
they were likely to react, she was going to need all
the energy she could muster just to get through the
upcoming conversation.

Tripp made up for his transgressions by clean-
ing up the kitchen as the rest of them enjoyed
their coffee and pie. When he finished and rejoined them at the table, the mood shifted from
relaxed to serious. On cue, two spiral notebooks
came out, signaling the two cops were ready to get
down to business.

Gage and Ben exchanged glances, maybe to verify which of them would start. When Ben nodded,
Gage took charge. "Okay, Abby, what's going on?"

Just that quickly she regretted eating such a big
meal. "Madam G came to see me this morning."

"You mean the psychic you spoke to at the fair
on Sunday?"

"That's her." She paused to sip her coffee, hoping to ease her dry throat. "It's funny—just yesterday Ben and I were talking about the dark auras and that path she warned me I would do well to avoid."

Just remembering Madam G's warning sent a shiver of apprehension dancing across Abby's skin. She might be sitting in her own kitchen, but with two cops sitting at her table and her badly shaken friend upstairs, she was pretty certain she'd already taken a few steps down that path.

"Just in case you haven't heard, Gage, she announced that she will be selling a limited number of tickets at the fair this weekend to a special séance. The proceeds will be donated to the town in Josiah Garth's memory. It was announced at the fair committee meeting yesterday, and I didn't think much about it at the time."

Ordinarily, the addition of the séance wouldn't be of any concern to her or the three men currently staring at her in confusion. But before she could finish explaining, Tripp asked the obvious questions. "What makes this séance so special? And what does it have to do with us?"

"Right after you left for school this morning, Madam G came by to tell me about the séance herself." She got up to get the tickets Greta had given her and passed them out. "Evidently I'm already heading down the path she warned me against. That's why she insists I have to attend the séance as her special guest. She also gave me tickets for the three of you and Dayna, too."

Ben looked thoroughly disgusted. "That woman has left message after message for me. I've already verified she didn't see or hear anything useful the day of the murder." He slid the ticket back toward Abby. "I have better things to do with my time than listen to a bunch of mystical mumbo jumbo."

Abby pushed the ticket back in his direction. "Ordinarily, I would agree with you, Ben. But here's the thing—she plans to use the séance to call the spirit of Josiah Garth, so he can identify his own murderer. Seems he won't rest in peace until his killer is brought to justice. All things considered, I thought you might want to be there for that."

Chapter 13

After dropping that little bombshell, Abby really wanted to let loose with a string of those special words that Tripp always apologized for using in front of her when things didn't go well. She bit her lip in an effort not to give in to the temptation, but then he saved her from having to say them herself by mumbling a few choice selections under his breath.

"Thank you, Tripp."

Frowning and looking confused, he asked, "For what?"

"For saying what I'm too much of a lady to say myself."

One side of his mouth quirked up in a small grin. "You're welcome. Happy to be of service."

Ben's expression made it clear he either didn't get the joke or he was too caught up in his case to appreciate any attempt at humor. Too bad. Gage might have kept his expression equally somber, but he winked at her when Ben wasn't looking.

The homicide detective remained laser focused on the matter at hand. "When you and I talked about Madam G, you didn't mention the two of you had become friends after she gave you that reading."

For Pete's sake, what on earth was he accusing her of now?

"We didn't, Ben. It was just as I told you. In case you've forgotten, let me refresh your memory." Then she ticked off the salient points on her fingers. "When we first met, I explained I was just there as a representative of the city council and the fair committee. She insisted on giving me a reading. I left when she was done. I haven't spoken to her again until today."

"If that's true—"

She might not like Ben's tone or what he might be insinuating, but Tripp clearly took offense and cut him off mid-sentence. "Watch it, Detective. Abby didn't have to call you today, and I'm leaning toward being sorry she did. Maybe you should leave now and let Gage handle this."

"Okay, let's try this again." Ben set down his pen and drew a slow breath. "You're right, Tripp. I apologize if that came out wrong."

Knowing this was a tough situation for both her and Ben, she should let her anger slide away but managed only a half-hearted effort at best. "Fine, Detective Earle."

Ben clearly sensed that she still wasn't happy and paused as if trying to rephrase his next question. "I believe the only other time you spoke to the woman was at the fair. So why would she think you would be interested in anything to do with Garth's death?"

"She is upset that you wouldn't let her help with your investigation." Then she held up her hand to stop Ben from expressing his opinion on that subject. No use in wasting time stating the obvious. "I understand why that is, Ben. She doesn't, even though she readily admits that she didn't see or hear anything at the fair that might prove useful. I also know why you'd hesitate to take a statement from someone whose entire testimony would be based on tarot cards, a crystal ball, and reading palms."

She paused to see if any of the men wanted to comment at that point. Finally, Gage motioned for her to continue. "Even if she's trying to garner publicity for her skill as a psychic, that's not all it is. Josiah's death hit her hard. Evidently they had been *close friends* for over twenty years."

She used air quotes when she described their relationship to further emphasize that there had been more between Greta and Josiah than mere friendship. Judging from the way Ben went on point at that bit of information, the possible relationship between the couple had been news to him. "Seriously?"

"Yep. That's why his death has knocked her sideways. You might not share her belief system, but it's very real to her. She desperately wants to help solve the murder so that Josiah can finally rest in peace."

Abby waited for Ben and Gage to get caught up taking notes before continuing. "By the way, that's Greta's description of her motivations, not mine. As to why she thinks I need to be there, she had a few things to say on the subject. Evidently people have told her that I'm friends with the two of you. Maybe she thinks that connection will increase the likelihood that at least one of you will attend the séance. She also heard I have experience in dealing with homicide cases. I don't know who told her that last bit, but I wish they would've kept their mouths shut."

Tripp lifted his coffee as if making a toast. "Amen to that."

She clinked her cup against his. "That aside, she is convinced that solving his murder is the path she warned me to avoid. According to Madam G, it's too late now, and I must follow it to the end. She claims that path leads straight through her séance, leaving me no choice but to attend."

Gage leaned back and crossed his arms over his chest. "And what does she think she can accomplish at the séance that Ben's investigation hasn't already covered?"

By that point, Abby felt more than a little foolish for laying it all out there. "I swear I did my best to discourage her from getting involved. Needless to say, Greta didn't listen."

By that point, Ben was already shaking his head. "I can't believe I'm about to ask this, but just who is Madam G planning to interview?"

Really, he knew the woman was a psychic and he still had to ask that?

She didn't bother to dial back the sarcasm. "Well, Ben, she's not going to interview your witnesses, and it's too late to look at the crime scene. She only has one avenue to pursue that you haven't. She going to contact Josiah Garth himself and ask who murdered him, since he's the only one who knows. Well, other than the killer, of course."

She pointed toward the invitation to the séance

Ben had left lying on the table. "Hence, the ticket. I thought you might like to be there when she solves the crime for you."

Ben stared at the brightly colored piece of paper as if it were a rattlesnake poised to strike. Finally, he picked it up and stuck it in his pocket along with his notebook. "My superiors are not going to like this."

She laughed just a little. "And you think I do? The last thing I want to do is sit in her tent and listen to a bunch of woo-woo stuff while she speaks to the spirit world."

Gage still hadn't touched his own ticket. Neither had Tripp, who studied his for several seconds and then said, "I think we're all in agreement that none of us take this stuff seriously."

Then he reached over to tap it with his fingertip. "But just because we don't believe Madam G will actually succeed in speaking to the dead, that doesn't mean the killer feels the same way. More likely, he or she figures the lady already knows something about the circumstances surrounding Garth's death and is just using the séance as a cover to reveal that knowledge in the most dramatic way possible."

Gage picked up his ticket and tucked it away. "You've got to wonder if it even occurred to Madam G that she might be putting herself in the killer's crosshairs."

Not to mention everyone else who showed up for the séance-slash-fundraiser. Abby swallowed hard. That thought hadn't even crossed her mind. "I have no idea how many tickets they were going to sell to the event, but I bet Bruce Redding will know. I have another fair committee meeting this afternoon. I can ask him then if you want me to."

Ben shook his head. "I'll check in with him myself. I'd rather you not get caught up in this mess any more than you already are."

"Thanks."

She meant that. "Somehow I doubt she's actually told the committee what she's really planning to accomplish. Do you think there's any way to cancel the séance altogether? That would seem the safest thing to do."

Gage jumped back into the conversation. "I doubt it at this late date, especially if the rest of the tickets have already been sold. Besides, even if we block her from holding the séance at the fair, there's nothing to stop her from holding it somewhere else. At least this way, we can have our people on hand in case there is a problem of any kind."

So much for that idea. She glanced at the clock. "Look, I hate to hurry this discussion along, but I have to be at my meeting soon."

All three men stood at once. Tripp started gathering up the leftovers. "I'll take care of the cleanup, Abby. After I'm done, I can hang out here until I have to leave, so I can keep an eye on Dayna for you. I'll text you if anything else comes up."

Ben and Gage headed for the back door. Before walking out, Ben stopped. She waited impatiently to see what he had to say now. At least he looked more like a concerned friend than a hard-nosed cop when he finally spoke. "I don't know what's going on with your friend upstairs, but be careful. We still haven't been able to track down Wendy

Larabie. There's been no sign of her at her house, her van is nowhere to be found, and she hasn't used her credit cards. For now, her disappearance is being handled as a missing persons case. My recommendation is the same as always—steer clear of the situation. Tell Dayna to do the same thing."

Good advice. But for Dayna's sake, she risked asking Ben one last question. "You already know that Wendy has a bunch of Dayna's pottery at her house. Well, unless she already trashed it."

"So?"

That came from Tripp. She really wished he would've stayed out of it, but that didn't keep her from answering the question since Ben probably wanted to know the same thing. "A gallery owner reached out to Dayna because someone is interested in buying a bunch of a particular style of vase that she makes, but only if she can deliver them right away. That leaves her no time to make more, so she needs to retrieve the ones that she left with Wendy. Dayna has a key to Wendy's workshop. Is there any chance that someone could supervise her letting herself in just long enough to find her vases?"

"And how would we know that they were hers and not Wendy's?"

At least Ben hadn't immediately rejected the idea. "They'll be signed on the bottom. I can even show you what her signature looks like since I have several of her pieces here at the house."

Ben joined Gage out on the porch. On his way out the door, he said, "I'll ask, but don't get your hopes up. It's not my case."

Then he was gone before she could even thank him. She almost hoped that the person in charge

of the case would say no. It would give her the perfect excuse to not go near the place. If only Dayna
would be that easy to persuade. That was a problem for later. For now, she had a meeting to attend.

Two hours later, Abby walked out of city hall in a
relatively good mood. As it turned out, the meeting was just to wrap up the last few details before
the final countdown started to the fair opening on
Saturday morning. According to Bruce Redding,
everything was moving along right on schedule, a
huge relief to everyone, including Abby. At least
one thing in her life was working right.

Dayna was gone when she got home. Tripp had
left a note that he'd tried to convince her to hang
around longer, but she had a class to teach. She also
needed to get her stuff organized for her booth at
the fair on Saturday. Hopefully, that would keep
Dayna busy and out of trouble for the immediate
future. So far, there had been no news from Ben,
which made Abby glad she hadn't had a chance to
tell Dayna about the favor she'd asked of him.
Rather than get her hopes up, she'd wait to text
Dayna only if he was able to work something out.

Having done everything she could for her
friend, she decided to take Zeke for a walk. If they
followed their favorite route, it would lead them
through the national forest and back around to
the park. That would give her a chance to see how
everything was going with Pastor Jack and his crew
of volunteers. Bruce had said they were already
hard at work getting things ready for the influx of

vendors who would start arriving anytime now. Since some had to travel quite a distance to get there, the city had made arrangements for them to park their motorhomes and campers at a nearby campground for the next few nights.

Zeke kept her moving down the path at a faster than normal clip. She finally gave his leash a sharp tug to slow him down a bit. "Come on, Zeke, we don't have to race down the trail. Let's relax while we can."

He grumbled a bit but slowed to a more reasonable pace, giving her more time to relax and appreciate their surroundings. She never got tired of the amazing natural beauty that surrounded Snowberry Creek, starting with the tall cedars and Douglas firs that were everywhere. The cool, damp air was heavy with their rich scent. She also loved the peek-a-boo glimpses through the trees of the Cascades as well as Mount Rainier, the snow-capped volcano that formed the backdrop to the entire area.

All too soon they reached the park. Normally, they would take a quiet stroll along the river there, but that wasn't going to work this time. Bruce Redding hadn't exaggerated when he said that Jack and company were already getting everything set up. The booths had popped up like mushrooms all across the park. Even from a distance, she could see several members of the veterans group hard at work, including Tripp and Gil Pratt.

She wasn't the only one. Zeke lunged forward hard enough to rip his leash out of her hand. As soon as he realized he'd won momentary freedom, he was off like a shot to join two of his favorite people in the world. "Zeke, darn it, come back here!"

No dice. He kept right on going, finally coming to a screeching halt in front of Tripp, who chastised the dog for taking off. By the time she joined them, huffing and puffing hard enough to be embarrassing, Zeke was seated at Tripp's feet, his head held down in shame.

He whined softly, his big eyes pleading for her forgiveness. Nope, she wasn't falling for it. The second she let him off the hook, he'd be back to his usual happy self. She picked up his leash and shook her finger at him. "You know better than to behave that way."

Next, Zeke tried to garner sympathy from Tripp and Gil, but the two men backed her play. Gil shook his head and looked mightily disappointed. "Sorry, boy, but the lady is right. You know better."

When the dog dropped to the ground with his big head on his paws and looked all kinds of pathetic, Gil turned around to hide a big grin. Tripp knelt down to stroke Zeke's fur. "Come on, buddy, apologize to Abby."

Zeke sighed and heaved himself back up to his feet. She waited for him to come to her and allowed him to lick her hand. As apologies went, it was sticky and a little bit gross, but heartfelt. She patted his head and gave his ears a quick rub. "You'll do better next time, won't you?"

His tail wag wasn't all that enthusiastic, which probably meant he wasn't sure he wanted to make that promise. Regardless, it was time to move on. She looked around at all the surrounding hustle and bustle. "How are things going?"

Tripp reassured Zeke all was forgiven by giving him a thorough scratching. "So far, so good. More vendors are showing up earlier than we were expecting, but we've been able to keep up."

"Well, we'll let you get back to it. Is it okay if Zeke and I take a look around and check things out?"

Gil patted her on the shoulder. "No problem. Just watch out for wires and cords on the ground. Wouldn't want you to take a header."

"Thanks for the warning. See you both later."

As she strolled through the area, she could see why Gil had felt it necessary to issue a warning. She was glad someone could make sense of the jumble of electrical cords and guide ropes for the canvas-topped booths that were being erected one right after another. Several friends from the veterans group waved or called out greetings, which she returned without stopping. They all had a lot to do and not much time to get it done. If she hadn't had Zeke with her, she might have even offered to lend a helping hand.

"Hey, Abby! Over here."

It took her a second to locate Pastor Jack among the workers busily stringing wires and unloading boxes off the back of carts. Finally, she spotted him standing next to a row of booths that were already in place and ready for use. She kept Zeke on a short leash as she carefully picked her way through the crowd. When she got close enough, Jack tossed her a bottle of water.

"Thanks, I could use a cold drink."

He pointed at Zeke. "He looks thirsty, too. Do you have his bowl with you?"

She pulled a collapsible bowl out of her pack. "Never leave home without one."

Zeke slurped up the water as if he'd been lost in the desert for weeks without a drop to drink. When he raised his head, streams of liquid dripped out of his jowls, which made Jack laugh. Abby didn't blame him and was about to warn him not to let Zeke get close until the last drop hit the ground. Sadly it was already too late. Hinting that he'd like to be petted, Zeke managed to wipe his face against Jack's jeans, leaving large wet streaks on the denim.

"Sorry, I should have warned you. Zeke means well, but his manners are seriously lacking at times."

The good-natured pastor just smiled and patted Zeke's head. "No apologies necessary. Doggy love isn't always neat and tidy, but it's always appreciated."

"So how are things going?"

He studied their surroundings. "For a first-time effort, things are going pretty darn smoothly. All of the advance planning we did has really paid off."

"That's great. I can hardly wait for things to get up and running. Especially the food court." She gave him a conspiratorial grin and leaned in close. "I spent last weekend chowing down on fair food, but all that did was whet my appetite for more. I know I'll regret loading up on funnel cakes."

Jack rubbed his hands together. "Personally, I plan to try out every single food truck that offers barbecue."

At that point, someone yelled that Jack's opinion was needed on an urgent matter. "Well, I'd better get back to work. No doubt I'll see you at some point over the weekend, maybe even at that séance on Saturday."

He was gone before she could respond. A séance didn't seem like it would be Pastor Jack's usual fare, but then it wasn't exactly Abby's either. As far as she could tell, it hadn't yet become widely known what Madam G had planned. That meant most of the crowd who'd bought tickets were expecting to be entertained, not to witness a murder investigation.

Despite the bright sun overhead, Abby shivered. Madam G could very well be putting herself in a lot of danger. After all, there was one person who for sure wouldn't find Madam G's big reveal entertaining—the killer.

There was no use in dwelling on things she couldn't control, so she led Zeke back the way they'd come. Before they got very far, she spotted someone she hadn't expected to run into at all. What was Jenny Garth doing there? Granted, her uncle had been scheduled to appear, but surely no one would've expected her to take his place. And had she cleared it with Josiah's attorney? It wasn't Abby's problem one way or the other. Regardless, she'd hate to see the young woman get into trouble for selling stuff that might not be hers to sell, even if she'd helped make some of it.

At that point, another thought crossed her mind. Had Madam G thought to give Josiah's family advance warning about the séance? She hoped so, but there was no way to know. That didn't mean she thought Jenny should attend or that Abby should be the one to break the news to her. Even so, she'd hate for Jenny to be the last one to know what Madam G had planned.

She'd taken several steps in Jenny's direction when the younger woman stopped to talk to a man whose back was to Abby. It wasn't until he turned to answer Jenny that she realized she was looking at Damon Wray. He was dressed in faded jeans and a Henley shirt, a far cry from his attire at the fair the previous weekend. She was too far away to hear what was being said, but it apparently had to do with a stack of boxes on a nearby cart. Damon picked up the one on top and followed Jenny into a nearby booth.

It was none of Abby's business what they were doing, but it was tempting to give Ben a quick call. Surely he'd want to know that Jenny was setting up shop. However, if Abby was going to make good on her promise to herself (and Tripp) that she'd stay out of police business, she had to start somewhere. This seemed like the perfect time to draw the line and walk away.

That didn't stop her from looking back one more time toward where the couple was hard at work unloading more boxes. So many questions bounced around in her head, but she finally forced herself to start down to the trail back toward the house. Tripp would be really proud of her. So would Gage and Ben. But the farther she and Zeke went, the more it felt as if she'd just taken a wrong turn on that path Madam G had warned her about.

Chapter 14

Abby made it home without anything else going wrong. That didn't mean that her misgivings about the rapidly approaching fair had gone away. Telling herself there wasn't anything more she could do to ensure everything went smoothly, she headed for her comfort zone upstairs in her aunt's sewing room.

Since moving into the big Victorian, she'd made enough changes, both large and small, that the house had gradually taken on enough of her personality that it had become hers. But one room had remained quintessentially Aunt Sybil's: the sewing room on the third floor. Abby missed having her aunt in her life and always would. But the time she spent working in what to her was the real heart of the house was always soothing. It was as if she could still sense Aunt Sybil's presence there and take comfort from it.

The last bit of her tension fell away as soon as she crossed the threshold and started working on her latest project, a baby quilt for Bridey's baby. All that remained to be done was the hand stitching on the binding along the edges.

She settled into the upholstered chair in front of the window and got comfortable. After only few stitches in, Zeke showed up in the doorway to check on her. He must have decided that she'd be there a while because he stretched out in a pool of sunshine on the other side of the room. His rumbling snores provided soothing background noise while she got lost in the rhythm of sewing.

The peace ended abruptly when her cell signaled an incoming call. She stuck the needle in the fabric so she wouldn't lose track of it, before reaching for the phone. Seeing it was Dayna, she hesitated before answering. She couldn't in good conscience ignore her friend's call, but she really hoped Dayna wasn't about to ask her to go with her to Wendy's place. Ben had been pretty clear that would be a bad idea, with or without an escort. She hadn't heard back from him yet, so either he hadn't had time to ask the officer in charge of Wendy's case, or the news hadn't been good and he was reluctant to tell her.

Knowing there was no way around the problem, she swiped right and took the call. "Hi, I was going to call you later."

For a heartbeat or two, there was nothing but silence coming from the other end of the line. Abby tried again. "Hey, what's wrong?"

Because something was. All she could hear was Dayna's breathing, a ragged sound as if it was a fight to draw air into her lungs. Abby was about to ask if Dayna shouldn't be calling 9-1-1 instead of her, when Dayna finally whispered, "I've screwed up, Abby. Really bad. I shouldn't be here, but I can't leave. Not without doing something to help. I think I should call the police or somebody."

"I'll make the call for you if you want. Just tell me where you are."

Although she suspected she already knew. "You went to Wendy's without me, didn't you?"

"I just wanted my vases. I swear that's all I was going to take. But there's blood, Abby. I can see a bunch of broken pottery through the window. It's on the counter in a pool of blood that's dripping onto the floor. There's no one in the workshop that I can see from where I'm standing. Before I called, I pounded on both the front and back doors and looked into all the windows I could reach, but there's no sign of Wendy anywhere. And she's still not answering her phone."

There was a pause, and then Dayna whispered, "Should I use my key?"

"Absolutely not, Dayna. That might just put you in danger, too. Let the police handle this."

"Will they get here in time? I'm so scared."

"I don't blame you. It is a scary situation. The safest thing you can do is wait in your van while I call it in. Don't touch anything, And don't even think about going inside that house. Just give me her address. Talk as you walk."

Dayna rattled off the address as well as some quick directions to the house's location. Her voice grew stronger as she put more distance between herself and the horrifying mess she'd seen in the workshop. A short time later there was the sound of a car door opening and closing.

Her own heart pounded in her chest as she struggled to remain calm for Dayna's sake. "Are you inside the van with the doors locked?"

After an audible click, Dayna said, "I am now. How soon will you be here?"

"I should be there in less than twenty minutes. I was upstairs in the sewing room when you called, but I'm on my way to the kitchen. I'll make the calls, grab my keys, and head out. Stay calm. Help will be on the way soon."

Even if Dayna's directions had been a bit slapdash, Abby found Wendy's house with little trouble. It helped that she could follow a county sheriff's car with its lights flashing for the last mile. When she was a block away, she parked her car and got out. There were too many emergency vehicles clogging up the street for her to get any closer.

She cautiously approached the center of all the action, scanning the crowd for a familiar face. Her preferred target was Dayna, but she'd settle for Ben or even Gage if he happened to be there. Either of them would be able to point her toward wherever they'd sequestered Dayna for the time being.

She was about to give up and ask the nearest officer when she finally spotted Dayna sitting on the step of an aid car from the fire department. It looked as if an EMT had given her a blanket to keep her warm while he took her vitals. Abby didn't blame him. Even from where she stood some distance away, she could tell that Dayna was pale and shaky. Realizing she'd just drawn the attention of one of the deputies from the county sheriff's department,

Abby picked up the pace in an attempt to reach Dayna, but the guy cut her off at the pass. "Ma'am, you need to leave. This is a crime scene."

"I know, Deputy. I'm the one that called it in. That's my friend over there, and I need to make sure that she's all right. If you would be so good as to tell Detective Earle that I'm here, I'd really appreciate it. My name is Abby McCree, and he's expecting me."

Okay, that was an out-and-out lie. Ben was one of those people who turned cold when he got mad. Really, really cold. He'd been quite clear when he ordered her to stay home and out of his way. Seriously, after all this time, didn't he know her better than that? Besides, she had no intention of setting foot anywhere near Wendy's workshop. Her only concern was Dayna.

Sadly, the deputy wasn't buying her story. She considered her options and decided to go with the truth. "Listen, my friend Dayna panicked and called me after she saw . . . well, whatever it was she saw. I called Ben. And, yes, he told me to stay home, but I'm understandably worried about my friend. I promise I won't go anywhere but right over there."

She pointed toward Dayna, who was now drinking the bottle of water the EMT had given her. "I'll stay only as long as she needs me. Once that EMT says it's okay for her to leave, I'll take her back to my house. Ben knows where I live."

Lord knows he'd been there often enough, especially lately.

The deputy studied her face and then looked past her to where Dayna remained huddled in a blanket. "I'll tell him. Don't either of you go wandering off. It won't go well if he has to hunt you down."

That was unfortunately true. Both she and Dayna needed to tread very carefully right now. Ben had clearly warned Abby to steer clear of Wendy's place unless the officer in charge of her case allowed them in with an escort. Abby hadn't wanted to get Dayna's hopes up unnecessarily, but she probably should've told her that she'd asked Ben to intercede for them. But even if she had told her, that was no guarantee Dayna would've stayed away even long enough for him to arrange for a deputy to escort them. Time was running out on her chance to sell those stupid vases.

She shouldn't think disparaging thoughts about Dayna's work and even understood why the potential sale was so important. But if it weren't for the vases, neither of them would be in so much trouble right now.

"I'll go find Detective Earle."

The deputy stalked away, stopping at the edge of Wendy's driveway until Abby reached Dayna, before disappearing from sight. She honestly hoped Ben was too busy to be bothered with them right now, but she suspected the two of them would be feeling the sharp side of his temper all too soon.

There wasn't much she could do about that, so she focused on the person who needed her right now. "Dayna, are you all right?"

"No, I'm not." She jerked her head in the direction of the EMT hovering nearby. "From what they've told me, I passed out as soon as the cops arrived."

Abby moved in close enough to give her friend a quick hug. "I'm sorry this happened to you."

That was enough to bring on the waterworks, and Dayna burrowed her face into Abby's shoulder and sobbed. "They still haven't found Wendy, and I'm so scared for her. I never wanted to see her hurt."

Did they even know for sure if it was Wendy's blood at this point? It was the most logical answer. She patted Dayna on the back and let her cry herself out. "I know, I know. But you can trust Detective Earle to get it all sorted out. Ben is good at his job."

A deep voice from behind her nearly had Abby passing out herself. "If I'm so good at my job, Abby, then why are you here? I told you to stay home."

Yes, he had, and she couldn't think of a single excuse that he would accept for her ignoring that particular order. She peeled herself free of the death grip Dayna had on her before turning to face him. "I only came to check on Dayna. I didn't go near your crime scene. Once you say she can go, we'll leave together."

He studied Dayna before responding. "Not a problem. I've already arranged transportation for the two of you."

His mouth quirked up in a smile that was anything but reassuring as he pointed down the street. "In fact, your driver just pulled up."

Abby looked back toward where she'd parked her car. An angry-looking Gage was just getting out of his cruiser. That was bad enough, but seeing Tripp climbing out of the passenger side made the situation so much worse. "Why did you call them? This isn't Gage's jurisdiction."

"I wanted to see if Gage had an empty cell I could borrow for a while."

Doing her best to fight down a sudden surge of raw fear, she forced herself to ask, "And what did he say?"

Ben looked incredulous. "What do you think he said, Abby? How many times have we threatened to lock you up for interfering? Clearly that hasn't worked. Maybe if we park you behind bars for real, you'll finally get the message."

She struggled to remain standing. "That explains Gage. Why is Tripp here?"

"He offered to drive your car back to the house. You won't be needing it for a while."

Dayna struggled to stand. "He's kidding, isn't he? We didn't do anything wrong."

Abby was pretty sure Ben was serious, and both Gage and Tripp wore grim expressions that said they would back his play. As far as them not having done anything wrong, that was debatable, too. Before Abby could explain her take on the situation, Dayna took a step toward Ben. "Is she in there? Wendy, I mean. Was it her blood?"

"There's no body, just the blood. No one called nine-one-one except Abby, so we don't yet know who was hurt or where they went. We'll be checking to see if the injured party was taken to a local hospital or emergency clinic."

His gaze was unwavering, but there was a note in his voice that said there was some question if Wendy could have made it to the hospital on her own. Had Dayna picked up on his underlying message? Abby got her question answered when Dayna crumpled to the ground hard before either the EMT or Abby could catch her.

Chapter 15

Much to her chagrin, Ben made good on his threat, and Abby ended up riding in the back of Gage's police cruiser. It was something she'd never expected to experience firsthand, and she hated the way the people they passed on the street stared at her. No doubt every one of them thought she was a lowlife criminal being hauled off to jail. All she could think about was how horrified her mother would be if she ever found out. No, make that *when* she did find out. From the way Abby's luck had been running lately, someone had already snapped a picture and posted it on social media or, worse yet, on the front page of *The Clarion*, the town's newspaper.

She could see the headline now: *Abby McCree, the newest member of the Snowberry Creek city council, hauled in for questioning.*

Who knows, maybe the ensuing scandal would get her kicked off the city council. It wasn't as if she'd wanted to be on it in the first place. For a few seconds, she let herself enjoy that happy thought, but she knew it was too much to hope for. Her organizational skills would buy her a lot of forgiveness from the mayor and her assistant.

At least there was one other small bright spot in the darkness. For the moment, their current destination was a nearby hospital and not an empty cell at the Snowberry Creek jail. She twisted around to look out the rearview window to reassure herself that Tripp was still behind them in her car. Gage had asked him to follow them to the hospital. Maybe that meant she'd be allowed to go home after Dayna was released. However, neither man had seen fit to inform her what the plan was, so she tried not to get her hopes up.

All she knew for sure was that Ben had taken charge of the keys to Dayna's van and said he'd have it taken to Abby's house. Again, did that mean that's where he expected that she and Dayna would end up? She hoped so. Leaning her head back, she closed her eyes to shut out the whole world. Seriously, all she wanted to do was drag herself upstairs to her room and barricade herself in there until this whole mess—Josiah's murder, the séance, and Wendy's disappearance—were all resolved. Too bad that when things weren't going right, nothing was ever that easy.

"Are you okay?"

She opened her eyes to meet Gage's somber gaze in the rearview mirror. "No, I'm not, but thanks for asking."

A large lump seemed to have lodged itself in her throat, making it hard to swallow, much less talk. "I promised myself I wouldn't get sucked into this kind of mess again. You probably have a hard time believing that, but I swear I've been trying."

She turned to face the side window, hoping he wouldn't notice the tears trickling down her cheeks. "Yes, a lot of this could have been avoided if I'd stayed home like Ben told me to. But, Gage, you should've heard Dayna when she called me. She was so scared. What kind of friend would I be to hide in my house while she's hurting?"

Gage huffed a small laugh. "I couldn't believe Ben actually thought you would leave Dayna to deal with the situation on her own, even if it would've been the smart thing to do. Seriously, what was he thinking? And that jail cell he mentioned? Locking you behind bars wasn't supposed to be a punishment."

That lump in her throat just got bigger. She'd been really hoping that whole thing was no longer on the table. "Then why do it?"

"So Ben, Tripp, and I could get at least one night's sleep this week without having to worry about what kind of trouble you've managed to get into when we weren't looking."

Okay, that wasn't funny, but then she suspected he hadn't been joking. Before she could decide if she should protest or apologize, he pulled into the hospital driveway and parked the car. He had to let her out of the back seat, since the rear doors evidently worked something like the child-proof locks on civilian cars.

Tripp caught up with them just before they walked through the door into the ER waiting room. He might not have been in the best mood at the moment, but that didn't keep him from putting his

arm around her shoulders and holding her close.
Thank goodness. His familiar strength gave her
something solid to hold on to in rough seas.

Gage pointed toward a row of vacant seats along
the far wall. "Abby, sit down before you fall down
while I see what I can find out about Dayna. Depending on what they have to say, I suggest we
head up to the cafeteria. I could use a bite to eat,
and you look like . . . well, let's just say a sandwich
might do you some good, too."

Tripp snickered. "Why don't you just flat out say
she looks haggard? I'm sure that will make her feel
a lot better about the situation."

"Very funny, you two. You're not the comedians
that you think you are."

Their assessment of the situation might not
have improved her mood, but the fact they were
both doing what they could to take care of her did.
She dropped into the closest seat. "A sandwich
does sound good about now. And, Gage, thanks
for checking on Dayna for me."

He nodded and walked away, leaving her alone
with Tripp. Once again, he put his arm around
her as he stretched his long legs out in an attempt
to get more comfortable. "The doctors will take
good care of her."

They could only hope. From what she could tell,
other than the brandy-induced nap she'd taken at
Abby's house, Dayna hadn't been sleeping. And if
she had to guess, her friend hadn't been eating
regularly either. Meanwhile, Gage showed his badge
to one of the admission clerks at the front desk and
explained the situation. She immediately started

typing on her computer and then made a phone call.

Abby couldn't hear what was being said, but it wasn't long before Gage was headed back in their direction. "Dayna's still being evaluated. They'll have to wait for test results to come back before the doctor will know anything for sure. I had the lady tell the ER nurse that we're heading up to the cafeteria for a while."

Tripp stood up and offered his hand to Abby. She let him tug her up to her feet. "I appreciate your being here with us, Gage, but you've probably got better things to do than babysit me."

"I'm actually off this afternoon, and Syd is going to a friend's house after school. I don't mind hanging around for a while. Besides, I promised Ben that I'd keep an eye on how things go with Dayna. He wants me to call him when she's up to talking. He'll either come here or meet us at your house if they decide to release her. From what he said, it seems likely he's taken over Wendy's case now."

Poor Ben. Didn't he already have too much on his plate dealing with Josiah Garth's murder, not to mention Madam G's stupid séance? Or had he learned something that made him think the two cases were related somehow? She opened her mouth to ask Gage if that were the case, but then realized what she was doing.

"Nope, I'm not going there. Not this time."

Tripp looked confused. "What are you talking about? It's just a cafeteria."

"Sorry, I wasn't talking about that." She winced

and decided to admit what she'd been thinking. "I was curious about something regarding Ben's cases. I was about to ask Gage a few questions, but then I reminded myself that wasn't a good idea. So that's what I was talking about."

The two men immediately exchanged glances. Gage actually patted her on the head. "See, she can learn with the proper motivation. All it took was the threat of a night in a cell to get through to her."

"Do you think we should take her on a tour of the jail to reinforce the idea?" Tripp gave her an assessing look from head to toe and back up again. "While we're there, maybe make her try on one of those tasteful orange jumpsuits? We might have to roll up the cuffs and sleeves to make them fit."

"That won't be a problem. I added a couple in her size the last time I ordered some, figuring I'd need them at some point. Even had her name embroidered on the pockets so she'd know she'd be an honored guest in our fine establishment."

Their matching grins made her want to punch them both. Right afterward, she should also probably hug them for trying so hard to cheer her up. Rather than get mad, she joined in the frivolity. "Just so you know, I would also expect fine cuisine from Frannie's diner on a daily basis."

Gage snorted. "Not happening, lady. The police department isn't in the business of making things too cushy for prisoners. They'd never want to go home if we did that."

"You let me bring Tripp treats when he was one of your special guests."

"Yeah, and we learned our lesson. If we hadn't

made things so comfortable for the idiot, we could've kicked him to the curb a whole lot sooner."

Tripp was looking a bit smug by that point. "You also let Abby bring Zeke by to visit, and you personally spent hours playing chess with me to make sure I didn't get lonely."

Abby moved to stand between them, looping her arms through theirs. "I'm making a mental note of all of this in case I need it. Throw me in the slammer, Gage, and I'll expect equal treatment. Failure to deliver will result in Riley Molitor getting a scoop about how the police department discriminates against women prisoners while showing favoritism to the police chief's friends. I'm sure a scandal like that will make the front page of *The Clarion*, with photos of all three of us."

Tripp looked at Gage over her head and stage-whispered, "Mean streak."

"Very funny, you two."

Which was nothing less than the truth. She was still smiling when they placed their order. Her problems hadn't gone away, but for a few minutes she could put them on hold.

An hour later, Abby stood in a small cubicle in the emergency room while Dayna sat on the bed with her legs dangling off the side as they waited for the nurse to bring Dayna's discharge papers. "Are you sure you feel up to leaving the hospital?"

"I'm fine. The doctor thinks I fainted because of lack of sleep and not eating right. I'm supposed to take it easy, drink lots of fluids, and follow up with my own doctor."

Abby stepped closer. "Just so you know, we're going to my house first. Ben wants to talk to you again, and he was having your van dropped off there, too. After he's done, you can go home if you feel up to it. Otherwise, you can stay over at my place tonight. We're close enough to the same size that you can borrow some of my stuff to wear."

None of that made Dayna happy, but the nurse walking in forestalled any more discussion on the matter. She quickly went over the discharge instructions one last time and then settled Dayna into the wheelchair she'd brought with her. Abby texted Tripp that they were on their way out. He'd already pulled up to the curb and was waiting for them as they walked out of the hospital door.

Abby was about to join Dayna in the back seat, but her friend waved her off. "I'll be fine by myself back here. You should sit up front with Tripp."

It wasn't worth arguing about it, so Abby did as Dayna had suggested. As he drove out of the hospital parking lot, she twisted around to look at her friend. "I can't believe I didn't think to ask if they fed you while you were there. Do we need to make a quick stop to pick something up?"

"I'm fine for now. They not only pumped me full of fluids, they brought me a full meal to eat." Dayna kept her eyes trained on the passing scenery. "Did your friend Gage tell you anything about what they found out at Wendy's house?"

Abby turned back around to face the front of the car. "Actually, he didn't. He drove me to the hospital right after the ambulance took you away, so there wasn't much of a chance for him to confer with Ben. All that I know is that Ben was going to stop by my house after we get there."

In fact, as it turned out, he was already waiting for them. Ben was sitting in one of the chairs on her back porch looking tired and frustrated. Tripp parked the car in Abby's usual spot and then stood by as Dayna got out of the car. He didn't touch her, but Abby knew he'd stick close by until he made sure her friend was capable of making it as far as the back porch on her own.

He waited until Abby fell into step beside him before speaking. "I'm going to come inside to see what Ben has to say. After that, I really need to head back over to my place and do some studying. I've got a hankering for some more of Owen's barbecue, and I'd be glad to call in an order for the three of us if it sounds good to you."

She was so tired by that point, there was no way she wanted to do any cooking. Even opening a couple of cans of soup would take too much effort. "That sounds great. We'll have whatever you're having."

He offered her a small smile. "And if he happens to have some of Frannie's pie on the menu tonight?"

"Do you really need to ask?"

Ben stood up at their approach. "Sorry I came without calling first."

He looked past Abby toward Dayna. "Your van should be here soon. A couple of Gage's men are going to drop it off."

"Thank you."

Dayna's words were said grudgingly, making Abby

want to shake her friend. Of course, that thought
was a bit hypocritical since in the recent past she'd
had her own issues with the man. Better to change
the subject. "You all might want to step to the side.
Zeke has a tendency to bolt out of the door, especially if he's been shut inside for any length of time.
His manners improve after he's had a chance to
take care of a few necessities in the backyard."

Everyone did as she suggested. Her prediction
proved true as Zeke tore past them on his way to
the cluster of bushes that would afford him a little
privacy. Tripp remained out on the porch to wait
for the dog to finish up and then make his usual
loop around the yard, nose to the ground and on
the lookout for any critters who might need a reminder of whose yard it really was.

Abby watched him from the kitchen window,
smiling as he stopped give one area a particularly
thorough sniff. A couple of minutes later, he headed
back to the porch to report in to his buddy that all
was well. She knew Tripp would reward Zeke for
his diligent efforts to make sure they were all safe
from squirrels, rabbits, and all manner of invasive
critters.

Meanwhile, both Ben and Dayna had parked
themselves at the table, quietly waiting for whatever came next. Time to play hostess.

"Tea or coffee? I also have iced tea, pop, and orange juice."

Ben's eyes showed a little more life. "Actually,
iced tea sounds good."

"Dayna?"

"I'd ask for some of that special brew you gave
me earlier. All things considered, that's probably

not a good idea. I'll settle for herbal tea if you have any."

That did sound good. She put the kettle on to boil and then fixed Ben's drink. When Tripp came in, she popped the cap off one of his favorite microbrews and set it on the table.

He grabbed a couple of Zeke's favorite pumpkin cookies and tossed him one before sitting down. He took a long swig of his beer before giving Zeke his other treat. "Thanks, Abs. That hit the spot."

Ben sipped his iced tea but still remained silent. Was he waiting for a special invitation or what? Before she could ask, he winked at her and then gave the cookie jar sitting next to the one that held Zeke's treats a hopeful look. Clearly he thought she was slacking off on her hostess duties. After fixing two mugs of tea, she set one in front of Dayna and the other where she usually sat. Then she made a show of getting out a small plate that she piled high with a mix of peanut butter and chocolate chip cookies. She also passed out some paper napkins.

Both men were already reaching for their fair share of the cookies before she was settled into her chair. "Okay, Ben. You've got your drink and the goodies to go along with it. Tell us what you can."

Dayna looked a bit pale as she glared at him. "Did you find Wendy? Was she in the house?"

The bite of cookie Abby had just taken turned to dust in her mouth. They all knew—or at least feared—there was a good chance she might not have survived whatever had happened in the workshop. He focused on the plate of cookies for a few seconds before finally looking up. "There was no sign of her in the house, but someone else had been there. That much was obvious. I talked to the officer who has been handling her missing persons case. He went through the house when she was first reported missing and then again today. All of her personal possessions had been rifled through like somebody was looking for something. Anyway, the place is a mess, and it wasn't when he'd been there before."

Abby used a sip of tea to wash down the cookie dust so she could speak. "Are you sure it wasn't Wendy herself?"

"It wouldn't make sense that she would have trashed the place like that." Ben glanced at Dayna. "You know her better than any of us. Would she have treated her own possessions with such blatant disrespect?"

"No, she always takes good care of her things, especially her workshop. She always kept everything in its rightful place. She was proud of her art, and there was no way she would destroy it for no good reason. She and I both make our living off our creations. You can't sell broken pottery. That would be like ripping your paycheck into little pieces and letting the wind blow it away."

Ben nodded as if she'd confirmed his own opinion. "The forensics people dusted for prints, and we're waiting for the results. We're also running DNA tests on the blood to see if we can confirm if it was Ms. Larabie's. I asked for everything to be expedited, but you have to understand things aren't like you see on television. It all takes time."

Out came his notebook and pen. "So, tell me what you were doing at Ms. Larabie's house in the first place. Especially since I'd already told Abby I would try to get the okay to escort you there my-self."

A surge of guilt had Abby raising her hand to get his attention. "That's my bad, Ben. I hadn't told her that there was a possibility that you would be able to arrange access for us. I didn't want to get her hopes up for no reason. She was still sleep-ing when I left the house, and I was hoping I'd hear something before I got back. By the time I re-turned home, she was already gone."

She turned to face Dayna. "I'm sorry, I realize now I should have woken you up to tell you. Maybe all of this mess could have been avoided."

"Don't sweat it, Abby. I knew it was a bad idea to go there, but I did it anyway." She drew a deep breath before turning back toward Ben. "I don't know what Abby told you about the situation, so I'll start at the beginning."

"Good idea."

"You already know that Wendy and I had a blowup because she was no longer interested in selling my pottery. I packed up my stuff and told her I'd pick it up later. When I went back, her booth was shut down just like Josiah's. There was no sign posted or anything, so I have no idea what was going on."

"Could she have been inside packing up when you stopped by?"

"I didn't hear anything. There was quite a crowd in the area, so it was noisy. I didn't want to risk going in for fear that she'd accuse me of . . . well, I don't know what exactly. It just didn't seem like a good idea, so I just left with Abby and Bridey."

Evidently talking was thirsty work for her, because Dayna got up to fix herself a second cup of tea. "I've tried calling Wendy a bunch of times since, but she never answered. I figured she was just blowing me off. I would've just let it drop, but I got a call from a gallery owner who markets my work. A customer wanted to buy twenty of my best vases. She needs them by this weekend, so no time to make new ones. I have a few at home, but I'd also given some to Wendy to sell."

As she sat back down, she offered Ben a small smile. "This sale would have been a big deal. The woman in question moves in pretty fancy circles in the area and has a lot of influence. Having someone like her promote my work could give my career a real boost."

Ben didn't comment on her motivations, but Abby thought she could detect a little sympathy for Dayna's situation in the quiet way he asked his next question. "So what happened when you got there?"

"I knocked on the front door and then tried to look in the living room window. The drapes were pulled so I couldn't see anything. From there, I walked around to the back and knocked on that door before trying the workshop. When there was no answer at either door, I started looking into all the windows I could reach from the ground. I don't think it really registered what a mess everything was until I finally looked into the workshop window. That's when I saw the broken pottery and the blood."

"And?" he prodded when she trailed off.

"I panicked and pounded on the door as I yelled Wendy's name. There was no sign of her anywhere, just that big pool of blood. I was too scared to use my key to her workshop to make sure Wendy hadn't passed out on the floor or something. I called Abby instead. She told me to go back to the van and wait there while she called you. I fainted twice and ended up in the emergency room. That's pretty much it."

Tripp spoke up for the first time. "How are you feeling now?"

"Tired, but I figure that's understandable with everything that's been going on. Barring any major setbacks, I should feel better with some rest."

She finished off her second cup of tea and set it aside. "And speaking of that, Abby. I think I'll take you up on the offer of a place to stay tonight. In fact, as soon as we're done here, I might just go up and rest for a couple of hours."

That sounded like a good idea to Abby as well, but she supposed it was up to the detective what happened next. He appeared to be lost in thought, though. To give him a minute, she filled Dayna in on the dinner plans. "Tripp has some studying to do first, but he offered to spring for barbecue from Owen's restaurant for the three of us. I hope that sounds good to you."

"Right now I'd eat an old boot as long as I don't have to do the cooking."

Ben snorted. "I might just have one out in my trunk. I'll trade you even for whatever Tripp brings back from Owen's."

Dayna gave Ben a narrow-eyed look. "I might be

tired, Detective, but I'm not stupid. Are we done here?"

"For now." He tucked his notebook back in his pocket. "I'll let you both know if I learn anything. And before I forget, we'll need to get your fingerprints at some point if they're not already on record. I'm guessing they'll be on at least some things in Ms. Larabie's workshop since she has some of your pottery in there. Don't get upset if someone calls and asks you to come in. Our primary goal is to identify any prints that shouldn't be there at all."

He grabbed a couple of the remaining cookies and slipped them into the same pocket as his notebook. "Thanks for the tea and cookies, Abby. Don't hesitate to call if either of you have questions or think of anything else I should know. Otherwise, I'll see you at the séance."

Tripp stood up at the same time Ben did. "I'm going to go hit the books, but I'll be back with dinner, probably around seven or so. Is that okay?"

"Perfect."

Dayna waited until the two men disappeared from sight before turning a puzzled look in Abby's direction. "What séance?"

It had already been a roller-coaster ride of a day that had left Abby's nerves stretched to the breaking point. Talking about what Madam G had planned was the last thing she wanted to do, but the problem wouldn't go away by ignoring it. The new surge of worry left her too jittery to sit still, so she started clearing the table.

"Ben refused Madam G's offer of help in solving Josiah Garth's murder, and so far the investigation doesn't seem to be getting very far. She decided to take matters in her own hands by holding a séance Saturday night at the fair."

Never let it be said that Dayna was slow on the uptake. She backed away several steps as if putting some distance between her and Abby would make any difference. "I've changed my mind. Don't tell me."

Maybe she should honor her friend's wishes, but denial wouldn't change a darn thing. "I don't have to spell it out for you. After all, you've known the woman a whole lot longer than I have. I bet you can guess what she plans to do."

Dayna didn't say another word. Spinning around, she almost tripped over Zeke in her hurry to hustle down the hall and up the stairs. A few seconds later the guest room door slammed shut. Zeke stood at the kitchen door and stared down the hall. He gave Abby a quizzical look as if asking her to explain what had just happened.

She stroked his fur, letting the small touch comfort them both. "She's had a rough couple of days, boy. Maybe a long nap will help her feel better. I'm pretty sure that's true for all of us. What do you think? Should we curl up on the sofa in the living room or head upstairs to stretch out on the bed? That might be more comfortable."

He stood stock still for bit while he considered the matter. Finally, he gave her hand a quick lick before leading the way down the hall and up the stairs toward her room. She just smiled and fell in step behind him.

Chapter 16

Only one more day until the fair officially began. Abby wasn't on anyone's list of volunteers, something that would normally make her happy. But with everything going on, she really, really needed something to do. Well, besides pacing the kitchen floor. It was tempting to do some baking, but her freezer was already overflowing with cookies, and she'd topped off Zeke's treat jar earlier that morning.

Maybe someone at the park could use an extra pair of helping hands. Surely Pastor Jack could find something for her to do. He'd also understand why she needed the distraction if she clued him in on everything that had happened lately.

It would be different if she had someone to talk to besides Zeke. While he was a great listener, he wasn't all that good at offering advice. And right now, that's what she needed, and on so many fronts. What could be done to help Dayna without treading on Ben's toes? And she had absolutely no desire to go to the séance. She didn't believe Madam G had a direct conduit to the afterlife, which would enable her to question Josiah Garth about his demise. But what if the séance was just a ruse to allow Madam G to reveal some actual evidence in the most dramatic manner possible? If the killer thought that was a real possibility, it could put Madam G and everyone who attended in danger.

Had Gage or Ben even thought of that?

She stopped mid-step and smacked herself on the forehead. Of course they had. No doubt they'd already made detailed plans to thwart any attempts to cause trouble. She had faith in both men; she really did. It was definitely time to put all this nervous energy to better use. Before leaving, she topped off Zeke's water bowl and knelt by his bed to give him a quick hug.

He blinked up at her sleepily and then closed his eyes as he dropped his head back down on the edge of his bed. It was hard not to envy his ability to shut out the world's problems and take a nap. Maybe if she worked herself to near exhaustion, she'd be able to do the same thing. One could always hope.

Already feeling better, she grabbed her keys and headed out the door.

Two hours later, Abby straightened her ponytail and finished eating a granola bar as she waited for Pastor Jack to finish a phone call. After he hung up, she said, "I flattened the last of the boxes. What else can I do?"

"I really appreciate your enthusiasm"—Jack stopped to flip through the pages on his clipboard—"but it looks like we've got everything covered for now."

Well, that was disappointing. She studied the neat rows of booths that had popped up all over the park. Earlier, the whole place had been barely controlled chaos, but now there was a sense of order everywhere she turned. "Know of anyone else who might need a hand?"

"Not right off the top of my head. Maybe one of the artists would appreciate some help unpacking."

"Good idea. Call me if something comes up where I might be of use."

Jack's phone rang again before he could respond. After he answered, he listened to what the person on the other end had to say while mouthing "I will" to Abby. She smiled and took off down the first row of booths, looking for anyone who might need some help. Even after hours of hard work, she still had plenty of energy to burn.

It wasn't long before Abby spotted Bonnie Simon, one of the artists she'd met over the past weekend. In fact, she'd bought two paintings from her, which were now hanging on her bedroom wall. The woman was busy sending a text message, so Abby hung back until she was finished before speaking. "Ms. Simon, I don't know if you remember me, but we met last weekend. I'm Abby McCree, a member of the Snowberry Creek city council."

The woman grinned as she dusted her hands off on her pants leg before offering one to Abby. "Of course. I might not remember every city official

I've ever met, but I do tend to remember the ones who buy my paintings."

Abby laughed and shook the woman's hand. "I was right about the roses. They were perfect for my bedroom wall."

"That's great. So, what can I do for you, Abby?"

"Actually, I was wondering if you could use a hand getting set up."

Bonnie's relief was obvious. "Are you sure?"

"I'm sure. Just tell me what needs to be done."

They fell to work unpacking all of the paintings and arranging them to Bonnie's satisfaction. While she finished hanging the last few, Abby went back to where Jack and his crew had set up their command center. "Hey, Jack, can I borrow one of the flatbed carts for a few minutes?"

After a quick peek at the schedule, he nodded. "Take the one on the end there. I'll need it back in a half an hour or so."

"Not a problem."

It took some careful maneuvering to get through the crowd without running over anyone's toes, but she finally made it back to Bonnie's booth. Once they had the boxes loaded, Bonnie insisted she could handle taking it back to where she was parked, by herself. "Thanks so much for your help, Abby. Please take one of my paintings as a special thank-you for your help."

"I couldn't do that, Bonnie. I was happy to help."

Bonnie ignored Abby's protest. "As I recall, you bought pictures of roses. But didn't you say those rhododendrons looked like the ones you have planted in your garden?"

"Good memory! I did say that, but it was actually

my late aunt who planted both the roses and the rhodies. They remind me of her."

"Even more reason for you to take one. Do you want the pink one or the purple?"

Bowing to the inevitable, Abby pointed to the purple one. "That one. It's absolutely lovely, and the flowers look so real."

It didn't take Bonnie long to get the picture wrapped up. "Stop by over the weekend if you get a chance."

"I will."

Abby left the booth and turned back toward the front of the park. It was past time for her to get back home. By now, Zeke had to be wondering what had happened to her. She shifted the package to her right hand as she checked her phone for any messages. She was hoping Dayna would've touched base at some point.

Sure enough, she'd left a message a few minutes ago to say that she'd be arriving to set up her booth in about half an hour. Abby stepped off the path and leaned the painting against her leg while she texted Dayna she'd meet her in the parking lot. Before she could hit SEND, something plowed into her hard enough to send her stumbling sideways into a nearby bench. With some effort, Abby managed to regain her balance and scoop up her painting before it could be damaged.

After a gasp, a female voice from behind her said, "Oops, sorry! The cart's heavier than I expected, and it got away from me. Are you all right?"

After taking a quick inventory, Abby decided there had been no real harm done. She picked up her painting and turned around to realize it was someone she knew. Sort of, anyway. "Jenny?"

Looking a bit puzzled, Jenny Garth manhandled her cart out of the center of the aisle before speaking. "Sorry, do I know you?"

It was no surprise that Jenny Garth hadn't immediately recognized Abby. After all, they'd only met the one time, and Jenny had been through a lot in the time since they'd crossed paths last weekend. Offering up a smile, Abby shook her head. "Not really. We met briefly at the fair last weekend when I bought some of those yard stakes you helped make."

Realizing she was no doubt stirring up some unpleasant memories for the other woman, Abby added, "I'm sure this has been a tough time for you and your family. I was sorry to hear about your uncle, and I'd like to offer my condolences."

After a second, the slight frown on Jenny's face eased. "I remember now. You're the lady from the council, aren't you? You gave me your business card for Uncle Josiah. Your name starts with . . . an A, doesn't it?"

"Right on the first try. It's Abby. Abby McCree."

"Nice to see you again." Jenny tightened her grip on the handle of the cart. "I'd love to chat, but I need to get this stuff to the booth. The fair committee stuck us all the way in the back. We were supposed to be featured right in the center, but for some reason they gave that spot to what's-her-name. You know, that whacko psychic."

Odd that she didn't use the woman's name. "You mean Madam G?"

"Yeah, her."

"Weren't she and your uncle friends?"

The question slipped out before Abby could stop it. After all, it wasn't really any of her business, and she only had Madam G's word on the matter. Jenny's response cast a lot of doubt on the situation. "She wishes. They might've been, back in the day, but I know for a fact that Uncle Josiah avoided her like the plague whenever possible."

Looking back, Abby still thought Madam G's pain over Josiah's death had seemed genuine when she'd been sitting in her kitchen. That didn't mean that he'd felt the same way about her.

Jenny was back to complaining. "Anyway, I can't imagine why they'd give her such a prominent position. It makes no sense."

It wasn't Abby's place to explain that no one had expected Jenny to show up so soon after her uncle's death. Besides, if she'd been both her uncle's assistant and his apprentice, that didn't necessarily translate into her having the legal right to sell his work. Again, that wasn't Abby's concern.

"I realize that this is the first time your town has held a fair like this, so there were bound to be some mistakes made. I just hope it doesn't have an adverse effect on our sales."

Rather than defend the committee's decision on where to place the various vendors, Abby kept her response simple. "I will convey your comments to the committee. I'm sure they'll appreciate your feedback."

Not.

Jenny clearly didn't care one way or another

what the committee thought about her opinion. "Well, regardless of how things go, I've got work to do. It was nice seeing you again. I hope you enjoy the garden stakes you bought."

"I'm sure I—"

Before Abby could finish what she was going to say, she realized she was talking to the back of Jenny's head as she charged on down the path at breakneck speed. Several people along the aisle had to jump out of her way to avoid being run over.

"Well, that was interesting about Josiah and Greta. And who is this 'we' Jenny kept mentioning?"

Abby grimaced when she realized she'd said all of that out loud, which probably had not been a good idea. She knew through Dayna that a lot of the people who sold their art at the fairs were a close-knit bunch. The last thing Abby wanted was for Jenny to find out that she'd been talking about her, even if it was only to herself. That didn't stop her from wondering what was going on.

It would be easy enough to satisfy her curiosity by following Jenny back to where her booth was located. That didn't mean it was a smart thing to do, especially since her partner was most likely Damon Wray. Considering she'd seen the two of them together yesterday afternoon, it was the most logical answer.

Not that she was going to follow Jenny to find out one way or the other. Curiosity didn't just kill the proverbial cat. It had also almost killed Abby a time or two since she'd moved to Snowberry Creek. It was time to remember the harsh lesson she'd learned staring into a killer's crazy eyes while wondering if she would live long enough to tell the tale.

Proud of her unexpected restraint, she sat down on the bench to rest a bit. Dayna should be arriving any minute and would need help unloading her van. They would also need one of the carts to haul everything, and it would speed things up if Abby had one ready and waiting. She'd enjoy the brief respite for another minute and then go hunt one down.

While she soaked up some sunshine, she studied the map that Jack had given her earlier. One side showed the layout of the fair. Each location was marked with a number that corresponded to a list on the reverse side of the map. She trailed her finger down the list until she found Dayna's name. The booth she'd been assigned was located on a side aisle near the front entrance. It was hardly Abby's area of expertise, but given Jenny's complaint about being located toward the back, she couldn't help but think Dayna's spot would draw a lot of traffic.

That should make her happy. Unfortunately, the booth was still listed under two names—Dayna's and Wendy's. Worse yet, the list wasn't the only place the names would be on display. As the booths were set up, the volunteers had posted a printed sign on each one to identify which vendor it belong to for the weekend. She thought about making a quick run to the booth to do something about the sign, but what was the point? All she could do was cross out Wendy's name.

On the other hand, a lot of the artists brought their own custom signs to mark their personal territory. With luck, Dayna would have one, too. For now, it was time to go looking for a cart. But before she'd gone two steps, her phone chirped to announce the arrival of a new text message. Sure enough, Dayna was waiting for her out in the parking lot, and she already had a cart. So much for being able to do even that much for her friend.

Abby texted back that she was on her way.

Chapter 17

Two hours passed before the two of them took a break to refuel. Dayna had continued unpacking her wares while Abby headed to the nearest food truck to buy their lunch. She spread the makeshift meal out on the small table Dayna had brought with her. As she pulled a folding chair over to sit on, she spotted the sign she'd meant to hide lying on the ground.

She picked it up and tore it in half. After stuffing it in the empty food bag, she said, "I'm sorry about the sign. If I'd thought about it sooner, I could have asked the committee to make the corrections on both the sign and the map."

Dayna shrugged. "Don't sweat it. I never thought to notify them of the change either. Besides, having someone cancel at the last moment isn't all that uncommon. If anyone comes looking for Wendy, I'll just tell them she had an emergency and couldn't attend. She posts her schedule on her website, so they can track her down at another fair or else e-mail her if they're that intent on buying something from her."

She stopped to root around in a portable file box, finally pulling out two matching small trays filled with business cards. She put hers on the table, but only set aside a few cards from the second one before putting it back where it came from. "I won't display Wendy's cards since I don't have any of her pottery with me, but at least I'll have them if anyone asks for one."

Even doing that much was far more generous than Abby might have been under the circumstances. "I'm guessing you haven't heard any more from Ben Earle or Gage about Wendy."

"Not a word." Dayna finally sat down and picked up her own sandwich. "I gave up and called the gallery owner and told her why I couldn't provide enough of the vases. She had me drop off the ones I did have in case the woman wanted them for some of the baskets. At least they'll both know I tried."

Despite Dayna's attempt to put on a brave face, Abby knew she had to be really disappointed to have such an opportunity slide through her fingers. "I'll keep my fingers crossed she'll think of you the next time she is putting together gift baskets."

"We'll just have to see."

A soft woof caught their attention. Abby's mood brightened as soon as she spotted Zeke standing outside the booth with Tripp right behind him. Considering how much of the stuff inside the booth was breakable, she decided the smart thing to do would be to join them in the aisle outside.

She knelt down to Zeke's level and wrapped her arms around his neck. He immediately gave her a flurry of slurpy kisses, which left her laughing. "Hey, boy, were you worried about me? Did I stay gone so long you decided to hunt me down?"

Tripp answered for him. "Pretty much. I went home to take a shower and change clothes after working all morning. When Zeke heard me pull in, he raised a huge ruckus. Since Jack had mentioned that you'd showed up to help, I figured you were probably still here. I could've called to let you know how much he was missing you, but he needed the exercise anyway."

"Thanks for bringing him."

Although she wasn't sure what she'd do with Zeke while she and Dayna finished unpacking. He was usually well-behaved, but accidents happened. "Dayna, would you mind taking our lunch out to one of the picnic tables? Zeke would never mean to break anything in here, but I'd rather not risk it."

After studying her surroundings, Dayna shook her head. "Actually, I'd better stay. Otherwise, I'll have to lug the cash box with us. I can handle the rest of the setup by myself. It will only take me an hour or so to finish."

"If you're sure."

"I am. I usually do it all by myself, so you've been a great help."

Abby picked up her sandwich and drink. "Okay. If I don't see you later today, I'll be here bright and early in the morning."

"See you then."

Tripp waited until they had put some distance between them and Dayna's booth before speaking. "How is she holding up?"

Good question. "On the surface, fine. But I suspect she's just putting on a brave face. She hasn't heard any more from Ben or Gage about the Wendy situation. She also had to tell the gallery owner and the woman wanting her vases that she couldn't fill the entire order."

Tripp cut between two of the booths to reach an open space in the park. They weren't the only ones looking for a quiet spot to escape the hubbub behind them, but at least there was one picnic table up for grabs. As they headed for it, he took Abby's hand in his. "I feel bad for her, but there doesn't seem to be much either of you can do about the situation."

"No, there doesn't. I just hate how unhappy she is right now."

When they reached the table, she took one bench while Tripp sat across from her. Zeke seemed a bit undecided where he should be, but quickly made up his mind as soon as she unwrapped her sandwich. "Sorry, but no mooching today, Zeke. I'm starving."

Unfortunately, the dog knew full well that she'd never stand up to his brown eyes coupled with a slow wag of his tail. "Fine, but one bite. That's it."

She broke off a piece of the bun along with a scrap of ham and held it out. After a quick sniff, Zeke accepted her offering while managing to look both disappointed and a little bit hurt. She found herself tearing off another chunk of her sandwich before she even realized she'd just been played. Tripp laughed. "Boy, he's got your number."

She ruffled the dog's fur as she shot his buddy a dirty look. "I'm not the only one who can't resist him when he looks at you with those puppy dog eyes."

Tripp didn't bother denying it. They both knew

who held all the power in their little threesome, and it wasn't either of the two humans. It didn't take long for her to finish her sandwich, especially when she tossed Zeke the final bite. She drank the last of her iced tea and wiped her hands on a napkin. "That hit the spot. I really worked up quite an appetite today."

"About that. What's going on with you?"

Where on earth did that question come from? "Nothing. Why?"

He shifted a bit as if finding either his seat or the subject of conversation uncomfortable. "Pastor Jack appreciated that you pitched in to help today. But I got the impression he was worried about you, not that he actually said so. He did mention how you charged from one task to another. Even when he ran out of jobs, you still asked for more to do."

All of that was true, but what was wrong with it? After all, she was the official liaison between the fair committee and the city council. It was her duty to keep an eye on how things were progressing. When she pointed that out to Tripp, he gave her one of those looks—the kind that said without words that she was lying, if not to him, then at least to herself.

She got up to toss her empty cup and sandwich wrapper in the trash, using the time to come up with a coherent explanation. "Okay, fine. I'm all tied up in knots for no good reason. I thought the fresh air and exercise might help."

"And did it?"

To keep her hands busy, she pulled the tie off her ponytail and then ran her fingers through her hair. "Not even a little. I'm worried sick about Dayna, Madam G and her séance, Wendy, and even the victim's niece, but there's nothing I can to do to help any of them."

Her confession didn't make him happy, but at least he didn't immediately launch into a tirade about none of those things being her problem. "You've been there for Dayna every step of the way since this mess started, so you have helped her. I have firsthand experience with how much your kind of support means when life goes off the rails. With your help, Dayna will get through whatever happens."

He obviously had more to say, but at the moment he seemed to be waiting for some response from her. She settled for saying, "She'd do the same for me, just like you would—and have."

He remained silent for another few seconds before he finally moved on. "I shouldn't have to point out that worrying about Wendy is Ben's job, not yours. As far as I know, you've never even met the woman. Other than what Dayna has told you, you don't know anything that would help Ben and company track her down."

Boy, she hated when Tripp lectured her. He was right, but no one liked a know-it-all. She also knew better than to say that. Feeling a bit foolish, she shook her head and hoped he'd made his point and was ready to move on to some other subject.

Instead he offered her a sympathetic look. "I know it's easier said than done, but let Ben shoulder the burden of what happened to Wendy. It's not just his job, but he's good at it."

Then without warning, Tripp stood up and reached for Zeke's leash. "Come on, let's walk."

As they made their way back over to the fair, he pointed toward the gaudy red-striped tent that held pride of place near the front. "As far as the séance goes, that's another job for Ben and Gage. I don't know what they said to that woman, but I know they had a long talk with her this morning. Judging from their expressions when they walked out of her tent, neither of them were happy with how the discussion played out. You do not want to get dragged into whatever is going on between the three of them. In fact, free tickets or not, it would be better if we stayed home tomorrow night."

"I've thought about it."

"Well, think about it some more. If you're not there, that will mean one less person that Gage has to worry about if everything goes to heck in a handcart."

There was a note in his voice that she found puzzling. "Are you afraid of what the psychic might say?"

"No. I'm more worried what the killer might do."

The same thought had occurred to her. "Well, at least we agree on that."

"So you'll stay home?"

He didn't sound the least bit hopeful that she'd answer in the affirmative. She wished she could assure him that she had no intentions of going. "I can't stop wondering why she decided I needed to be there as her special guest. Well, other than somehow my palms magically had told her that Ben and Gage would show up on my doorstep. She obviously thinks I have some special tie to the situation."

Tripp caught Abby by the arm and spun her

around to face him. "But you don't. Think about it. You didn't know Josiah Garth. You had no idea he'd been killed until Ben insisted on telling you in person, which was an idiot move on his part. The man says he wants you to stay out of his business, and then he brought it right to your doorstep. A simple call would have answered his questions about the business cards."

"That's true, and I wish that was how he'd handled it. Regardless, I do think he wanted to minimize my involvement. Besides, it's Wendy's connection to Dayna that's complicated the situation."

Tripp pointed out the obvious. "Unless there's something you know that I don't, there's no reason to think that Wendy's disappearance has anything to do with Garth's murder."

That might be true, but it all seemed to be too much of a coincidence that she shut down her booth at about the same time that Josiah did, and then disappeared. What were the chances that there would be two events in the same location, which would result in an unrelated murder and an unexplained disappearance?

When she said as much to Tripp, he glowered at her. "Even if Ben is thinking along the same lines, that doesn't make it your concern. And why on earth would you be worried about Garth's niece? She had a perfectly good reason for being out of touch for a few days. Yeah, learning what happened to Josiah after she left had to be hard, but you don't even know the girl."

Boy, he was really on a roll. "Did I tell you that I ran into her earlier? Well, actually, she ran into me—literally. I was standing off to the side of one of the aisles sending a text to Dayna, when I got hit from behind with one of those carts everyone is using to haul stuff around. As it turned out, it was Jenny Garth with a load of what looked like some of her uncle's work, or it could have been hers. I didn't ask."

But she might have if Jenny hadn't charged off before she had a chance. Not that she'd share that little tidbit with Tripp. They moved on down the path, letting Zeke take charge of their walk. Since he'd be stuck at home by himself over the weekend, she wasn't in any hurry to end their walk. Tripp paused at the intersection of two aisles and looked around. "The fair is a lot bigger than I thought it would be, especially for the first time out. You know, more vendors, more food trucks, and stuff."

She felt the same way. "The fair committee did an incredible job getting all of this organized, and the people in town have really stepped up to help whenever something needed to be done. Now we'll just have to wait and see if it draws enough of a crowd to make all the effort and expense worthwhile."

He pointed toward the package she was carrying. "Looks like you've already done some early shopping. Do you want me to carry it for a while?"

She handed the painting to him. "Actually it was a gift from Bonnie Simon, that artist I bought pictures from last weekend. After I volunteered to unpack stuff for her, Bonnie insisted I accept one of her watercolors as a thank-you."

"That was nice of her."

"It was. She even remembered which one I'd admired."

By that point they'd reached the back end of the fair. Zeke turned the corner onto the aisle that crossed from one side to the other. Abby had been so lost in her conversation with Tripp that she hadn't noticed how far they'd come—or that they were walking right toward where Jenny Garth was busy setting up for business. Just as she'd suspected, the other person inside the booth was Damon Wray.

Seeing the two working together was one thing, but it was the sign on the front of the booth that caused Abby to stumble. Thankfully, Tripp caught her before she actually fell. "Are you okay?"

She nodded and kept walking, needing to put some distance between them and Josiah's niece. After they turned the corner and headed back toward the front of the fair, she stopped to catch her breath. "Did you see that?"

Tripp looked behind them. "See what?"

"All of that wrought iron artwork. That woman is Jenny Garth, Josiah's niece. The guy was the one Josiah was arguing with last weekend while I was there."

"What's the problem? Shouldn't they be here?"

"I knew she was here, since I saw her earlier. I wasn't sure what she was going to be selling. Ben said he wasn't sure who would end up with all of Josiah's artwork, that it was up to the lawyers and whatever provisions he'd made in his will or trust. That is, if he had one."

Tripp was finally catching up with what was

bothering her. "And you're thinking it's too soon for any of that to have gotten sorted out. After all, it's only been a week since he died, and the case is still open."

"That's part of it, but the sign she has posted at the front of the booth makes no mention of her uncle's name. It just shows hers. She said she helped him with his work, but it looks like maybe they might be marketing Josiah's work as hers."

"I'm with Ben on this one. It's something for the attorneys to sort out. Or maybe they already know that she's his sole heir or something."

"Maybe."

Tripp turned his back on the scene and gave Zeke's leash a tug to get him moving, which left Abby no choice but to fall into step next to them. "I shouldn't call Ben."

She didn't phrase it as a question, but Tripp looked as if he had something to say on the subject. Before he could launch into another lecture, she added, "Because it's none of my business. I know that, Tripp. I just can't help be curious about what's going on, but that doesn't mean that I have to act on that curiosity."

"That's right."

The next intersection led to the designated food court area for the fair. Not all of the food trucks and carts were set up, but several were already doing a brisk business. Tripp cruised to a stop as he studied the various offerings. "What sounds good?"

She pointed out the obvious. "I've had lunch."

His grin was positively wicked as he drew a deep breath. "So have I, but I didn't have dessert. Neither did you, and it sure smells like the elephant ear stand is open."

Darn the man anyway, he knew her weaknesses. "Fine, but you're buying."

He was already reaching for his wallet. "I'll get them, but you might want to get Zeke some water if you can. He's panting pretty hard."

Tripp handed her the painting. While she looked around for a place to get water, he and Zeke headed across the circle of trucks and carts, following the enticing scents of fried dough and cinnamon to their source.

Luckily, Pastor Jack's command center was close by. When she'd last seen him, he'd still had several cases of water for his volunteers. With luck, he'd have some left and wouldn't mind her snagging one for Zeke. The pastor was once again on the phone when Abby approached him. She didn't want to interrupt him, so she picked up a bottle of water and gave him a questioning look. He grinned and nodded without missing a beat in his conversation.

By the time she got back to the food court, Tripp was already seated at one of the tables with Zeke lounging at his feet. She was headed straight for them when she realized that she didn't have Zeke's bowl and detoured toward the closest food truck. Luckily, it belonged to Owen Quinn, barbecue connoisseur and her mother's boyfriend.

"Hey, Abby, how is it going?"

"Just fine, Owen. Tripp and I were headed back home when he was lured in by the smell of elephant ears." She shook her head. "Poor man, no willpower at all."

Owen gave her a skeptical look. "That might be true, but it appears he bought two of them. Unless you're going to feed that much sugar to Zeke, I'm guessing the extra one is for you."

She laughed. "Yeah, guilty as charged. I was hoping you might have something I could borrow to use as a water bowl for Zeke."

"I might have just the ticket."

He disappeared for a few seconds and then was back with a paper bowl. "It's a little on the small side, but will this do?"

"It's perfect. Thanks. Now, I'd better get over there before Tripp finishes off his elephant ear and starts on mine."

As she took a step backward, she ran into a solid mass that hadn't been there just seconds before. This was definitely not her day. "Sorry, I should really watch where I'm going, especially when I'm backing up."

The man behind her chuckled. "That's all right. It's my fault, really. I was so focused on the chance to get some of Owen's famous barbecue, I practically ran you down."

"His barbecue has that effect on people." She finally turned around and then took a quick step back as soon as she recognized who it was she'd collided with—Damon Wray.

Realizing she'd actually said his name out loud, she clapped her hand over her mouth and wished she could simply disappear.

Chapter 18

Abby wanted to walk away and get back to Tripp and Zeke as fast as possible. But even if she could've convinced her feet to move, she still had the problem of the gallery owner standing in her way. When in doubt, fall back on blustering. "Well, no harm done."

She managed to slide two steps to the right, but the man echoed her movements as if they were doing one of those line dances where people faced their partners. She tried to pretend that blocking her wasn't a deliberate move on his part. She slid back to the left. "Sorry, I've got an elephant ear waiting for me. Also, my dog is thirsty."

By that point, Damon Wray was looking at her as if she were a blithering idiot. Sadly, she was pretty sure he was right. That didn't keep him from blocking her once again. "I'm sorry, have we met before? Because I rarely, if ever, forget a pretty woman's name."

The compliment had her blushing as she stammered, "Not really."

He stared down at her, his eyes crinkling in good humor. "So you only pretended to know my name, or did you think I just looked like a Damon Wray?"

Could this get any worse? She could only imagine how well it would go over if she confessed she'd learned his name from a homicide detective. "Someone told me your name."

He edged a bit closer. "So we have a mutual acquaintance?"

Rather than confess she'd been talking about him with the police, she settled on a different part of the truth, hoping to distract him. "I've met Jenny Garth a couple of times."

Just that quick, his smile was gone. At least he looked more puzzled than concerned. "When?"

"I saw her earlier today."

True, but that wasn't the real point. Couldn't the stubborn man just let it drop? "Now, if you'll excuse me, my friends are waiting for me."

She caught a flash of movement out of the corner of her eye and winced. Actually, Tripp and Zeke were no longer waiting. They were headed straight for her. Time to make her escape before the situation only got worse. "Enjoy your barbecue. My favorite is the brisket burnt ends."

If Damon still had questions, at least he didn't chase her down to ask them. That didn't mean he wouldn't come looking for her once he had a chance to talk to Jenny about her. Rather than dwell on something she couldn't control, she hustled toward Tripp and Zeke, pretty sure that the man she'd left behind was still watching her.

When she finally reached Tripp, he wrapped his arm around her shoulders as if staking his claim. Or more likely, making sure the other man knew that she was under his protection. Either one was all right with her as long as it kept Damon Wray at bay for the time being.

"Who was that guy? Was he bothering you?"

"Can we wait until we're out of here before we continue this discussion?"

He studied her face and frowned, but at least he didn't force the issue. "Your elephant ear got cold. Do you want a new one?"

"No, I can reheat it at home."

"Okay, let's go."

They paused when they got to the parking lot, to give Zeke a badly needed drink of water. As they waited for him to finish, she looked back over her shoulder to make sure the gallery owner was nowhere in sight. Might as well get the discussion started. Postponing it wouldn't make it any easier. Besides, it wasn't as if she'd gone looking for the man. It wasn't her fault that she couldn't seem to control her unruly mouth.

"Remember me telling Ben that I saw Josiah Garth arguing with another man the day of the fair?" She plunged on without giving Tripp a chance to respond. "Jenny Garth never told me who he was, just that it wasn't a good time to interrupt them so I could meet her uncle. It wasn't until later that Ben showed me a picture of the guy and told me his name was Damon Wray. He owns a local art gallery and acted as Josiah's agent or broker. You know, something like that."

"And?"

"And when I turned to walk away from Owen's truck, I ran right into him. Instead of just apologizing, I was so startled to see him that I blurted out his name without thinking."

"So, what's the problem?"

Seriously? Couldn't he figure that out? "The problem is that he's never seen me before. He wanted to know if we'd met. Even said that he never forgot the name of a pretty woman."

Okay, she probably shouldn't have shared that last bit. Tripp muttered something under his breath, which she ignored. "When I said we'd never actually met, he thought it was more amusing than worrisome. I admitted someone told me his name, but I didn't say who. When he pushed a bit, I panicked and said I'd met Jenny Garth a couple of times."

"That's true."

"He doesn't know my name, but she will probably realize it was me if he describes me well enough. Then he'll find out that she definitely wasn't the one who told me his name. I'd rather he not find out that I ratted him out to the police for having a heated argument with Josiah less than an hour before the man was murdered."

The sheer stupidity of it all had her wanting to kick something. "Even when I try, I can't seem to avoid these kinds of situations. Should I call Ben and tell him?"

Zeke slurped up the last of his water and was antsy to get moving again. She picked up the empty bowl and started walking, skirting the fairgrounds to reach the entrance into the national forest. She didn't know about her two companions, but she needed to spend some time in the soothing quiet of the trees. Tripp had yet to answer her question, but she'd give him all the time he wanted to mull it over.

"Do you want me to call him for you?"

Darn, she was really hoping Tripp would tell her that she was overreacting. As tempting as it was to take him up on his offer, letting him run interference for her seemed cowardly. "No, I'll do it, but I'm going to need a cup or two of your special brew to get through the rest of the day."

"You got it. I'm sure it will go perfectly with a re-heated elephant ear."

Abby sat in her favorite chair in the living room. She was trying to read, but mostly she sat and stared morosely at her cell phone. Her call to Ben had gone straight to voice mail. That had been over two hours ago, and she was still waiting for him to respond. She knew he was a busy man and would get back to her as soon as he could. Maybe she would've heard something by now if she hadn't ended her message by saying it wasn't urgent.

By the standards of what the man dealt with on a daily basis, that was true, so she'd done the right thing. But, darn it all, she really wanted that special drink that Tripp had promised her. However, knowing how the brandy-laced tea affected her, she'd thought it was smarter to hold off until after she reported in to the detective. Once she did, she had every intention of brewing a full pot of the stuff. She might even share some with Tripp.

Her phone finally rang, startling her into dropping her book. "Hi, Ben. Thanks for calling me back."

"No problem. What's up?"

Looking back, she suspected that she'd blown the whole incident out of proportion. But since she had Ben's attention, she might as well tell him what had happened. After describing the run-in, she added, "I didn't want him to know I'd learned his name from you."

"He won't hear it from me." At least Ben didn't reject her concern out of hand. "He already knows he was seen arguing with Josiah and that I asked multiple witnesses to identify him using a photograph from his website. I didn't mention any witness names, though. You might have been the first person to tell me about their encounter, but you weren't the only one who saw them."

"Thanks, that helps." Although she wished his reassurance made her feel better than it actually did. Another thought occurred to her. "While I've got you, I was wondering how you feel about the séance tomorrow night."

Without hesitation, he said, "That it's idiotic, but we can't stop Madam G from holding it. Why are you asking?"

His simple question broke the dam of all the things that had been whirling through her brain. The words tumbled out at an alarming rate. "I know she wants me there for some inexplicable reason. But when Tripp and I were talking about it, he said—and I agree—that doesn't mean I have to go. Maybe she thinks I'm connected to the investigation into Josiah's death because of the reading she gave me."

But there was one other connection to the whole situation, one that was purely incidental. "Yeah, admittedly my business cards were found at the scene, but that's all. On the other hand, Madam G is donating the proceeds to the city, and she knows I'm the liaison between the fair committee and the council. Maybe she thinks an official representative of the city should be there."

Realizing she was babbling, she closed her eyes and tried to regain control of the words pouring out of her mouth. "I guess my question is, do you think there is a good reason that I should be there?"

"I think that's up to you, Abby. I'm sure there will be other members of the fair committee there to represent the city. Gage and I will be there to keep an eye on things. I don't really expect her to come up with anything that will prove useful to my investigation, but weirder things have been known to happen. Let me know what you decide."

"I will, and thanks for calling, Ben. I'm sorry to take up so much of your time, especially when I suspect you've been putting in a lot of long hours."

"Not a problem. And back to Damon Wray—don't hesitate to call if you do run into problems with him."

"I will. For now, I'm going to head for the kitchen and make a cup of tea."

The detective chuckled softly. "I could use a big cup myself, especially if it's the kind Tripp makes for you. Too bad I'm driving."

Chapter 19

At least one thing was going right on Saturday morning—the weather. While it was an exaggeration that it rained in the greater Seattle area all the time, unexpected showers were always a possibility. But the sun was out, the temperature mild, and it was supposed to stay that way through the weekend. In addition, the Cascades provided a stunning background for the event. The beautiful mountains and gorgeous weather were the perfect combination to encourage people to spend their time outdoors.

As Abby and Tripp walked down to the park, the traffic moving through town in that direction was gratifyingly heavy, which boded well for a successful fair. Her plan was to spend the morning browsing the booths and then have lunch with Dayna. The one place she planned to avoid was the red striped tent in the middle of the fair. She was sure Madam G would be doing a brisk business, but Abby wanted no part of it.

She still hadn't made up her mind whether or not to attend the séance and didn't want to give that woman a chance to harass her about it. Tripp thought she was crazy for even considering it, and she couldn't fault his logic. It wasn't smart, it wouldn't accomplish anything, but regardless some small part of her kept insisting that she should stand witness to the great revelation, whatever it turned out to be.

For now she set all of that aside to enjoy the day. As they walked past the food court along the edge of the fair, Tripp took her hand and steered her toward Bridey's booth, where she was selling coffee and other drinks. "Let's get some coffee before we go our separate ways."

Then he tugged her in close and grinned down at her. "If you play your cards right, I'll even spring for a couple of whatever pastries she brought."

She smiled right back at him. "And exactly what would that entail?"

"Not to sound like an eight-year-old, but that's for me to know and you to find out. I promise you won't regret it."

What was he up do? Not that she was going to even think about refusing his offer, not with Bridey's goodies on the line. "It's a deal. I'll have a tall decaf with cream. Pick whatever treats that strike your fancy."

There was a definite wicked gleam in Tripp's dark eyes that had her blushing as he leaned in close to whisper, "Trust me, I plan to."

Before she could stammer out a response, another person joined the conversation. "Hey, you two, Ben and I have a table over there if you'd like to join us."

Tripp gave her a wink before answering Gage. "Give us a minute. We were just discussing what kind of goodies we were in the mood for."

After getting a closer look at Abby's face, Gage retreated a step, his mouth curving up in a big grin. "Or maybe you'd rather find your own table. I think there are some more private ones up the hill inside the tree line."

Okay, now he had her blushing big-time. "No, we'd be glad to sit with you. In fact, I'll go join Ben while you and Tripp get our stuff."

Then Abby took off like a shot, leaving both men in her dust. She was pretty sure they were laughing at her cowardice, but too bad. When she made it over to where Ben was sitting, he motioned for her to have a seat while looking past her to where she'd left Tripp and Gage. "I'm tempted to ask what's going on, but somehow I think you'd rather I didn't."

"I always knew you were a smart man." She dropped down on the bench and let out a slow breath. "So, how are things with you?"

He didn't answer right away, as if unsure what she really wanted to know. "Are you asking about me personally or about the investigations? Because I can't really talk about those."

As if she didn't know that. "Sorry, Ben, I was just trying to make conversation. I'm actually a bit surprised to see you here with everything you have going on."

"Even cops get days off occasionally, but you're

right. I only stopped by to touch base with Gage about tonight. Then I'll be off and running again."

He paused to sip his coffee. "But because it's you, I will tell you this much. Still no sign of Wendy Larabie. None of her friends or family have heard anything from her. No record of her at any of the hospitals or emergency clinics in the area. We've got bulletins out looking for her van."

"Thanks for telling me even that much."

She noticed he hadn't mentioned whether or not the blood that Dayna had seen through the window had belonged to Wendy. She wasn't going to ask. Ben would expect her to keep any information he shared with her confidential. If Dayna were to ask if she'd heard anything, she'd hate to admit she had but that she couldn't tell her. Still, that didn't mean she couldn't ask about a related subject. "I'm guessing you're still planning on attending the séance tonight."

He nodded but didn't look all that happy about it. "Don't really have any choice, although I really don't appreciate spending my evening hours listening to a bunch of hooey. I don't know what that woman's thinking, but she could be putting herself in danger. That's why Gage is going to be my date for the evening."

The man himself had just walked up. "For the record, Ben, I expect to be taken somewhere nice for dinner afterward."

That had Tripp laughing as he joined Abby on the bench while Gage slid in on the same side as Ben. "Heaven forbid that anyone think you were a cheap date."

The detective shrugged. "You mean like the time Gage offered to buy me a special lunch and we ended up eating burgers at the bar?"

Gage looked insulted. "Hey, I threw in onion rings as a special bonus. And don't forget, I let you beat me at pool that afternoon."

Abby perked up. "Are you any good, Ben? I've beaten both Gage and Tripp. Liam, too, for that matter. You know, the guy who owns the bar."

There was a new look of respect in Ben's expression. "I knew about these two, but I hadn't heard that you'd beaten Liam. That's impressive. Not many get the best of him. When things settle down a bit, we'll have to play a few rounds."

"You're on! Loser buys lunch, including the onion rings."

Then he looked past her and frowned. Abby glanced back over her shoulder to see what—or who—had caught his attention. She wasn't surprised to see Jenny Garth walking across the food court, but it appeared that Ben was.

"You knew she was setting up a booth, didn't you?"

He looked puzzled. "Not actually, but I probably should have since you mentioned seeing her and Wray here. I thought she'd been told that she couldn't market Josiah's stuff until the estate is settled."

Yikes, she really hoped the girl wasn't treading on the wrong side of the law with what she was doing. "Her assigned booth is near the back of the fair. She thought she would be given the prominent spot that would have been Josiah's. She wasn't happy that Madam G got it instead. When Tripp and I were walking Zeke around the park yesterday, we saw her setting up. The sign she posted made no mention of her uncle's name, so maybe she's only selling her own creations."

Although the stuff Jenny had been unpacking had looked a lot like what Josiah had on display at the fair last weekend. "This is none of my business, but what are the chances that Damon Wray got permission somehow to market the pieces that Josiah had given to him on consignment?"

Both Ben and Gage were looking pretty doubtful about that, and she tended to agree with their assessment. "Can you do anything to stop them?"

"Abby."

The one word conveyed Tripp's displeasure on the turn the conversation had taken. He was right. "Never mind. Forget I said anything."

She turned her attention to the two mini-muffins Tripp had bought for her, one blueberry and the other one peach. "Tripp, after I finish these, I'll be heading off to see if Dayna needs any help. Where will you be?"

"I'm scheduled to work at the information booth for the next couple of hours. After that, I'm done until the séance tonight."

Okay, that last bit surprised her. He'd been pretty clear about his thoughts on that subject. He picked up on her confusion and shrugged. "I know you don't want to go, but I also know you feel like you should. That means I'll be there sitting right next to you."

She reached over and took his hand in hers. "Thanks, Tripp. I'll feel a whole lot better with you there."

Gage and Ben both managed to look insulted. "You do know we'll be there, too, Abby."

"I know, but with Tripp there to make sure I'm safe, you two won't have to worry about me. You can concentrate on Madam G and her other guests."

She popped the last bite of her peach muffin in her mouth and washed it down with coffee. "And on that note, I'll see you gentlemen later."

Tripp walked with her as far as the information booth. "If I haven't seen you by the time I get done here, I'll come find you at Dayna's booth."

Then he gave her a quick kiss that resulted in several hoots and wolf whistles from a few of his fellow veterans in the area. Seriously, were they all stuck in high-school-boy mode? Rather than let them know they'd managed to embarrass her, Abby stood on her tiptoes and gave Tripp a kiss that left both of them breathing a bit hard. Proud of herself, she waved at the guys and sashayed on down the aisle to find her friend.

Abby didn't get far before trouble found her. After turning onto the side aisle that would take her in the right direction, Jenny Garth stepped out of the crowd right in front of her. When Abby tried to back away, she ran right into someone else. She looked back to apologize only to realize she was now sandwiched between Jenny and her buddy Damon Wray.

Fighting to remain calm, she attempted to side-step around Jenny, but the younger woman blocked her way. Trying escape was futile unless she wanted to make a huge scene. Saving that for a backup plan, she calmly asked, "Is there something you wanted?"

"I saw you sitting with those two cops. You know, the ones who keep sniffing around my personal business."

"They are our friends and invited us to join them for coffee."

That didn't go over well at all. Jenny was glaring big-time, and Damon crowded closer to Abby as he took control of the conversation. "I'm not buying it. From what Jenny said, the detective's attention zeroed in on her as she walked by. After you realized who he was looking at, the pair of you launched into quite a discussion about her."

They didn't just talk about Jenny. After all, Damon Wray had also been a topic of conversation as well. Not that she was going to admit that. It was time to bluff, or better yet, tell a different version of the truth. "Actually, the four of us were talking about Madam G's séance tonight. We're all going."

That didn't help the situation at all. Instead of lessening the tension, she'd just dumped gasoline on the fire. Jenny was now vibrating with fury. "I can't believe anyone would let that stupid cow do something like that. Have they no respect for the dead? She's just trying to get rich off my family's pain. I'm thinking about suing her."

Abby didn't point out that any money brought in by the séance was being donated to the town in honor of Jenny's uncle. Somehow she suspected it wouldn't do anything to calm the waters. Far better to keep her mouth shut.

Damon looked far more rumpled than she'd

seen him previously. "You lied about how you knew who I was. Jenny never told you my name."

"Someone else must have told me." Ben Earle, not that she was going to point that out.

At least Damon didn't ask her to name names. "Whoever it was, don't make a habit of discussing either of us with other people, especially your cop buddies. If it happens again, I'll be calling my attorney. And for the record, just like I told the police, I left Josiah shortly after you saw us."

Interesting he felt compelled to tell her that. She had to wonder why he had. She also noticed he didn't make the same claim about Jenny. It was definitely time to make a run for it. "If you'll excuse me, I'm supposed to be somewhere right now."

Since both Jenny and Damon were now standing in front of her, she simply reversed course and headed straight back to where she'd left Tripp at the information booth. It was tempting to break into a run, but that would only draw more attention in her direction.

She was so focused on finding Tripp that she failed to notice help was much closer at hand until Gage stepped right in front of her. He took one look at her and pulled her out of the aisle to stand in a narrow gap between one booth and another. "Abby, what's wrong?"

"I ran into Jenny and her buddy Damon. Evidently she noticed Ben watching her earlier and decided the four of us were plotting against her somehow."

He immediately scanned the surrounding area for the offending pair. "Did they threaten you?"

"Not exactly, but Damon did tell me I shouldn't be talking about either him or Jenny with anyone, especially you or Ben."

The more she thought about the confrontation, the madder she got. "It's not my fault the two of them are tangled up in the aftermath of Josiah's death. And I can talk to my friends any darn time I want to."

Her anger was a thin disguise for her fear, one that Gabe saw right through. "Maybe I'll go have a chat with them."

As much as she'd love to see Gage rip into the pair, it could backfire on her at some point when he wasn't around to intercede.

"Please don't. I'm probably overreacting."

He cocked his head to one side and studied her for several seconds. "No, I don't think you are. You've always had good instincts when it comes to people. If you were scared, there was a reason for it even if you can't immediately put your finger on why."

"I don't want to think anyone is out to get me, Gage."

"No one ever does, Abby." He gave her a quick hug.

When he finally released her, he crooked a finger and used it to tilt her chin up to better meet his gaze. "I won't talk to them now, but only if you promise to call me if they even look at you wrong."

She'd rather fight her own battles, but not when it came to murder. Even if agreeing to Gage's demands was also scary, they both knew it was the safer choice. Swallowing hard, she managed a small smile as she held up her hand and said, "I promise."

Chapter 20

"Why did you need a police escort?"

Abby waited to answer until she finished wrapping up one of Dayna's vases for a customer. "We just happened to be going in the same direction."

Dayna rolled her eyes and shook her head. "Liar. You were pale and shaky when you got here. Still are, for that matter."

Abby wished like heck that a whole bunch of people would descend on the booth, thereby providing a legitimate excuse for her to ignore her friend's comments. Sadly, they had no customers who required their attention.

"Fine. On my way here, I ran into Jenny Garth and that gallery owner I saw arguing with Josiah at the fair last weekend. They had the idea that I'd been gossiping about them with my 'cop buddies.' Their words, not mine."

Dayna rearranged items on a nearby display table. "And were you?"

"Well, yes, but it wasn't my fault. When Tripp and I stopped at Bridey's booth, Gage invited us to sit with him and Ben. Right after we sat down, Ben spotted Jenny walking by and was surprised that she was here today. He'd thought she wasn't supposed to be." Abby didn't figure she should add the reason for why he thought that.

"And how does that translate into her being mad at you?"

"She was pretty sure he asked me something about her and that I answered. I tried to avoid admitting that was true by saying we were actually talking about the séance tonight. That all four of us were going to be there."

Dayna cringed. "I'm guessing that wasn't the best topic of conversation to bring up with Jenny. Several of my friends heard her having a hissy fit because Madam G has a better location here than poor Jenny rated. The fact that the woman is hosting a séance to talk to Jenny's dearly departed uncle just makes it worse."

Abby's responding laugh had little to do with humor. "Tell me something I don't know. Although, to be honest, I have some sympathy for her feeling that way. It's been less than a week since Josiah was killed, and the family hasn't had any time to come to terms with Josiah's death. Now the public is going to be entertained by a psychic attempting to talk to the man from the other side of the grave."

Not that there'd been a funeral yet as far as she knew.

"Any new leads?"

"Not that Ben has told me about, but then he wouldn't."

Luckily, the crowd she'd been hoping for finally arrived, even if a bit late. At least it kept the two of them too busy to talk about anything but Dayna's pottery until it was time to take a break for lunch. Tripp arrived just in time to join them. She'd been worried Gage would've snitched about what had happened. One look at Tripp's face answered that question for her.

She didn't wait for the interrogation to start. "I'm fine, and Gage is a big tattletale."

That last part didn't go over well. Tripp definitely had his soldier game-face on full display. "No, you're not fine, and you should've told me yourself."

There was a hint of hurt along with the anger in his voice. Was he jealous that Gage was the one to offer her some comfort before escorting her to Dayna's booth? "I was on my way to find you, but Gage spotted me first and offered to escort me to Dayna's booth. I had every intention to tell you what happened."

While they were talking, she was fully aware of Dayna listening to their conversation, her gaze bouncing back and forth between them as if she was watching a tennis match. Meanwhile, Tripp finally let go of his frustration and held out his arms. When he gathered Abby in close, her own fear faded away.

Dayna made some shooing motions with her hands. "If you two are done being adorable, I would appreciate it if you would go have lunch. You're clogging up the works, so my customers can't get in."

Abby jumped back and looked around. Sure

enough, there were several people lined up at the entrance to the booth. She even knew a couple of them, the ones who were now sporting big grins. Great.

Trying for dignity and failing miserably at it, she turned her full attention toward Dayna. "What about you? You've got to be starving by now."

"I'd rather see to my customers. Bring back something if you're that worried about me." She gave Tripp another appraising look. "There's no rush. Take your time and enjoy yourselves. I'll be here."

Then she dropped her voice. "That is, if you get back. I'll understand if Tripp feels like you need to continue your discussion at home. You know, in private."

Rather than encourage any more teasing, Abby headed for the exit with Tripp trailing along in her wake. "We'll be back."

He didn't say anything until they'd put some distance between them and Dayna's booth. "Are you really okay?"

"Yeah. I just really wish Ben would find some answers about what happened to Josiah Garth and Dayna's friend . . . or ex-friend . . . Wendy. I don't like looking at people and trying to decide if they're the kind who could shove a yard stake through someone's chest. You know what I mean?"

"You know I do." Suddenly he had that look in his eyes that often sent him out to prowl in the backyard late at night. It usually meant that something from his time in the military was haunting him. "It would be nice if bad guys always looked the part."

Before she could think of a response, he some-how shook off his dark mood. "So what sounds good for lunch? I'm not picky, just hungry."

They settled on the gyros and iced tea. Then they followed it up with a frozen banana dipped in chocolate and served on a stick. Tripp claimed it was a healthy dessert, and Abby didn't argue. They took their time wandering back toward Dayna's booth, stopping occasionally to check out a booth if something caught their attention. Half an hour and several purchases later, they arrived at Dayna's booth, only to find it closed.

When Abby attempted to peer inside, Tripp im-mediately stopped her. "Let me."

She froze in position and let him take the lead. That didn't mean it was easy for her to stand there and do nothing while her heart slammed around in her chest in fear of what might have happened to her friend. After all, the last time she'd encoun-tered a similar situation, the artist had been mur-dered. Tripp stepped back out of the booth a few seconds later.

"Dayna's not in there, and I don't see her cash box. There's no way to know if she took it or hid it somewhere." Tripp studied their surroundings and then pointed off to their right. "There she is, safe and sound."

Abby handed off her purchases to Tripp and then plowed her way through the crowd to reach Dayna's side. When she and Tripp got within hear-ing distance of her friend, Abby snapped, "Where did you go wandering off to?"

Dayna looked more confused than offended by

Abby's brusque demand. "Potty break. I was only gone for a few minutes."

"Well, you scared the heck out of us." Abby added, "Me, anyway. Tripp remained pretty calm."

He stood to one side, keeping an eye on the people passing by. "I thought one of us should keep a level head. Unfortunately, seeing the booth closed when she expected it to be open sent Abby into a bit of a tailspin. You know, because of what happened last weekend."

Dayna immediately wrapped an arm around Abby's shoulders. "I'm so sorry, guys. I didn't even think about that. I should've waited until you got back and could cover for me. I never thought about how it might look to you."

Abby's pulse finally slowed back down to somewhere close to normal, and she held out the bag containing Dayna's lunch. "Don't worry about it. Here's your lunch."

Dayna took the bag and peeked inside. "How much do I owe you?"

"Nothing. Tripp said it was his treat." She gave him a narrow-eyed look. "Something about your willingness to babysit me while he was working at the information booth."

When Tripp nodded to confirm that was right, Dayna laughed. "Yeah, it's like they say, it takes a village to raise a child. Or in this case, to keep Abby out of trouble."

"Hey, no fair in ganging up on me. It's not my fault."

Neither of her friends seem to believe that, and trying to convince them any different at this point was probably futile. "Do you want me to hang around long enough for you to eat your lunch in peace?"

"No, that's okay. I'll be fine."

Abby lowered her voice. "Are you going to the séance tonight?"

"I'm almost afraid to, but I might since I'm guessing you'll be there. Depends on how tired I am."

Surprisingly, Tripp didn't try to convince them to change their minds. "Just in case, we'll save you a seat next to us."

"Thanks, I'd appreciate that. Now, I'd better get back to work. Those vases and bowls don't sell themselves, you know."

Then she was off and running, leaving the two of them watching to make sure she got back to the booth safely. When Dayna disappeared inside, they took the most direct route back home. Well, actually it was really two homes since Tripp lived in the one-bedroom mother-in-law house in Abby's backyard.

Be that as it may, it didn't surprise her one bit when he asked her to wait on his porch while he gathered up his laptop and textbooks so he could study in her dining room. It's what he often did whenever he thought she might be in danger. She wanted to tell him that she would be perfectly safe in her own house, especially with Zeke there to stand guard, but she didn't bother. First, she knew Tripp would just dig in his heels and refuse to leave. Second, and more importantly, she'd feel a whole lot better with him there.

She unlocked the back door and let Zeke out to stretch his legs. While Tripp waited out on the porch for the dog to finish his rounds, she put on a pot of coffee and then momentarily debated whether to get out some cookies to go with it. Then she huffed a small laugh. This was Tripp she was talking about. Of course he'd want some cookies. She piled some on a plate along with a few doggy treats for him to dole out to Zeke.

The coffee had just finished when Tripp and his buddy came inside. Abby poured two cups and handed Tripp his as she pointed toward the plate of goodies on the table. "That's for the two of you to share. I'm going to curl up with my book in the living room. I'm hoping to sneak in a nap at some point."

"Sounds like a plan. What time do you want to head back to the park for the séance?"

"About five thirty."

When he nodded, she added, "I need to be there, Tripp."

"Did I say any different?"

"You've been pretty clear about your opinion on the subject."

He didn't deny it. "We've already told Dayna we'd be there. Besides, Ben and Gage agree that Madam G wants you there for some reason, crazy as that seems."

She hated that he worried so much about her. "I don't mean to make things so hard for you, Tripp. I know I'm your landlady, but I'm pretty sure rental agreements don't usually include guard duty."

He stepped close enough to brush a lock of hair back from her face. "They don't, but this is something I've willingly volunteered for, Abs."

Just that quickly, it was another one of those moments that seemed to be happening more frequently between them—the kind where they hovered right at the edge of becoming something more than just tenant and landlady, even more than just friends.

"Tripp, are we . . . you know . . . do you want?"

She wasn't sure what she was really asking him, but he seemed to understand anyway. "The answer to what I think you're asking is yes, but we should probably save that discussion for a day when things are a bit calmer."

"Okay, then."

She took a big step back in more ways than one as he picked up his coffee and cookies and started down the hall with Zeke hot on his heels. "We'll be in the dining room if you need us."

She watched until they were out of sight. What had she been meaning to do? Oh, yes, coffee and her book. And if her hands were a bit shaky as she made her way to the living room, she blamed it on her concern about the upcoming séance. Nothing to do with the way Tripp had looked at her right before he left the room.

Nope, not at all.

Abby had drifted off to sleep while reading her book. When she finally woke up, a glance at the clock told her that she'd been napping for the better part of two hours. It was time to get moving if they wanted to get to the séance on time. Tripp went back over to his place to get ready while she ran upstairs to change into something warmer and touch up her makeup. It was bound to get a bit chillier after sunset, so she left her dark hair down loose rather than in a ponytail. Satisfied with her appearance, she headed back downstairs to wait for Tripp. Zeke looked disappointed that he was once again being left behind, but she promised him extra treats when they returned.

At the park, Tripp held her hand as they strolled along the river toward where the fair was still going strong. They'd only gone a short distance when Abby's phone rang. After glancing at the screen, she held it out for Tripp to see. "The caller ID is blocked. Should I answer it?"

He shrugged. "It's up to you. I'd let it go to voice mail. If it's important, they'll leave a message."

He was right, of course. It rang another eight or nine times before the phone finally went blessedly silent. With no little trepidation, she forced herself to check if whoever had been on the other end of the line had left a message. It was disappointing to see that they had. She didn't want to listen to what they had to say, but there was really no choice. If she deleted the transcript unheard, she'd spend a whole lot of time wondering if she'd done the right thing. Better to find out for sure. If it was a spam call, she could relax and send it to the trash.

Regardless, her sixth sense was sure she wouldn't like whatever the person had to say. She hit the PLAY button and braced herself for the worst. The caller's voice sounded robotic rather than human, sending a shiver straight through her. The message was short, but terrifying just the same.

Ms. McCree, listen well. You should learn to keep your

nose out of affairs that are none of your concern. You will come to regret it if you fail to heed this warning. Just ask Madam G what happened because she didn't listen. Wendy Larabie, too.

Tripp was already dialing Gage's number before the last word faded away. As he waited for the police chief to answer, he grabbed her hand. "Don't delete the message. Gage and Ben will both want to hear it."

She very much wanted to delete the call, but he was right that Gage and Ben should hear it first. What kind of horrid person would threaten her like that? How did they get her number? And finally, would this give Ben confirmation that Wendy's disappearance was connected to Josiah's murder? If so, surely that would finally clear Dayna from any involvement in the whole affair.

She listened to Tripp as he filled Gage in on what had just happened. He finished up with his take on the message. They'd resumed walking toward the fair as he talked. Then he fell silent as he listened to what Gage had to say. They talked for what seemed like a long time, as Tripp kept his gaze pinned on Abby, his expression getting darker and darker. "Okay, keep us posted. We're almost there. We won't go inside the tent until either you or Ben gets there."

Abby didn't bother asking which tent Tripp was talking about. They were headed straight for the one with red stripes that belonged to Madam G. Before they even got near it, Abby's heart was back to marching double time. The entrance was open, but it was dark inside. "Uh-oh, there's a sign posted."

Tripp squinted as he tried to read it from a distance. "It's about the séance. Something about it being moved to an alternate location. Evidently they needed a larger tent to hold the size of the crowd they're expecting."

"That makes sense. Her tent is more suitable for the individual readings she does."

Still, she would have thought that Madam G would've zipped the entrance closed if she was away setting up for her performance at the new venue. It took everything Abby had to keep walking toward the red-striped tent. "Did Gage say how soon he'd arrive?"

"He was in his office at city hall when we talked. He was going to clue Ben in on the call and then head right over. It shouldn't take long for them to get here. Parking might take a few minutes, but I doubt either of them wants to come roaring up with lights and sirens blaring. No use in setting off a panic if there's nothing wrong."

"What do you think the chances are of that being the case?"

When he didn't immediately reply, she said, "That's what I thought."

She turned her back to the tent and watched for one of her favorite cops to show up. It took Gage surprisingly little time to arrive. From the way he was huffing and puffing, she suspected he'd run all the way from his office.

He headed straight for them, his phone pressed against his ear as he finished up a call. He was breathing a little easier by the time he made his way through the crowd circulating near the entrance to the fair. Abby handed over her phone as soon as he held out his hand.

When he was done listening, he muttered a few curses under his breath. Tripp jerked his head in the direction of the tent behind them. "We waited out here as promised."

Gage nodded. "Let's see what we're dealing with, if anything."

Tripp clicked on the flashlight app on his cell phone and followed Gage into the darkened tent. Should she follow them or wait outside for Ben to arrive?

She'd never felt so alone in a crowd even though she could hear Tripp and Gage talking through the canvas wall of the tent. They kept their voices too low for her to make out more than the occasional word. All of them on that list were worrisome: "blood," "emergency," "hurry," and "ambulance."

She risked a peek inside but only saw a rolled-up rug. Just as she realized there was a woman's foot sticking out one end, she heard one last word that was the scariest of them all—"dead."

Chapter 21

The impact of that single word, combined with what else she'd seen, left Abby nauseated and pretty sure she might embarrass herself right in front of a whole bunch of people if she didn't sit down soon. She'd told Tripp that she'd remain rooted to the spot where he'd left her, but sometimes dignity won out over promises. Luckily for her, the tent was next to a small brick building that belonged to the parks department and had a bench by the door.

Right now she was just grateful for having a place to sit while she waited for the ground to stop rocking and rolling beneath her feet. Ignoring the people passing by, she leaned into the cool surface of the bricks, closed her eyes, and hoped that the dizziness would soon pass. When she opened them again, Ben was closing in on her location.

When he got close, he asked, "Abby, are you okay?"

She nodded and then pointed toward the tent.

"Gage and Tripp are waiting for you inside. I'm pretty sure someone needs to call nine-one-one."

He patted her on the shoulder. "Gage already did. Will you be all right if I leave you out here while I touch base with him? I need to see what we're dealing with before the rest of the crew arrives."

When he glanced back over his shoulder, she turned to see what had caught his attention. The parking lot was rapidly filling up with emergency vehicles of all kinds.

"I'll be fine."

No, she wouldn't, but Ben had enough on his plate without having to babysit her. She did her best to maintain a calm façade. It couldn't have been more than a minute before Tripp charged back out of the tent. He waited until he had her wrapped up in his arms before he spoke. "Ben said you needed me. He didn't say why."

There went the tears again. And any words she would've used to explain the situation tangled up in a big knot in her throat, making it impossible to talk. Rather than press for details, Tripp stroked her back and gave her all the time she needed to regain control. Finally, she managed a rough whisper.

"I overheard you and Gage talking. Not everything. Just enough to know something bad happened inside the tent. I should have stayed outside, but I looked in the door and saw the foot. The one sticking out of the rug."

Not that she really needed to add that last part. After all, how many random feet could there be in one tent? So not the point. "I'm sure I heard the word 'dead.' The combination sent me into a tail-spin."

"I'm going to take you home. We don't need to get caught up in this any more than we already are. Besides, the séance is canceled, even if the fair committee doesn't know that yet."

"What happened in the tent?"

"Not now, Abby. Like I said, we're out of here."

She dug in her heels. "Ben will want our statements. You know, about the call and what we saw here."

"Ben wants a lot of things. He can talk to us at the house later." He tugged on her arm again. "If it's up to me, it will be much, much later."

They'd only gone two steps when the detective came out of the tent. "Where are you taking her?"

"Anywhere but here." Tripp shoved Abby behind him to prevent Ben from getting anywhere near her. "But home is where we'll be if you need to talk to us."

His words sounded as if they had been chipped from stone. Ben responded in kind. "Don't you mean *when* I need to talk to you, Blackston? It might be easier if we got it over with."

Maybe for him, but she really didn't feel up to talking right now. Luckily, a sudden, if not unexpected, onslaught of first responders finally arrived. Tripp took advantage of the momentary chaos to resume hauling Abby back toward the parking lot to his truck. She didn't even try to protest. Ben would figure out where they'd gone, and right now the crime scene had to be his priority.

They reached the truck without interference, so

she had at least one thing to be grateful for. Tripp practically lifted her up into the seat and made sure she was safely buckled in before hustling around to the other side to get in. It would be tricky maneuvering around all of the emergency vehicles crowded into the lot, especially with the bunch of curious bystanders starting to gather. Two of Gage's men were directing traffic and actually helped facilitate their escape. Tripp lowered his window to talk to Deputy Chapin, whom they both knew from past cases.

"Tell Gage and Ben we're not waiting around. We'll be at the house." If Tripp thought he sounded calm and in control, he was sorely mistaken.

His blunt statement had the deputy frowning as he stepped closer to the truck. He laid his hands on the doorframe as he looked past Tripp to study Abby. "Were they expecting you to hang around?"

She managed a small nod. "There's a body."

Maybe more. She still didn't know what else Gage and Tripp had been dealing with inside the tent. Deputy Chapin cringed, clearly torn between doing his duty and his sympathy for her. It was a relief when he finally nodded. "I'll tell them she needed to lie down for a while."

That wasn't far off the truth. Meanwhile, Tripp let out a slow breath. "Thanks, man. I owe you."

Chapin patted the side of the truck door and stepped back. "Just take care of her."

Then the deputy headed out into the street and stopped traffic long enough for Tripp to pull out of the parking lot. When they had driven a couple of blocks, the tension in her chest started to ease up. Just putting even that much distance between them and the park made it easier for her to breathe. "I'm sorry, Tripp."

"There's nothing for you to be sorry for. None of this is your fault."

Maybe that was true, but it sure didn't feel that way. All too often it seemed like the world went spinning out of control around her. That didn't keep her from bringing up a subject Tripp wouldn't want to talk about right now. Maybe ever. "What happened in the tent?"

No answer. From the stubborn set to his jaw, he was going to pretend he hadn't even heard her question. His refusal to discuss the matter only made it that much scarier. She tried again. "I need to know. No matter how bad it is. You know Ben is going to bring it up. I'd rather be prepared than blindsided. I also shouldn't have insisted on going to the séance. If we'd stayed home, we would have heard about the situation on the news. We wouldn't be in the middle of it."

Tripp slammed his fist against the steering wheel. "I'm mad, but not at you. None of this is your fault. You didn't put that dead body there where anyone could stumble over it, and you sure didn't conk Madam G over the head inside her own tent."

"Is she all right?"

"She was coming around. Gage tried asking her a few questions, but he wasn't getting much in the way of answers. The EMTs had just gotten there when Ben told me you needed me. My guess is they'll take her to the hospital to get checked out. Gage will try to take a more complete statement once the doctors give him the okay to talk to her.

Then they'll either keep her overnight for observation or send her home."

What a scary thought. "Should she be alone? Even if she doesn't have a concussion, whoever did this to her is still out there."

"No doubt she'll have one of Gage's people parked on her doorstep."

That was a relief. So was the fact they were back home. She didn't wait for Tripp to help her out of the truck. When her legs agreed to support her, she headed for the back porch. He matched his longer strides to hers, hovering just close enough to offer support if it was needed.

Trying to lighten the moment, she gave him a sideways glance. "I don't suppose it would be a good idea to knock back several cups of your special tea before Ben finally shows up. I'm guessing he wouldn't be particularly thrilled about taking a statement from someone who reeks of booze and keeps nodding off midsentence."

Tripp chuckled. "I'm betting it wouldn't be the first time he's had to do that. He might even enjoy it."

"Why?"

He finally looped his arm around her shoulders. "Because you're cute when you're tipsy. He could probably use some cute in his life about now."

Should she be insulted by that assessment? Probably a little, but it was nice to see Tripp smiling again. "Maybe we could temper the effects of the brandy with food."

"Good idea. Should we order in?"

They'd been doing that a lot lately, but right

now she simply didn't have the energy to cook. "Yes, your choice."

"I'll take Zeke for a quick run if you'll call Frannie's. I'd suggest two dinner specials, and don't forget the pie. It's been that kind of day."

"It's a deal. I'll have it delivered."

She unlocked the door and stood back to let Zeke come barreling out to greet his people. While he and Tripp tussled a bit on the ground, she took Zeke's leash off its hook just inside the door and waited for the excitement to die down before handing it off to Tripp.

"I think I'll order extra in case Ben hasn't had a chance to eat. If he doesn't want it, it will make for an easy dinner tomorrow."

"Better make it two. There's a good chance Gage will tag along with him." Tripp clipped on Zeke's leash. "We won't be gone long. Zeke and I'll pick up my to-go bag and schoolbooks on the way back. I'll be sleeping on your couch tonight."

She'd already assumed that would be the case, not that she minded at all. Both of them would be happier knowing he was close by if something happened. Not that she was expecting trouble, but she wouldn't sleep well until Ben and Gage got to the bottom of what was going on.

By that point, Zeke was all but dragging his buddy around to the front of the house, clearly eager to head off on their adventure. Tripp called back, "Lock the door."

Like she wouldn't have thought of that herself. Rather than point that out, she went back inside, dutifully locked the door, and then headed for the phone. She knew the number for Frannie's by heart, a testament to how often she gave in to the temptation of letting someone else do the cooking.

Once that was done, she made herself a cup of tea, sadly without Tripp's not-so-secret ingredient. She'd save that treat for later after the police had come and gone. For now, she was going to curl up in her chair and wait for the next disaster to hit.

As it turned out, Tripp had been right on the money. She and Tripp were just finishing up their own meal when both Gage and Ben came knocking at the back door. One look at the exhaustion etched in their faces and she pointed at their usual chairs. "Park it."

When they were seated, she set the rules. "No business will be discussed until you've eaten something. We ordered enough for everybody."

That had the pair sitting up straighter, and Ben made a passable attempt at smiling. "Woman, I'd kiss you if I thought Tripp wouldn't deck me for it."

She pulled the plates, which she'd already dished up, from the fridge and put the first one in the microwave to heat. When it was done, she set it in front of Ben and heated up the second one for Gage. Both men dug right in while she and Tripp finished off their desserts. While she waited for her guests to get caught up with them, she made herself a cup of herbal tea and put on a pot of coffee for everyone else.

It didn't take very long for both Ben and Gage to polish off their meals, and now looked a lot less like roadkill. Tripp cleared their plates and poured the coffee. When he sat back down next to Abby, both lawmen pulled out their spiral notebooks as Ben took charge of the discussion. "Okay, tell me what happened from when you left home."

When she didn't immediately launch into their story, Tripp reached over and took her hand. "Take your time. They're in no rush."

That wasn't true, but his calm words helped center her. "I got the phone call we told you about. After Gage listened to it, he and Tripp went inside Madam G's tent while I waited outside. Mostly, anyway."

When she paused, Tripp pushed her teacup closer, encouraging her to take a sip. Meanwhile, he picked up where she'd left off, making quick work of his part of the narrative. That's when she rejoined the conversation. "I peeked in the tent saw a woman's leg sticking out of a rolled-up rug."

"How did you know it was a woman?"

She closed her eyes in a futile attempt to shut out the grim images playing out in her head. "By the style of slacks and shoe."

Ben's voice was gentle as he attempted to make this as easy for her as possible. "And what happened next?"

"I backed away and sat down to wait for you."

Her throat was dry again, so she finished the last bit of her tea. "After you arrived, we talked briefly, and then you went inside the tent to see what was happening in there and sent Tripp out to me."

She squeezed Tripp's hand. "He brought me home because I still wasn't feeling all that good. That's pretty much it."

Gage put his notebook away, but Ben skimmed

over his notes again. "I'm sorry to tell you that we've tentatively identified the deceased as Wendy Larabie, your friend Dayna's former business associate."

It felt as if the floor was about to collapse beneath Abby's chair. It wasn't as if the idea hadn't crossed her mind. She'd been really hoping that it was some random stranger, not that it would make the death any less tragic.

"We're not releasing any details until we've confirmed the identity."

By that point, Tripp had her hand in a death grip. "Is it a safe assumption the cause of death wasn't an accident or natural causes?"

Abby had been staring down at the table, but she slowly lifted her gaze to meet Ben's again as she waited for him to answer. He was a handsome man in his late thirties or maybe his early forties. But right now, the grim expression in his eyes made him look decades older. She wanted to bolt from the room, to run anywhere to avoid hearing his response to Tripp's question, but it was already too late. He might not have yet said the words, but the answer was already hanging in the air between them.

"I'm sorry, but no such luck. She was murdered, most likely within the past twenty-four hours."

Chapter 22

That was the bad news. Abby could only hope that Ben wasn't about to share something far worse—like who his main suspect might be. She wasn't going to ask and really hoped he wasn't going to tell.

"We'd better get going." He tucked his notebook away and stood. "Thanks for dinner, you two. I might just make it through the day after all."

Abby remained seated. "Any word on how Madam G is doing? Or what the fair committee is going to do about the séance?"

Gage joined Ben by the door before he answered. "They're going to keep her overnight just to be on the safe side. At her request, the committee has already rescheduled the séance for tomorrow night. Since all of the tickets have been sold, they didn't feel like they had any choice as long as Madam G feels up to hosting it."

Clearly neither of the two men was happy about that decision, but the situation wasn't under their control. It seemed foolhardy at best, at least on the part of Madam G. She'd already come under attack once. Did she think whoever had conked her on the head was going to be any happier about her simply rescheduling the séance?

Gage was already out the door, but Ben stepped back into the kitchen. "I would appreciate the two of you keeping anything we just discussed under your hats for now. Everything will be made public soon enough, but I'd rather prevent any leaks until we officially confirm the identity of the victim."

Once again, Tripp answered for both of them. "We won't tell anyone."

Evidently that wasn't good enough for Ben. "Abby?"

They both knew he was worried that she'd call Dayna with the news as soon as he walked out the door. "Like he said, Ben, we won't tell anyone. We're staying in tonight."

"Thanks. I guess we'll see you at the séance tomorrow."

He was gone before she could respond. It was just as well. She wasn't sure she wanted to go or if Tripp would let her. Yeah, she was an adult and capable of making her own decisions. But she wasn't sure she'd find the courage to go if he wasn't there with her.

She gave him a smile. "I don't know about you, but I could really use a cup of that special tea about now."

He patted her on the shoulder as he got up to put on the kettle. "To heck with a cup. I'll make a whole pot."

"Perfect."

* * *

After the tea was done brewing, they headed for the living room, where Zeke curled up on a thick fleece blanket that Abby had bought specially for him. Tripp suggested that they watch a sci-fi movie they both enjoyed. When she dug out the DVD and put it in the player, she started to sit in her favorite chair, but Tripp stopped her. He patted the cushion next to where he was sitting on the couch. "Come sit with me."

Although they frequently watched movies together, sitting side-by-side on the couch wasn't what they usually did. What was going on? Deciding she was overthinking things, she hit the play button on the DVD player and then walked around the coffee table to take her assigned seat. Most likely it was as simple as Tripp thinking she needed some comfort after all they'd been through.

But when she started to sit down, he suddenly took her by the waist and dumped her on his lap. She flailed a bit at the unexpected maneuver, but he settled her against his chest. "I want you closer than that. Just relax and let me hold you. It will do both of us some good."

Neither of them were paying the least amount of attention to the movie credits rolling across the screen. Instead, she studied the man who held her with such care. His gentle touch did far more than the brandy-laced tea had to soothe away the stress of the day.

"I thank the day that Aunt Sybil picked you as her newest tenant."

He grinned. "I still remember the look on your

face when we first met. You thought I'd be some twenty-year-old kid."

She didn't bother denying it. "I'm guessing I wasn't exactly what you were expecting either."

"True, but as it turned out, you're exactly what I needed."

He gave her a quick kiss and then pointed at the television. "Now quiet. I don't want to miss my favorite part."

Her head was spinning again, but this time the source of her confusion was sitting right there on the couch with her. She smiled and cuddled in closer and let the man watch his movie while she wondered if she'd eventually be renting the mother-in-law house to someone else. After all, Tripp already spent a lot of his time hanging out with her in this one. She'd like to have him closer. A lot closer, in fact. As in no more sleeping downstairs on the couch.

But that was a discussion for another day. They still had a séance to get through and two murders to solve.

Sunday morning dawned sunny and bright. Abby did her best to adjust her mood to fit the day, but it was a struggle. Tripp was working at the information booth again as soon as the fair opened. Rather than lurk around the house alone for hours, she decided to go with him. He had looked relieved when she asked if that would be okay, probably because it meant he could more easily keep an eye on her.

All things considered, she couldn't blame him

for wanting to do that. Not that she'd come under attack herself. However, there was no denying there had been two murders and an assault, all connected to fairs in the past week, and she'd come into at least indirect contact with all three victims. Rather than focus on that, she did her best to get lost in a book. After only half an hour or so, she realized she'd been staring at the words on the page without absorbing their meaning. Rather than give up entirely, she decided maybe a cup of coffee would help clear out the cobwebs.

She waited until Tripp finished answering a question before telling him her plan. "I'm going to go get a cup of coffee and a snack. What can I bring you?"

He studied her for a few seconds before answering. "Whatever you're having will be fine. If you stop to chat with anyone, let me know."

She ruffled his hair. "Anyone ever tell you that you're a bit of a worrywart?"

He rolled his eyes and quietly grumbled, "Anyone ever tell you that I have good reason to be?"

Abby conceded the point. "Fair enough. I'll come straight back."

She made it all the way to Bridey's booth without mishap. The woman herself stepped up to take Abby's order, motioning her to join her at the far end of the makeshift counter.

"What can I get you?"

"Two tall coffees, one black, the other with two sugars and a lot of cream." She paused to study the display of baked goods. She tried to hide her disappointment that there was no gooey butter cake in sight. "I'll have two of the cheese Danishes."

Bridey made quick work of her order and counted out Abby's change. Keeping her voice low, she asked, "How are you doing? I've heard some of what's been going on. Not all the details, of course, but enough to know you've probably had a rough time of it."

Abby looked around to see if anyone was listening in on their conversation. "Yeah, it's been bad. I really hate getting sucked into these kinds of things. It never gets any easier to deal with."

"It won't help a lot, but try to focus on the positive things. Like what a success the fair has been despite it all. The attendance has already far surpassed even the most optimistic predictions."

"I hadn't heard that, but that's wonderful. The mayor and the city council will be thrilled with that news."

Bridey leaned in closer. "Are you going to the séance tonight? We thought about it, but Seth thinks I should stay home and get some rest. I haven't spent the entire weekend here, but enough that I can't wait to put my feet up for a while. Besides, tomorrow is another workday."

"I don't blame you. But, yes, Tripp and I will be at the séance. Madam G even showed up at my house to personally invite me to attend."

"Why would she do that?"

"I don't know for sure, but I suspect her excuse is that stupid reading she gave me right before I went by Josiah Garth's booth. You know, where she told me that two men would show up on my doorstep bringing darkness with them."

Her friend shivered despite the warmth of the

day. "Looking back, I'm sorry Dayna and I let you meet with that woman by all yourself that day."

"It's not your fault, Bridey. Besides, I still think she was just making stuff up. Like I told Ben, or maybe it was Gage, what she told me could have just as easily applied to Tripp and Zeke, who snuck out to the bar to play pool and eat pub grub while I was gone."

By that point, Bridey was laughing. "What on earth were they thinking?"

"Apparently Zeke was sulking because I was gone, and Tripp hoped the outing would cheer him up."

"Are you sure it was only Zeke who was missing you?"

Tripp had already admitted that the dog wasn't the only one who had missed her, but she wasn't sure he'd appreciate her sharing that with anyone else. It was time to get back to Tripp before he came charging after her. "I'd better get going before the coffee gets cold."

Outside of the booth, she stopped to text Tripp that she was on her way back. That he answered before she'd taken five steps made her glad she'd made the effort. No use in worrying the man for no reason.

As she cut across the grass to the path that led back to the information booth, she caught sight of a familiar figure. Why on earth was Madam G at the fair so early? Even though the séance had been rescheduled for that evening, surely the woman wasn't there to do readings. Abby and Tripp had avoided walking past the medium's red-striped tent on their way to the information booth, so she didn't know if it was still cordoned off with crime scene tape.

Even if Ben Earle had given Madam G the all-clear to go ahead with her plans, the thought of Madam G doing readings there so soon after she'd been attacked—not to mention the dead body—gave Abby the heebie-jeebies. If it was her tent, Abby would have it incinerated and got a new one.

Regardless, the woman looked pretty darned perky after spending the night in the hospital. Abby slowed down just long enough to see where the psychic was headed. After studying her options, Madam G got in line at one of the food trucks. Rather than risk being seen, Abby picked up speed again.

Before turning the last corner, she glanced back one last time. The lady in question had already gotten her meal and was seated at one of the picnic tables. That was nothing out of the ordinary. However, it was interesting to see who had just sat down across from her. It was tempting to see how Madam G reacted to Damon Wray interrupting her meal.

There were no immediate signs of fireworks between the pair, but their body language looked anything but relaxed. What could the two be talking about? Greta wasn't an artist and had no need for a gallery owner to sell her wares. Of course, if Greta and Josiah had indeed had a long-term relationship, it was likely that she and Damon had crossed paths in the past.

However, Damon was working with Jenny Garth, who clearly hated her late uncle's self-proclaimed girlfriend. Somehow Abby rather doubted seeing Greta and Damon together would make the younger woman happy. Why would Damon risk setting off Jenny's volatile temper?

When he suddenly sat up taller and scanned the surrounding area, Abby took cover behind a cluster of people. She hesitated a few seconds before peering around the edge of the group to see if the coast was clear for her to make a hasty exit from the area. Madam G's attention was now aimed at a legal-sized envelope in Damon's hand. He said something and waited for her to respond. When she nodded, he tossed the envelope down in front of her and left.

Rather than risk being caught spying on the pair, Abby hustled back to the comparative safety of the information booth and Tripp. After all, the exchange between Damon and Madam G wasn't any of her business.

But it sure was curious.

Chapter 23

Abby had hoped that by some miracle Ben and Gage would've solved both murders and learned who attacked Madam G before she and Tripp had to leave for the séance. That would have saved everyone from having to sit through the performance the woman planned. But if they'd progressed on that front, they hadn't chosen to share it with her.

Now there was no choice but to head back to the fair one last time. When they reached the park, the food trucks and most of the vendors were already packed up and gone. Once again, they strolled along the river, enjoying the last few minutes of peace before they had to head for the one remaining large tent. As far as Abby was concerned, they could be the last two to arrive and the first two to leave. No doubt Tripp felt the same way. She tried skipping a stone with only marginal success. As she hunted for a flatter specimen to use next, she made a confession. "I have a bad feeling about this evening."

Tripp sent a rock skimming across the surface of the water, counting off five skips before it finally sank into the river. "Me too, but we're expected."

He turned to face her. "I don't know why that idiot woman insists on doing this or why she wants you there. My gut feeling is that everything is coming to a head. At least, Gage and Ben will be there to handle the fallout. My job is to protect you."

What could she say to that? That it wasn't his job? It wouldn't do any good. They both knew he'd taken on that role from the first time she'd crossed paths with a killer. He would always stand between her and any threat, no matter the risk to himself. He was that stubborn or maybe simply that determined. But what if something happened to him because of her . . . how would she ever live with that?

Surrendering to the inevitable, she took his hand and started the long walk back to the tent where the séance would take place. "Fine. We'll go, but we'll sit near the exit. And just know this, Mr. Blackston, we run for cover at the first sign of trouble."

"It's a deal."

They'd only gone a short distance when he spoke again. "So who do you think is behind all of this? I know that busy brain of yours must have some kind of theory by now."

Abby didn't bother denying it. "It's absolutely not Dayna, no matter what Ben and his people might think. Admittedly, she was an idiot for going anywhere near Wendy's house, but she stuck around until the police came. She wouldn't have done that if she'd done something wrong."

Tripp bumped her shoulder with his. "I believe you about Dayna, Abby. You can't blame Ben for having questions, though, especially since she and the victim had a very public disagreement right before Wendy disappeared. But once you eliminate her from the list of suspects, who else is left?"

Good question. She pondered it as they continued walking. "I can't help but think that it all circles back to Josiah Garth. After all, Wendy's booth was right next to his. It was right about the time he was killed that she packed up her stuff and left. Even if she was just upset because of her fight with Dayna, that wouldn't explain why she'd leave early when it would cost her sales. It's also strange that she didn't let anyone know why she was leaving or where she was going. Even if Wendy was in a hurry, it wouldn't have taken her long to tell one of her other friends at the fair what was going on."

Tripp walked on in silence for a few seconds before finally speaking. "Something must have spooked her into taking off like that. What could have scared her that much?"

Abby had been wondering the same thing herself. "Again, it had to be something to do with Josiah's death. Maybe she saw or heard something that she shouldn't have. I'm guessing Ben had that same thought since he was so intent on finding her as soon as possible."

By that point, Tripp looked pretty grim. "It would be interesting to know where she was hiding since he was killed. That is, assuming she only died in the last day or so. Did Ben say anything about the time frame of her death?"

The discussion made it seem as if the temperature had just dropped several degrees, making Abby wish she'd dressed warmer. "No, but I doubt he'd had time to learn anything definite when we talked to him yesterday."

They walked on in silence for a while, finally stopping just shy of the tent where people were starting to gather for the séance. Neither of them was in a hurry to go inside. Instead, they hovered a short distance away as they scanned the crowd for any side of Ben or Gage. When she finally spotted them in the distance, she leaned into Tripp's side and crossed her arms over her chest.

Trying to sound calmer than she felt, she whispered, "You always hear about artists' work increasing in value upon their deaths. It's hard to know if that's true or just an urban myth propagated by TV mysteries. But regardless, if I had to guess, it could come down to figuring out who would benefit the most from Josiah's death."

As she spoke, the line started snaking into the tent. Tripp nudged her forward. "Come on. It's showtime."

It didn't take long for the tent to fill to capacity. Tripp saved the two seats beside him for Gage and Ben while Abby saved another one for Dayna. Madam G had definitely gone all out for the affair. There was a table along the far side of the tent that displayed an array of refreshments. Most of the guests seemed happy to take advantage of the offerings, but right now Abby's stomach was too tied up in knots to eat anything.

Tripp also eyed the table. "I'm going to grab a cup of coffee. Would you like something?"

"Some tea would be nice."

When Gage left with Tripp, Ben slid over next to Abby. "How are you doing?"

She shrugged. "As well as can be expected. I almost skipped out on coming tonight, but that felt a bit cowardly. Any idea what Madam G is trying to accomplish?"

The detective didn't look any happier about having to be there than she did. "No, and I think doing this is especially idiotic considering what happened yesterday. I also don't want people to think that either I or Gage condone such interference in matters best left to the professionals."

"I don't blame you." She'd learned that lesson the hard way. "I haven't seen Madam G yet. Have you?"

Ben smiled and shook his head. "She's probably waiting to make a grand appearance."

Abby sat up straighter to get a better look around. She and Tripp had been so intent on claiming seats in the back row that she hadn't paid much attention to the rest of the tent. As soon as she spotted the large circular table at center front, she groaned. Given the crystal ball sitting in the middle, she had no doubt that was where the real theatrics of the night would take place. Worse yet, she suspected those small, folded pieces of brightly colored paper in front of each chair were place cards.

"What's wrong, Abby?"

She swallowed hard before answering. "Look at that circular table up front. It has a crystal ball in the middle and a folded card sitting by each chair. I'm guessing those cards have specific names on them."

He stood up long enough to study the scene. Never let it be said that Ben wasn't quick on the uptake, because he was already looking a bit sick when he sat back down. "My boss will bust me back to writing parking tickets if I get dragged up there to actually participate in this circus."

By that point, Gage and Tripp were on their way back. She exchanged glances with Ben. "Are you going to tell them or shall I?"

"Be my guest."

"Gee, thanks, Detective Earle."

She injected enough sarcasm into her words to make sure he understood full well she didn't appreciate being the bearer of bad news. "Did you guys notice the table up front? Ben and I were just wondering if any of our names are on those fancy place cards."

Gage immediately looked as aggravated about the situation as Ben did, but Tripp only appeared a bit confused. "What are you talking about?"

Abby tried again. "I suspect that Madam G decided to invite some special guests to join her at the table for the actual séance. Everyone else will be just spectators."

He went from confused to furious in a heartbeat. "There's no way you're going to sit up there, especially if I'm not invited, too."

Before she could respond, the lights strung along the back walls dimmed as Madam G finally made her appearance. She swept up the center aisle headed straight for the bright lights focused on the front of the tent. She wore a long, flowing gown done in shades of black and silver. Her nails were painted a deep red that matched her lipstick. If she had suffered any ill effects from yesterday's attack, they certainly didn't show.

Upon reaching the front of the tent, she paused and then spun back around to face the audience, her elegant gown swirling around her legs. "Ladies and gentlemen, thank you for coming. As you can see, a highly select group of guests will be invited to join me at the table. Once they are seated, we will begin. I do ask everyone to remain as quiet as possible. To get the best results, I need to be able to clear my mind and concentrate. Holding a séance is far from new to me, but it is the first time I will attempt to solve a tragic murder."

She paused for dramatic effect. "I'm speaking of the recent death of my dear friend Josiah Garth. In order to assist the police investigation, I will ask Josiah himself to identify the vile person who ended his life much too soon."

The tent went totally quiet as if everyone had stopped breathing for the space of three heart-beats. Even having suspected what the psychic had planned, Abby still had trouble getting her head around the idea. Yes, she understood why the woman wanted to see justice done. But why make a public spectacle of the whole affair?

The murmurs of conversation started up again, but all it took was one hard look from Madam G to restore order. "I will now call out the names of the people who will be assisting me at the table. Some choices will make immediate sense to you. Others, perhaps not so much. Please believe that each one was carefully chosen for what their energy will contribute to this evening's effort."

By that point, heads were spinning like tops as people tried to guess who had been lucky enough to make the cut or, to Abby's way of thinking, unfortunate enough. The psychic sure knew how to work her audience. Maybe it was her imagination, but Abby could have sworn Madam G looked straight at her. She did her best to hunch down far enough that she couldn't be seen over the rest of the crowd.

The ruse failed miserably. She'd no sooner ducked her head than her name rang out across the tent. "Would the following people please join me at the table? Abby McCree, Dayna Fisk, Detective Ben Earle, Chief of Police Gage Logan, Jenny Garth, and Damon Wray."

At that point, Jenny Garth rose from her seat on the outside aisle near the front of the crowd. "This is obscene, Greta. You have no right to put my family's pain on public display. What makes a charlatan like you think you can find Uncle Josiah's murderer when the police haven't been able to figure out what happened?"

Much to Abby's surprise, Madam G didn't look upset about Jenny interrupting her . . . performance, for the lack of a better word. No, she actually looked triumphant, as if somehow Jenny confronting her actually played right into her scheme.

Looking sympathetic, Madam G offered Jenny a smile, one probably meant to be conciliatory and comforting. Abby didn't know about Jenny, but it actually put her own teeth on edge.

By that point, people were watching to see if Abby and her companions would dutifully file to the front of the tent. So far, neither Ben nor Gage had made any move to leave their seats. As long as they remained rooted in place, Abby refused to do anything different. It wasn't as if any of them had asked to be invited to be an active participant in the Madam G show.

Meanwhile, the two women's conversation had grown even more heated. It was evidently Jenny's turn to lob another retort in Madam G's direction. "It's bad enough you make a living by suckering people into thinking you have some phony magical power that will help guide their lives." She glanced around the tent. "These folks came here tonight expecting to be entertained. Instead, they're witnessing you using my uncle's name for your own gain. You claim he mattered to you. If that were true, you wouldn't be playing games with his death. Sadly, it's just a cheap publicity stunt."

Then Jenny met Madam G's creepy smile with one of her own. "No wonder he dumped you."

Wow, that scored a direct hit. Madam G gasped and staggered back a step before catching herself. "How dare you, young lady! Your uncle and I shared a special relationship for longer than you've been alive. All couples have their ups and downs, but he and I always came back to each other."

Then she pointed one of her blood-red nails at Jenny. "You, young lady, are the one who profited off of his artistic talent. He generously shared the gift of his art with you. And how did you repay him? With treachery."

Jenny gasped in outrage and charged toward

the psychic. Gage was up and running to plant himself between the two women before they could do any real harm to each other. When Jenny tried to do an end run around him, Ben joined the fray and prevented her from reaching her target.

He glared down at her. "That's enough, Miss Garth."

Then he glanced back over his shoulder at Madam G. "You too. Any more of this, and you'll both be seeing the inside of one of Gage's jail cells."

That pronouncement immediately took all the wind out of their sails. Ben held Jenny's gaze while Gage rode herd on Madam G. "It's time you got this show on the road. All of these fine people deserve better than to watch the two of you tear into each other. I suggest you get back to business."

Madam G finally took a step back and nodded after giving Jenny one last hard look. "My apologies, ladies and gentlemen. I haven't been quite myself since learning of Josiah's death, and there have been other events over the past two days that have also taken their toll."

Then she briefly tilted her head to the side to acknowledge her nemesis once again. "Jenny, we have our differences, but I would greatly appreciate it if you would take your seat at the table. The sooner we get started, the sooner all of us will get the answers we seek."

Jenny remained glued to the spot for several more seconds before finally moving. She didn't say a word as she circled the table before stopping in front of a chair situated with its back to the audience. Next, Madam G held out her hand as if to guide Gage and Ben to their seats. Instead of following her unspoken order, Ben headed toward Abby. She'd so hoped they would have forgotten about her in the kerfuffle, but no such luck.

Ben stopped at the end of the aisle, all of his attention focused on Tripp rather than Abby. "I'll make sure she's seated between me and Gage."

There wasn't much Tripp could do about the situation. Turning to her, he said, "I'll be right here. At the first sign of trouble, I promise I'll get you out of here no matter who I have to run over to do it."

She kissed his cheek before she accepted Ben's help in making her way to the front of the tent. Madam G started to say something when Ben rearranged the place cards to make good on his promise to Tripp about where Abby would be sitting. One look at Ben's expression, the psychic gave up the fight and moved to stand behind her own place at the table.

There were two chairs left to be filled. After glancing around the tent, Madam G called out, "Ms. Fisk, are you here?"

No answer. Abby looked around in case she'd missed seeing Dayna arrive, but there was no sign of her. If she'd changed her mind about coming, why hadn't she let Abby know? She had known that Abby would be worried. She quickly sent a text and hoped her friend would answer.

Meanwhile, Madam G tried to locate the second missing person on her list. "It would seem that Ms. Fisk chose not to attend tonight. But Damon Wray, I know you're here somewhere. Please quit being childish and come to the table."

Once again silence reigned supreme for several

seconds before the man in question finally stalked into the tent. Abby didn't know what he'd been doing, but this was the most unkempt she'd seen him look. His hair was rumpled, and his flannel shirt and jeans had certainly seen better days. Damon ignored everyone except their hostess. "Greta, stop this farce. I thought we'd already settled this."

Settled what? Sadly, Madam G didn't explain. Instead, she patiently waited until he reluctantly took his designated spot between Jenny and Gage. With her last guest finally in place, Madam G removed the chair that had been reserved for Dayna and set it out of the way. Then she turned on a small stereo located in the corner. The soft sound of a flute filled the silence as she returned to the table.

"All right, everyone, please remain silent. I am about to invite the spirits to join us, which requires concentration on my part."

Then she sat down, and smiled at each person in turn. "Please lay your hands on the table and do not move them. That will help all of us to focus on sharing our energy."

One by one, they all complied. Abby doubted anyone other than Madam G really thought hand placement actually accomplished anything. At this point, she'd do anything to get this whole thing over with as fast as possible.

Madam G gently swayed from side to side in time to the music, a slight smile on her face. "You may close your eyes if you wish."

Abby wasn't about to do that, not when it would leave her vulnerable to attack if things went wrong. Since no one else took the woman up on her suggestion, she wasn't the only one who felt that way.

"Come, welcome guests. Please make your presence known."

The sudden chill in the tent was probably due to Abby's always overactive imagination kicking into hyperdrive. That didn't make the goose bumps on her arms any less real. Even Gage shifted uncomfortably in his chair as they all waited for some kind of response to Madam G's invitation. The moment seemed to drag on forever, the only sound besides the music was the restless stirrings of their greater audience.

When Abby's nerves were stretched to the breaking point, Madam G's head fell forward and then jerked back up, her eyes wide and unfocused. She stared into the distance as she stage-whispered just two words.

"They come."

Chapter 24

"Who comes?"

Abby was wondering the same thing, but it was Jenny who asked. Madam G aimed a dark look in her direction but didn't respond. Evidently taking questions from the audience wasn't part of her shtick. Instead, the psychic closed her eyes and drew several slow breaths. When she spoke again, her voice had dropped nearly an octave.

"As we hoped, it is Josiah who approaches. He's not alone."

Ben slid his hands to the edge of the table and gripped it hard enough to turn his knuckles white. It was hard to figure what was going on in his head right now, but Abby bet that it wasn't a bunch of happy thoughts bouncing around in there. Gage looked much the same, while Damon Wray looked a bit ashen. Jenny actually glanced up at the peaked roof of the tent as if expecting to see her uncle's ghost descending from above.

By that point, Madam G sounded more like her

normal self. "We welcome you both to our gathering. We have come here to learn the truth of your passing and to see that the guilty parties are brought to justice. Only then will you be able to rest in peace."

She went back to swaying. "Josiah, your death has left a huge hole in all of our lives. I miss you so much."

The woman's voice cracked a little right at the end. It might have been another bit of theatrics, but Abby was inclined to believe the emotion was genuine. After pausing to regain control, Madam G continued. "Speak through me, Josiah, and tell us what happened that tragic day."

Then she threw her arms out to the side, and her head fell back as if her neck would no longer support it. The sudden motion caused Abby to jump, and she wasn't the only one spooked by the woman's ever more dramatic actions.

"We beseech you to answer, Josiah. You too, Ms. Larabie, if that is you I sense."

Ben muttered "Oh, brother" under his breath.

His comment pretty much summed up Abby's feelings on the subject. She'd give this another couple of minutes, and then she was going to break the circle and march right on out of the tent. It was a sure bet that Gage, Ben, and Tripp would join her determined parade. Unfortunately, Madam G upped the ante.

"Ms. Larabie, I do believe that you were just in the wrong place at the wrong time. I fear perhaps it was your curiosity about what happened inside Josiah's tent that proved to be your downfall. Running as you did set the killer on your trail."

At that point, Madam G tilted her head to the side as if straining to listen. "You say you were held prisoner where no one would think to look. Can you be more specific? Ah, yes, that's much better. I see woods. A stream. A narrow road. Mountains in the background to the east. Do you know how they found you?"

There was another long pause as if she were listening to someone before her narration resumed. "You thought it was safe to return home, but they were watching. There was a struggle before they managed to drag you out of your workshop. You were injured in the process and bled quite profusely. That's all you remember until you woke up to the sound of an argument."

Madam G frowned as she pretended to listen to something no one else could hear. She addressed her next comments directly to Ben Earle. "Detective, the young lady wants you to know that her younger captor hoped to find some way to let her go. The second one insisted they couldn't risk letting a witness live. In her weakened state, it didn't take much effort to end her life. She's starting to fade now and can't remember anything more specific."

A slight movement on each side of Abby drew her focus away from Madam G and toward the two members of the police seated beside her. She had no idea when they'd each brought out their spiral notebooks. They might not appreciate Madam G turning their investigations into the equivalent of one of those true crime shows on television, but it wasn't stopping them from taking notes.

"Thank you, Ms. Larabie, for sharing your tragic story with us. Please be at peace."

Abby hoped that Wendy was at peace as well, but she still wasn't buying into Madam G's one-sided conversation. Once again, the psychic raised her face toward the top of the tent, her eyes tightly closed as she waited for the next guest to speak. From the length of the wait, it seemed Josiah wasn't in the mood to chat. That was assuming he'd even made an appearance at all. From the whispers from the audience, Abby wasn't the only one who was getting bored with the whole situation.

Picking up on the growing discontent, Madam G flung her hands upward in supplication. "Josiah, speak to me this one last time. Help bring your killer to justice. Let those who betrayed you and used your talent for their own benefit be exposed for the thieves they are. Only then you will be able to rest in peace."

Jenny Garth shoved her chair back from the table and glared across at the psychic. "This is ridiculous. And why am I not surprised? I'll tell you. It's because you're ridiculous and always have been. I'm out of here."

Madam G wasn't having it. "Sit back down, young lady."

"Are you going to make me, old lady?"

Jenny had definitely hit a hot button. Madam G huffed in disgust. "Just because you act like a child, that doesn't make me old."

"Uncle Josiah must have thought you were, because the women he's dated lately were a whole lot younger. They also had better taste." She pointed at the other woman. "Seriously, who wears a ridiculous outfit like that in public and still expects to be taken seriously?"

This was getting uglier by the minute, but the audience was getting its money's worth, even if the spirits weren't currently the ones putting on the show. It was doubtful that anyone other than those at the table could see the sheen of tears in Madam G's eyes. The woman herself paid no attention to them, not even to blink to clear her vision. Instead, she rose to her feet with great dignity and met Jenny glare for glare. "Leave. Your negativity helps no one. Not you, not me, and certainly not your uncle."

Jenny's angry veneer cracked just a little. "There is no help for Uncle Josiah. Dead is dead. Nothing will change that."

She walked out of the tent, head held high as she ignored the rows of gawkers she passed on her way out. When she was out of sight, Madam G once again turned her attention to the matter at hand. "If you will all please do your best to clear your minds of that unfortunate incident, we will continue."

At that point, Damon Wray shook his head and clenched his hands into fists. "Jenny's right. Greta, this is insane. End this now, or you will regret it."

Was that a threat? From the way both Ben and Gage tensed up, they sure thought so. Both men were braced for action if the gallery owner made even the slightest move in the wrong direction.

The lady herself was made of stern stuff. She raised her eyebrows and calmly stared down Damon. "Leave if you want, but that won't stop the truth from coming out. Josiah knows what happened. Once I have learned the facts of the situation, I will take appropriate action against the guilty."

"Seriously? Who appointed you judge and jury?" He gestured toward Ben and Gage. "In case you've forgotten, these men are the professionals, which is why you invited them. It's their job to figure out what happened to Josiah and the other victim. You should have never gotten involved. I doubt you ever met the girl who died, and you have no way to prove the two cases are even connected."

Damon then offered her a chilling smile. "For the record, Jenny was right about how Josiah felt about you. He complained to anyone who would listen that you wouldn't accept the fact that whatever it was you two had shared was over. And like Jenny, I'm out of here."

Before walking away, he once again pointed at Gage and then Ben. "I will be contacting whoever holds the other end of your leashes to make sure they know how you're wasting tax-payer dollars."

Abby's pulse pounded a heavy rhythm in her head. Was he going to turn on her next? She really hoped his tirade had run its course. But no such luck. If anything his temper burned even hotter by the time he got to her. "And you, I don't know how you managed to get yourself sucked into this circus, but you have no business poking your nose in police business. Sneaking around and spying on people isn't just rude; it's dangerous."

With that grim pronouncement, Damon took a step back from the table and turned to leave. At the last second, he turned back one last time to look at her. "Think about this, Ms. McCree. Maybe there's a lesson to be learned from what happened to that potter."

His attack left her shaken to the core, but right now Damon had a lot bigger problem on his hands. Tripp was up and moving, charging toward him with furious determination. She was dimly aware of people scrambling toward the exit. Smart move on their part, and Abby heartily wished that she could join the exodus. But right now there were four riled-up men between her and the exit.

Madam G slid over into Gage's empty seat and took her by the arm. "Best we let the men sort things out."

Meanwhile, Ben took charge of Damon Wray while Gage tried to head Tripp off at the pass. The gallery owner might be physically fit, but it was unlikely that he had the right kind of training to take on someone who had spent twenty years as an elite soldier. Like Tripp, Gage had served in the Special Forces and was well equipped to keep him from doing something stupid. While she appreciated Tripp's support, she didn't want him spending the night in a jail cell. That didn't mean she wouldn't like to punch Damon in the nose herself.

Gage planted himself in front of Tripp. "Back off, Blackston. We'll deal with this guy. You have other priorities. If you haven't noticed, you're scaring Abby right now."

His words hit home, because Tripp froze mid-motion to look right at her. "Are you all right?"

With some effort, she managed to sound far more calm than she actually felt. "He upset me. He didn't hurt me. I'll be fine."

He nodded but made no immediate move to

close the distance between them. Instead, Tripp returned his attention to Damon Wray. The man had taken cover behind Ben, showing a bit more common sense than Abby would have given him credit for at that moment. After all, what kind of idiot threatened people right in front of two police officers?

Tripp made no further move toward him, but it wouldn't take much to stir him into action. His voice was low and so, so cold when he spoke. "You don't ever threaten Abby again. Not now, not ever."

He didn't say what would happen to Damon if he did, but there was no need to spell it out. The threat of violence was all too clear in Tripp's rigid stance and the way he'd squeezed out each word through clenched teeth. Having made his point, Tripp gave the man a dismissive look and headed straight for Abby.

He knocked a couple of stray chairs to the side to reach the table. From the way he latched on to her, Abby suspected he needed a hug even more than she did. "I'm sorry I let him treat you with such disrespect. I kept thinking that either Ben or Gage would shut him up."

"It's not your fault, Tripp. His words don't mean anything."

Okay, that wasn't true. He'd sure made it sound as if he knew something about why Wendy had been killed. If Ben or Gage noticed that, too, Damon might have some hard explaining to do. Even if he had no direct involvement, they wouldn't appreciate him not coming forward with any information he had on the subject.

"Let's go home."

Tripp eased his ironclad hold on her. "Good idea."

Before making a move, though, he spoke to Madam G. "How about you? Would you like us to escort you to your car?"

How like him to worry about someone else who might be vulnerable to attack tonight. His concern for her had Madam G smiling. "Thank you, but I'll be fine. I need to finish packing up a few things before I can leave. There's also a good chance the detective or the chief of police will have a few questions for me as well. If so, I'm sure they'll make sure I reach my car safely."

She looked around at the scattered chairs and sighed. "I have to confess that not everyone is happy with the results whenever I give a reading or do a séance. Having said that, I've never had the entire audience bolt out the door before. I'm not sure whether this disaster will hurt my reputation or enhance it."

With that, she walked away, shaking her head as she packed up the stereo and crystal ball. Abby hated to leave the woman alone, especially now that the sun had gone down. That didn't keep her from willingly following Tripp when he headed for the exit. Gage caught up with them just outside of the tent.

"Are you two all right?"

When Tripp didn't respond, Abby stepped into the breach. "We're fine. Really, we are. Everyone's emotions were running hot tonight, so it's no surprise that things got said that shouldn't have."

Gage ran his fingers through his hair in frustration. "We should have found a way to put a stop to this farce when Madam G first floated the idea. It doesn't matter whether or not she really has some magical connection to the afterlife. Whoever killed Garth, Ms. Larabie, and attacked Madam G is still out there. How could folks not realize pulling a stunt like this makes as much sense as poking a beehive with a stick?"

He patted Tripp on the shoulder. "Sorry I had to go all hard-nosed on you in there, but I couldn't let you unleash your temper on Mr. Wray. That would be like letting a Chihuahua face off against a Great Dane."

That image had her laughing, and even Tripp cracked a little bit of a smile. "Even assuming I'm the Great Dane in that scenario, I'm not sure that was exactly a compliment about my fighting prowess, but thanks for stepping in."

Abby tugged on Tripp's hand. "Let's get going. I promised Zeke a walk when we got home, and we still have to do something about dinner."

"How about we pick up Zeke and head for Gary's Drive-in for cheeseburgers and shakes. We can walk along the river afterward."

It would do them all some good to get away from everything for a while. "Good idea."

Gage was looking pretty wistful by that time. "Dang, that sounds good. Unfortunately, Ben and I will be working for a while yet. Have fun." He disappeared back inside the tent.

Abby asked, "Should we offer to bring them something from Gary's?"

Tripp didn't hesitate. "Not this time. Let them fend for themselves for once. We both know if we show up at city hall with burgers for the two of them, everyone else in Gage's department will be upset we didn't bring them anything. And if we invite them over to the house, we'll end up talking about this entire fiasco for hours."

She couldn't argue with his logic. "Okay, burgers for three it is, and then we'll head home and then the two of us will head straight to bed."

As they made their way down the path toward Main Street, she tried to figure out what Tripp was thinking as they walked. And what was behind the very odd expression that had briefly appeared on his face after hearing her plans for the rest of the evening?

Chapter 25

After the debacle at the séance, Abby really appreciated that Monday hadn't presented her with any new drama. Of course, the respite would've been better if she wasn't sure it was only a matter of time before the other shoe dropped. A great big one. With spikes, the kind that would do some serious harm when it landed.

Tuesday was starting off in much the same way, but at least she wasn't alone. Tripp had spent the last two nights on her couch. But even with that extra layer of protection so close at hand, she'd only slept in fits and starts. Somewhere in the neighborhood of three in the morning, Zeke had given her a disgusted snort and stalked out of her bedroom in search of someplace quieter to sleep.

She hadn't blamed the dog one bit.

He stood waiting for her at the bottom of the steps when she'd finally given up on sleep altogether and trudged downstairs. Tripp was still asleep in the living room, so she patted the dog on the head and motioned for him to follow her down the hall into the kitchen. She waited until after she'd set the coffeepot in motion before turning to face her roommate.

Zeke immediately sat down at her feet and hung his head, which made her feel even worse than she already did. The poor boy obviously felt guilty for abandoning her during the night. She knelt and wrapped her arms around him. "It's all right, big guy. There was no reason both of us should lose sleep. I still love you."

That earned her a slurpy lick up the side of her face, making her grateful she hadn't yet showered. Zeke's doggy kisses tended to be a bit sticky, not that she ever complained about it. Such devoted love was a gift to be cherished. Their hug continued until the sound of shuffling footsteps headed their way caught Zeke's attention. When Tripp appeared in the doorway, the dog wagged his tail but made no move to leave Abby's embrace in favor of his best buddy.

The man looked as if he were sleepwalking with a bad case of bed head. Not to mention he could really use a shave. "Is the coffee ready?"

"Almost."

"Good." He frowned and blinked several times as if trying to figure out what he needed to do next. "Can you pour me a to-go cup while I grab a quick shower over at my place? I have a big exam this morning, and my study group is meeting to review for the test."

Abby released her hold on Zeke and pushed

herself back up to her feet, ignoring the creakiness of her back and legs. "Do you want some breakfast before you go?"

"No, but thanks for the offer. I promised to pick up a bunch of breakfast sandwiches at a drive-thru on my way over to the college. I could also get the coffee there, but yours is better."

"So I've managed to turn you into a coffee snob."

"Yep, it's all your fault. I'll be back in a few."

Should she point out he was barefoot and the grass was wet from an overnight shower? Too late. He was already out the door and heading for home. "Guess I got my marching orders, Zeke. One coffee to go."

It wasn't quite done brewing, so she fed Zeke before hunting down one of the to-go cups that seemed to migrate from Tripp's house to hers. She decided to wait until he was on his way back before fixing his drink. In the meantime, she got out a tub of yogurt for her own breakfast. She lacked the energy for anything more elaborate. Rather than sit at the table, she ate over the sink so she could watch out the window for Tripp.

She was just finishing her makeshift meal when he finally reappeared. His coffee was poured and ready to go before he made it in her back door. He'd made good use of his time. The man definitely cleaned up quite nicely, but he also now looked alert and ready for the day. It occurred to her that he hadn't gone for his early morning run, a rarity on his part.

"How come you didn't go pounding the pavement for your usual five or ten miles this morning?"

He grabbed the cup out of her hand and took a sip. "No time and no energy. If I live through my exam today, maybe Zeke and I will head out for a run when I get back. What are your plans for the day?"

She'd been pondering that herself. "Not sure I really have any. I'll probably catch up on some chores or finish the quilt I've been working on for Bridey's baby. If I can muster up the energy, I might even do some grocery shopping. The fridge is pretty empty."

Tripp set his cup aside and stepped closer. "You be careful. In fact, hold off on the store. We'll go together after I get back."

His tone made it more of an order than a question, but she answered anyway. "I don't expect you to babysit me wherever I go."

He cupped her cheek with his hand. She leaned into his touch, taking comfort from the warmth. "Lock the door behind me, and I'm not babysitting. I'm protecting what's mine."

Then he was gone, leaving her standing there sputtering in shock. As she did as ordered and locked the door, she looked to Zeke for advice. "What am I to make of that last comment? If I'm his, does that make him officially mine?"

Because she really liked that idea a whole lot.

Instead of expressing any opinion on the subject, Zeke opted for a diversionary tactic by staring up at his treat jar with a hopeful look. She didn't really blame him for not wanting to tread a potential minefield between his two favorite humans. As she tossed him one of his favorite pumpkin cookies, she apologized. "Sorry, Zeke. I know you don't like to take sides. Why don't you go take a nap while I vacuum?"

At the mention of that last word, Zeke tore out of the kitchen and charged up the steps to take sanctuary as far from the hated noisemaker as possible. She tried not to laugh, but his fear of the vacuum cleaner just seemed ridiculous. At ninety-five pounds, Zeke far outweighed the vacuum cleaner and could easily outrun it. Still, everyone had their foibles. He was fearless when confronting spiders, no matter their size, while Abby cowered in fear until Tripp ushered the eight-legged terrors outside where they belonged.

Although housework was never at the top of her list of favorite things, today it was soothing to do something that didn't require a lot of thinking but kept her too busy to brood. She was just finishing up when she got a text message from Dayna. Whew! She'd tried calling her several times since the séance but with no luck. She'd left a message for her to call, so it was nice to finally hear back from her.

Hey there! Sorry I've been missing in action. I wasn't feeling well and didn't hang around for the séance on Sunday. Still under the weather. Any chance you could bring me some chicken soup from the diner? I've been craving it all day, and I live outside of their delivery area.

Abby didn't immediately leap into action. Tripp hadn't wanted her to go out in public alone, but surely she'd be safe enough picking up an order at the diner. Since she was going there anyway, she'd also get soup for her and Tripp to go with sandwiches for dinner.

First, though, she'd let him know where she was going and about what time she should be back. Most likely he'd have his phone muted while he was taking the test, but he'd check for messages as soon as he was done.

Hi! I hope your test wasn't too hard. Dayna finally texted. **She's sick and asked if I could drop by with some of Frannie's chicken soup. I'll pick up some for us while I'm at it. I don't plan on hanging out at Dayna's. I'm also craving a latte from Something's Brewing, and I promised Zeke some treats. He wants me to get something for us, too, so we don't eat his. See you soon.**

"Zeke, I won't be gone long."

She gave his head a quick rub and headed for the kitchen to grab her purse and keys. Using the diner's app on her phone, she placed a to-go order for the chicken soup. While she did that, Zeke parked himself by the door and gave her a hopeful look. Evidently she wasn't the only one who was getting restless. "This won't be much of an outing. Mostly you'll be waiting in the car, but at least you can give the wind a good sniff as we drive through town."

He woofed happily and bolted for the car as soon as she opened the back door. Careful to lock it on her way out, she joined Zeke at the car. Once he was comfortably ensconced on his blanket in the back seat, she lowered both back windows for him before heading toward the diner. After stopping at the diner, she'd head straight for Dayna's house to drop off her soup while it was still hot and then stop by Something's Brewing on the way back home. If she'd heard from Tripp by then, she'd ask if he'd like a latte, too.

Once again she wondered what degree her handsome tenant was working toward. Eventually he'd have to tell her. After all, he did plan to graduate at some point. "Zeke, has Tripp ever told you what he was studying to be?"

As soon as she asked the question, Zeke snorted and went back to drooling on the outside of the car as he checked the wind for interesting scents. She laughed and shook her head. "I'm guessing you wouldn't tell me even if you could talk. You two are thicker than thieves."

That just earned her another snort.

She whipped into a parking spot in front of the diner and rolled up Zeke's windows, leaving just a three-inch gap at the top to keep the air circulating while she ran inside. When Zeke protested, she met his gaze in the rearview mirror. "Don't worry. I'll be right back, big guy."

When she stepped inside the diner, the owner herself was packing up Abby's order. Frannie held out the bag. "I had them double-check the order when I didn't see any pie listed. That's not like you, especially when some of this is probably for Tripp."

She was right to wonder about that, but Abby couldn't very well tell her that they were going to get their sugar fix from a different source, without risking offending Frannie. The woman didn't react well when she thought someone wasn't treating her wares with the right amount of respect.

"Actually, I'm baking this afternoon. Zeke is getting low on treats."

The explanation was pretty weak, but at least Frannie seemed satisfied. "Well, tell the fur ball hi for me."

"Will do."

With that, Abby picked up the bag and headed back out to the car. It didn't take long to reach Dayna's place. Her small van was parked in the driveway. No surprise there since her garage had been converted into the studio where she made her pottery. Oddly, though, the house had an empty look about it, and there were no lights on. Granted, it was early afternoon and light outside. Add in the fact that it sounded as if Dayna wasn't feeling at all well, she was probably holed up in her bedroom at the back of the house.

"Zeke, this won't take long."

For that reason, she didn't bother rolling up his windows when she got out of the car and headed for the front door. She rang the doorbell and waited to see if that got any response. If Dayna had fallen back to sleep, she might not hear it. When there was no response, Abby tried again, this time pushing the button three times in quick succession.

Still nothing.

After knocking several more times, Abby tried the studio. It seemed unlikely that Dayna would be working if she'd been sick enough to ask her to deliver chicken soup. Just as she expected, the door was locked, and the lights were off. Fortunately, there was enough sunshine filtering in through a skylight for her to see inside. Dayna was nowhere

in sight, but there was what looked like an unfin-
ished vase slumped over on the potter's wheel.

That had Abby stepping back, a frisson of fear
running through her. No matter how sick Dayna
might be, she wouldn't leave a mess like that even
if she didn't feel up to finishing the piece. Except
for there being no overt sign of violence, the scene
reminded her of what Dayna had encountered at
Wendy's house.

It was tempting to get the heck out of Dodge.
But before hustling back to where she'd left the
car, she veered across the yard to peek in the windows on the back of the house. Dayna's bedroom
curtains were drawn, blocking any chance of seeing if she was in there. The vertical blinds on the
sliding door that led into the kitchen were closed,
too.

The good news was that the ones over the kitchen sink were open. The bad news was the window
was out of reach. As much as she wanted to simply
walk away, she'd never forgive herself if she did,
only to find out that Dayna had really needed her.
With some effort, she dragged an old-fashioned
Adirondack chair across the patio and positioned
it under the window. Standing in the seat didn't
help, so she grabbed on to the windowsill and put
her right foot on one arm of the chair and then
lifted her left one onto the other arm. Shading her
eyes with one hand against the glass, she peered
through the window and immediately spotted Ben
Earle lying on the floor. He wasn't moving, and his
head was facing her with a streak of dried blood
on his cheek.

She started to pound on the window to get his attention, but stopped before her fist made contact with the glass. Her heart slammed in her chest with the realization she could be putting both of them in more danger. If whoever had done this to Ben was still around, she couldn't chance drawing their attention in her direction. She needed to call 9-1-1, but not until she reached the relative safety of her car. Silently apologizing to the detective, she scrambled back down off the chair.

Making a run for the car was an excellent plan, one Tripp would definitely approve. He was a firm believer in her ducking for cover whenever trouble raised its ugly head. Sadly, the bad guys always found a way to derail her best intentions.

Chapter 26

Abby reached the corner of the house before her luck ran out. So close, but she had no choice but to come to a screeching halt when Jenny Garth stepped out from behind the garage with a gun pointed right at her. The younger woman's clothes looked as if she'd been sleeping in them, and her ponytail was skewed to one side with several strands of hair hanging down around her face. Unfortunately, disheveled didn't mean she wasn't dangerous.

When Abby dared to take one more step, Jenny shook her head. "That's far enough. I don't particularly want to shoot you, but that doesn't mean I won't. Back up."

Having no choice, Abby slowly retreated. With each step, she cursed her bad luck. Why hadn't she called for help the second she'd spotted Ben? Or better yet, left as soon as she suspected Dayna might not actually be home? Her captor remained strangely silent as she matched Abby step-for-step until they both reached the patio. When Jenny didn't issue any more orders, Abby asked the obvious question. "What now, Jenny? So far, you haven't hurt me. Why not walk away while you can?"

"Because I have no intention of going to prison. The second you call the police—and don't bother denying that's exactly what you will do—they'll be on my trail."

She wasn't wrong about that, so Abby changed topics. "Are you the one who hurt Ben?"

When Jenny only looked puzzled, Abby tried again. "You know, the homicide detective who is investigating your uncle's murder. It looks like someone knocked him out in Dayna's kitchen."

Rolling her eyes, Jenny gave Abby an incredulous look. "Seriously, do you really think I'm that gullible?"

"See for yourself." Abby gestured toward the chair she'd left parked under the window. "You'll have to climb up there to be able to see inside. That's what I did."

Jenny wasn't buying it. "Again, I'm not stupid. The second I climb up there, you would be off and running."

Abby wanted to scream in frustration. This discussion was getting them nowhere. "So why are you here if not because of Ben?"

"I could ask you the same thing."

"That's simple. It's because I thought Dayna wanted some soup." She slowly reached down to pull a container out of the bag she'd left on the patio. "I received a text from her saying she was sick and wanted some chicken soup from the diner in town."

As she spoke, there was a faint scraping noise coming from the front of the house. Not sure if she was right about what she'd heard, she kept talking. "Frannie's chicken soup tastes really good when you're under the weather. I bought her a double order if you'd like to give it a try. I don't mean this as an insult, but you look like you haven't slept in a while. If that's true, I'm guessing you've also missed a few meals."

Jenny snorted. "Seriously, woman, are you for real? I'm standing here with a gun pointed at you, and you're trying to feed me. Who does something like that?"

No one Abby knew, but right now she'd offer anything to keep Jenny's attention focused on her. "Well, you can't blame me for wanting to stay on your good side."

"If you wanted to do that, you should have kept your busybody nose out of my business from the start."

At that point, Jenny had lowered the barrel of the gun slightly, but she brought it back up as she spoke. Abby recognized how much danger she was in, but she had no idea what else she could do to de-escalate the situation. "I never meant to cause you any problems, Jenny."

The girl shrugged as if Abby's intentions meant nothing to her. "But you did."

The chill in her words matched the dead look in her eyes. The combination had Abby having to lock her knees to remain upright. "So what happens next?"

Not that she really wanted to know the answer to that question. Fortunately, Zeke intervened before Jenny could share her evil plans. He charged around the end of the house headed straight for them. "Get her, Zeke!"

At the same time, she heaved the soup right at Jenny's face. It was no longer hot enough to burn, but the combination of being hit with it at the same time the dog plowed into her had Jenny down on the ground and screaming. She dropped the gun as she swiped at her eyes, trying to clear her vision.

Abby lunged forward to grab the gun up off the ground and train it on Jenny as she called Zeke to her side. "Good boy!"

When Jenny started to push herself up from the ground, Abby snapped, "No, you stay down there."

She made sure her prisoner was going to comply with her orders before pulling out her cell phone to call for help. Before she'd done more than dial the first "one," another person joined the party. "Jenny, why am I not surprised to see that you've managed to screw up again?"

Jenny shot a nasty look in Abby's direction. "She threw soup at me and sicced that vicious dog on me."

Damon Wray finally moved into Abby's peripheral vision. "And which of the three of you had the gun? Seems to me that would have given you a distinct advantage."

He kept his own gun pointed right at Zeke.

Smart man. He'd evidently guessed Abby wouldn't put Zeke at risk to save herself. Looking disgusted, Damon studied his partner in crime for several seconds before returning his attention back to Abby. "Do I really have to tell you to drop the gun?"

When she carefully set the pistol down on the ground, he motioned toward it with his own. "Pick it up, Jenny."

She struggled up to her feet, still blinking to clear her eyes of the soup. When she retrieved the other gun and retreated to a safer distance, Damon gave Zeke a considering look. "Keep that dog under control if you want him to live through the day."

Abby latched on to Zeke's collar and did her best to angle her body so she stood between him and Damon. This wasn't the first time a killer had threatened her dog, and she didn't like it any better this time. She noticed Damon hadn't said anything about *her* surviving this encounter. "If I'm going to die, I'd like to at least know what Josiah did to deserve one of his yard stakes through his heart."

Jenny was doing her best to wipe the rest of the soup off her face with the hem of her T-shirt. "I wouldn't know. I didn't kill him."

"Shut up, Jenny. There's no reason to satisfy Ms. McCree's curiosity. We would've all been better off if you'd simply avoided talking to her in the first place."

Jenny stamped her foot and glared at Damon. "None of this is my fault."

He sighed. "I've had enough of your temper

tantrums. No wonder Josiah was planning on ending your apprenticeship."

She gasped. "That's a lie! He couldn't keep up with the demand for his work without my help. He made a lot of money off my talent while he paid me a mere pittance."

Damon scoffed at her high opinion of her role in her late uncle's life. "Face it, kid. We both know that your real talent was your ability to copy Josiah's work. It's not like you ever had an original thought of your own."

If the situation hadn't been so dire, Abby would have made some popcorn and pulled up a chair to enjoy the spectacle. But with both combatants armed with guns, and tempers running hot, she was well aware that it wouldn't take much for the situation to turn deadly. Meanwhile, Jenny went on the attack. "Do the police know why Uncle Josiah had decided to sever his relationship with you? That's what the two of you were fighting about that day at the fair."

She sneered at Damon before turning to face Abby more directly. "Uncle Josiah had figured out that Damon here has been cheating him on the pieces he sold through his gallery. He accused him of lying about how much he got for them and then taking a higher percentage of the money than he was entitled to."

Her smile turned malicious. "It would've ruined Damon's reputation and put his precious art gallery at risk if Uncle Josiah had gone blabbing that stuff around in the art community. And that's exactly what he would've done. We both know that."

Damon's face flushed red-hot as he raked his fingers through his hair in frustration. "Don't go sounding all high-and-mighty, Jenny. You've got no room to talk. Just imagine how your dear uncle would've reacted if he learned that you had me sell some of your pieces, but under his name so they'd fetch a higher price. Is that why you killed him?"

Jenny jerked as if Damon's accusation landed a physical blow. "For the last time, I wasn't even there. It's more likely you came sneaking back around after I left for the cabin. That Larabie woman must've seen you and probably tried to blackmail you. That's why you ended up killing her, too."

Abby's fingers itched to be taking notes about all of this. Both Gage and Ben would have loved to have been included in this conversation. She only hoped she could survive long enough to tell them about it.

The growling sound Damon made as Jenny continued to hurl accusations in his direction would have done Zeke proud. Abby continued to stroke the dog's head while she tried to come up with a viable plan to get the two of them out of the danger zone. Meanwhile, the argument continued.

Damon took two determined steps toward Jenny, which had her backpedaling like crazy. "Quit trying to pin his death on me, Jenny. Your uncle and I knocked heads plenty of times over the years, but we always got past it. This time would have been no different. You saw me leave the fair. The police have questioned everyone and their brother. Not one person has claimed that I came back. And as far as the Larabie woman goes, I never saw or spoke to her that day."

By that point, Jenny looked more confused than angry. "But if you didn't kill them, then who did?"

For the second time, a new arrival joined the conversation, this one far more welcome. Abby's knees finally gave out, and she abruptly dropped to the ground next to Zeke as Gage Logan's voice rang out over the backyard. "That's a good question, Miss Garth, one we'd all like to learn the answer to. Considering we have the place surrounded, why don't the two of you put down your guns, and we'll continue this conversation down at the police station."

Damon muttered a few choice words as he very slowly set his gun down on the ground and then raised his hands high over his head. Jenny remained frozen in position for the longest time before she finally followed suit. Everyone breathed a huge sigh of relief, or at least Abby assumed they did. She remained seated on the ground with Zeke, content to let Gage and his people take charge of the situation.

It wasn't long before a large pair of feet appeared in front of her. Zeke woofed happily as Tripp squatted down to her eye level. "Are you hurt?"

"No, just resting."

From the concern in his dark eyes, she figured her smile was as unsteady as her knees had been a few minutes before. "Can we go home?"

It was Gage who answered her. "Not quite yet. Ben wants to talk to you."

Tripp immediately stood and then offered her a

hand up off the ground. "I thought the EMTs wanted him to go to the hospital to get checked out."

"Yeah, they did, but the stubborn idiot refused to go. He's really ticked off that someone got the drop on him. Heaven help whoever conked him on the head when he finds them."

That was surprising. Well, not that he felt that way. Just that he didn't know who had attacked him. "He didn't see who it was?"

"Why don't you sit down until we get done here?" Gage pointed toward the chair under the window. He waited until she was seated before he answered her question. "If he saw them at all, maybe it will come back to him."

She hoped Ben recovered his memories, but she also had a more pressing issue on her mind. "I'm actually more interested in what he knows about Dayna."

Before she could launch into an explanation of everything that had happened, Ben joined them. He was sporting a bandage on his forehead and an attitude that made it clear that the next person who crossed him would regret it mightily.

"Abby, I'm sorry I wasn't of more help with those two idiots. I had just regained consciousness when I heard Jenny and her buddy arguing. I was in no shape to rush to your rescue. Heck, I barely had the strength to call in the cavalry."

He still looked as if a stiff breeze would send him cartwheeling across the yard. "I wondered how Gage managed to show up just in the nick of time. Anyway, why were you here anyway? And where is Dayna?"

Before responding, Ben took one of the other two chairs, wincing as he did so. "I'm not sure. I got a text that she had important information for me. When I got to the house, the front door was ajar. When I called out Dayna's name and got no response, I came inside and started looking around."

He stopped to rub the back of his head. "The last thing I remember clearly was walking into the kitchen where someone must have clocked me from behind. I woke up on the floor not remembering how I got there."

That matched with what she'd seen. "All the doors were locked when I got here. I knocked and knocked and got no answer. When I saw you through the window, I was headed back to my car to call for help. That's when I ran into Jenny. She must have been lurking behind the garage, but I have no idea where Damon had been before he joined us out here on the patio."

Ben might not be up to full strength, but he wasn't going to allow that to interfere with his need for retribution. "Don't worry. I'll sort out those two idiots when I get to the station."

Ben was pale and shaky before he sat down. That was nothing compared to how he looked when he tried to stand up again. If Tripp hadn't been so quick on the move, the man would've face-planted on the patio. She'd known the good detective was a bit on the stubborn side, but this was ridiculous.

Abby stood up with a great deal more grace and style than he had. "Ben Earle, go to the hospital and get checked out. You won't be any good to anyone if you pass out and hurt yourself worse than you already are."

He glared at her. "I have prisoners to interrogate."

Hands on her hips, she glared right back. "Seriously? Just how intimidating do you think you'll be when you can barely stand up straight?"

Ben was even more unhappy when Tripp laughed, then immediately held up his hands in apology. "Sorry, Ben, I wasn't laughing at you. I just get a kick out of it when Abby let's her mean streak come shining through."

Now she was the one frowning at him. "I'm not mean. I'm concerned."

Gage had stepped away for a couple of minutes but came back just in time to offer his own opinion on the subject. "She's right, Ben, and you know it. Go see what the docs have to say. I've got enough information to ensure Jenny and Damon will still be parked in one of my cells whenever the doctors release you. If you won't let the EMTs transport you, I'll have one of my people take you."

"Fine. I'll see you in a couple of hours."

He marched off under his own steam, his back rigid as if he was struggling to hold his head upright. Gage gave one of his men a nod and then jerked his head in Ben's direction. Having made sure his friend would be watched over, he turned back to Abby.

"Sit back down and give me the short version about what happened here today." He took the chair that Ben had been sitting in. "When we're done, Tripp can take you home. Stay there."

She normally didn't appreciate being ordered around, but she was in no shape to argue. Well, except maybe she was. "Wouldn't your time be put to better use getting Jenny or Damon to tell you what they did with Dayna? Doesn't it seem weird to you that both Ben and I got texts from her when she's not here? And why would either of them still be hanging around here once Dayna was gone?"

Gage pinched the bridge of his nose as if praying for patience. Tripp intervened, probably fearing Abby would only make an already tense situation even worse. He placed his hand on her shoulder and gave it a tight squeeze. "Yes, Abby, we're all concerned about your friend. Gage needs to gather all the pertinent facts before he can know how best to proceed. He knows how to do his job."

Her eyes felt the sting of tears. "I'm sorry, Gage. It's just that I'm so worried about her."

"I know. We all are. But like Tripp said, I need the facts. I can trust that you're telling me the truth. It will give me something to measure against what Jenny and Damon have to say."

Abby took a deep breath and started talking as fast as she could. After all, the sooner Gage got his precious facts, the sooner the hunt for Dayna could get started.

Chapter 27

"You okay?"
"I will be."
She wasn't so sure about Tripp, though. Abby pried her eyes open long enough to study him. Gage had promised to see that someone would drop Tripp's truck off back at the house so that Tripp could drive her car for her. Neither man was ready to stop fussing over her quite yet, so she hadn't bothered pointing out that she was capable of driving herself home.

As soon as they'd left Dayna's place, it had occurred to her to wonder how Tripp had gotten there so fast. As it turned out, he'd gotten her message about where she was heading and when she'd get back. When she hadn't show up on time, he'd gone on the hunt. After confirming with Frannie that Abby had stopped at the diner, he'd headed right for Dayna's. He'd arrived just as the police came roaring up.

He hated that she'd been caught up in another

hostage situation. Reaching out, she rested her hand on his arm. "I'm sorry about all of this."

"You didn't plan this."

No, she hadn't, but that didn't keep her from feeling bad about it. "I know, but I hate that I did everything I could to keep you from having to worry about me, and I failed miserably."

He patted her hand. "You were trying to take care of a sick friend. There's no way you could've known there was something else going on."

That didn't make her feel any better about the situation. "I'm so worried about her."

Tripp bypassed the turnoff to their place, continuing on toward Main Street, where he pulled up in front of Something's Brewing. After shutting off the ignition, he twisted in the seat to face her. "I'm guessing you have some doubts that Jenny Garth or Damon Wray killed Josiah, or Dayna's friend."

He was right. However, she struggled to put her finger on exactly why she felt that way. "Jenny has a temper, and she resented Josiah getting all the glory and most of the money. She probably exaggerated how much of the creative work was hers. But if she was anywhere as talented as her uncle, surely she could've simply gone out on her own at some point."

"But what about Damon? Josiah was in a position to destroy his entire career."

"Damon didn't exactly deny Jenny's accusations and lobbed a few dandies back in her direction, so neither of them is innocent. That doesn't mean they're killers."

"You'd think all of that would've driven them

apart. Instead, they joined forces to sell a bunch of stuff at the fair over the weekend. It seems likely they were passing her uncle's work off as Jenny's." After a brief pause, he added, "If so, it was a heck of a way to jumpstart her solo reputation in the local art community."

"Thinking about all of this makes my brain hurt." Abby leaned her head back and closed her eyes. "I almost wish they had done it, because the culprits would be behind bars."

"I'll keep you safe, Abs."

Bless the man, he meant that. She didn't bother pointing out that he had classes to attend, obligations to the veterans group, a life to live. He might be able shuffle things in order to dog her footsteps for a few days, but it couldn't go on forever. Sheer stubbornness on his part meant he'd try, but she wouldn't let him.

She changed the subject. "So we're parked in front of Something's Brewing. Are we going in or just sightseeing?"

"I'm going in. You're staying here while Zeke stands guard. I'll be right back." He held up his phone. "I've got Bridey's new app. Our order is ready to pick up."

Then he was gone, leaving her staring after him. She'd been so distracted, she hadn't even noticed what he'd been up to. True to his word, he was already on his way back out. Just the sight of him had her relaxing. They'd go home and stay there just as Gage had ordered. Their soup would reheat just fine, and then they'd find something to watch on television while they ate their desserts.

There was no telling what tomorrow would bring, but at least there was a good chance they could catch their breath and maybe get a decent night's sleep. Crossing her fingers that was true, she forced a smile when Tripp got back in the car. One whiff of her coffee was all it took for the smile to feel more genuine.

"Ready to go home and lock the doors?"

The tightness around Tripp's eyes and mouth softened. "Yeah. I vote we let the rest of the world take care of itself."

He had to know that she wouldn't be able to forget about Dayna that easily. Tripp brushed his fingertips along her cheek. "Think you can do that?"

Her friend's fate was now in the hands of Gage Logan and Ben Earle. Luckily, Abby knew her friend couldn't wish for better men to be on the job. That knowledge had her nodding. "I can try."

As it turned out, she succeeded. To help keep the mood light, they'd ended up watching an animated children's movie together. It was one of her favorites, and they'd both needed the respite that the lighthearted film provided. They'd curled up on the couch and shared a huge bowl of buttery popcorn as they laughed at the antics on the screen.

Afterward, she'd trudged upstairs to bed, unfortunately alone. Zeke had evidently decided to share guard duty for the night. He'd been contentedly snoring away on the living room floor next to the couch where Tripp would sleep. While the dog

might have ignored her, at least his buddy had
given her a goodnight kiss that was sure to inspire
happy dreams.

And it had worked, at least for most of the night.
But just before dawn, her dreams took a dark turn.
Suddenly, she was back in the tent at the séance.
Except this time, it was just her, Madam G, and
Damon Wray, who waved an envelope in the air
as he yelled, "Why am I here? You promised this
ended it."

Meanwhile, Madam G kept trying to grab the
envelope, but she wasn't quite tall enough to
reach it. "You're here because you screwed up big-
time. You trusted the wrong person."

He sneered and tore the envelope in half.
"You're the one who screwed up, woman. How
many more people are going to have to die to
save—"

Abby desperately wanted to hear what he'd told
the psychic, but someone else started shouting.
She tried to shush them. "Be quiet! I need to hear
what's going on."

Big hands latched on to her shoulders as her
world started rocking and rolling. "Abby, wake up!
You're having a nightmare."

It wasn't until she heard a dog whining close by
that she finally was able to distinguish between the
dream she'd been caught up in and the reality of
Tripp and Zeke trying to wake her up. It took
some effort to pry her eyes open as she batted at
Tripp in an attempt to break free of his grip.

"I'm awake. I'm awake."

The chaos ratcheted down several notches at
that point, giving all three of them a chance to

catch their breath. Tripp stepped back to give Zeke enough room to get closer to her. She stroked his wrinkly head. "Sorry if I scared the two of you."

Tripp crossed his arms over his chest and kept a wary eye on her. "That must've been some dream."

"It felt so real. Like I was actually there."

"Where exactly?"

She pushed herself upright to lean back against the headboard. "I was back inside that stupid tent with Madam G and Damon Wray. I'm not sure either of them knew I was watching them argue. He kept waving an envelope up in the air and shouting that it was supposed to have finished something, but she claimed everything was his fault. That he'd trusted the wrong person. He asked her how many people had to die to save . . . something."

"Like what?"

"No idea. That's when you woke me up."

"Sorry, but the way you were moaning and groaning upset Zeke. He heard you all the way from the living room. He barked and then tore up the steps."

She finally checked the time—five o'clock was way too early for any of them to be conscious. "Why don't you two go downstairs and see if you can't go back to sleep?"

He glanced out the window. "I'm awake now. Maybe I'll go for a quick run instead. Will you two be okay if I take off for a little while?"

"Yeah. It was just a weird dream."

Although it didn't exactly feel that way. Maybe her subconscious was trying to tell her something.

But what? She closed her eyes and replayed what she could remember about the dream. As soon as she thought of the envelope, she was up and following after Tripp. "I remembered something. It's about Damon and Madam G. I saw them together at the fair on Sunday. I was surprised she was there, considering she'd just gotten out of the hospital. She bought something to eat and sat down at one of the picnic tables. A minute later, Damon joined her."

Tripp waited for her at the bottom of the steps. "There's nothing particularly odd about that. It's clear they've known each other for some time now."

"True, but he had an envelope like the one in my dream. I was too far away to hear their conversation, but he tossed it on the table and then stalked away after she nodded."

She winced, knowing how that sounded. "I didn't set out to spy on them. By that point, I was afraid if I moved, they might notice me. Once he left and she was busy eating, I hightailed it back to you at the information booth."

"Did you tell Gage or Ben about it?"

"I don't think so. It didn't seem like a big deal at the time. But when he went on that tirade at the séance, one of the things he was mad about was that he'd thought they'd already settled something. What if it had something to do with Josiah's death or whatever was in that envelope?"

Tripp mulled it all over for several seconds before nodding. "It's too early to make any calls, so I'll still go for a run. When I get back, we can decide what to do next. There's no way to know if the envelope had anything to do with what's been going on, but we should run it past Gage and Ben to be on the safe side."

It was a relief that he didn't think she was just grabbing at straws. "While you're gone, I'll grab a quick shower and get dressed. By the time you get back, I'll have breakfast ready and the coffee on."

"Sounds like a deal."

Abby followed him to the door. "I know this borders on the wrong side of the line when it comes to staying out of police business, and you're right that the envelope might not be connected to the case."

"But?"

"Gage told me I should trust my instincts when it comes to people. And right now, they're telling me that Damon knows more about Josiah's death than he's admitting. If I'm right about that, then he probably also knows what's happened to Dayna. I can't just let it slide."

Tripp sighed. "I know, Abby. Lock the doors behind me."

She hated to worry him, but right now it was unavoidable. She might not be able to make good on her promise to stay out of police business, but she could have breakfast ready and waiting when he got back.

At least that was something.

Ben was a bit brusque when Abby called him. She didn't take it personally. The man was dealing with two murders and now an additional missing person. It didn't help that both Jenny and Damon had lawyered up and weren't talking. He promised to share the information about the envelope with Gage, but that was all he could do at this point.

He mentioned they'd finished going through Dayna's house. There had been no other sign of violence except for what had happened to him. Abby wanted to find that reassuring, but it really wasn't. She thanked him anyway and hung up.

Tripp needed to take some paperwork to Pastor Jack at the park. After promising to be only gone for an hour, he'd taken Zeke with him, figuring the dog could use the exercise. While she missed their company, it was a relief to have the house to herself for a while.

The problem was that it left her alone with her thoughts, a messy tangle of questions about who did what to whom and why. Maybe it would help if she made a list of everything that had happened and what she did and didn't know about each occurrence.

Two cups of coffee and a few cookies later, Abby set her pencil aside and studied her notes. Under the section titled "Josiah's murder," she'd noted the time and the supposed whereabouts of the primary characters. It appeared that no one had a rock-solid alibi.

She started with Damon, who claimed to have left the fair before the incident. But as Abby thought back over her interactions with him, he'd chosen his words pretty darn carefully when it came to his alibi. The last time they'd spoken, he hadn't actually said he'd never come back to the fair, only that the police hadn't found any witnesses to prove that he had. His possible motive for the murder was pretty clear—Josiah could ruin Damon's reputation, and with it, his career.

According to Jenny, she had been on her way to the cabin. Even if that was true, no one knew for sure when she'd left the fair. In general, her behavior was puzzling. During their first encounter, the young woman had been warm, friendly, and helpful. She'd also been understandably proud of her art and no doubt hoped to build a successful career just like her uncle's. If so, working with him long-term seemed to be the most likely route for Jenny to reach her goal.

On the other hand, if her uncle really had been taking advantage of her talent rather than nurturing it, it would be no surprise if she'd come to resent him. Also, what if Damon was right when he claimed Jenny's only talent was her ability to copy Josiah's work? Had he just said that because it would hurt her? But if he was right and her uncle had actually admitted that he only kept her around to do grunt work, maybe her disappointment had festered to the point of violence.

So many questions and no clear answers. Personal relationships could be complicated, and it was nearly impossible to understand them when looking in from the outside. That was why she was struggling to guess what was the truth when it came to Josiah and Madam G. Both Jenny and Damon admitted the pair had been involved in the past. They also claimed Josiah had moved on while Greta claimed their problems were only temporary.

But what if something had happened that finally convinced her Josiah felt differently? After all, Jenny had claimed he'd been dating other women.

Younger ones, at that, if she was to be believed. Had Greta spent decades loving a man who then tossed her aside for the simple crime of growing older?

Beyond the mystery of Josiah's death, there were several other major questions left unanswered. Who had killed Wendy and why? And finally the one that was most troubling right now: Where was Dayna?

She took a drink of coffee, hoping to wash down the lump of worry lodged in her throat. It tasted cold, bitter, and didn't help at all. Those instincts Gage told her to trust were screaming that time was running out for Dayna if it hadn't already. Even if Gage and Ben were doing everything they could, it wasn't nearly enough. They all needed answers and needed them now. She'd promised everyone who mattered that she'd stay out of the investigation. But it seemed that Madam G had been right on target when she'd told Abby that once she'd started down the path, it would be imperative that she continue on to the end.

That left one last question to be answered: What should her next step be?

Before she could come up with a viable plan, it sounded like someone rattled the front door. She wasn't sure that's what she actually heard, but then it happened again. Was someone really trying to get in? Rather than give in to panic, she tried to think logically.

She needed to call the police, but Tripp might be closer. He answered on the first ring. "What's wrong?"

Smart man, he knew she wouldn't be calling for

no reason. She kept her voice to a soft whisper. "I think someone is trying to break in. How close are you?"

"Not far. We'll run the rest of the way."

When the rattling started again, she moved into the hall away from any windows. "I don't know who's out there, but they're impatient."

She could hear the sound of Tripp's feet picking up speed as they hit the pavement. "Hang up. I'll call nine-one-one and then call you right back."

When he did, she whispered, "Tripp, they're trying the back door now. They seem pretty determined to get inside."

"Where are you?"

"In the hallway."

"It's too late to get out of the house without being seen. Head upstairs to the third floor and lock yourself in the bathroom. Lie down in that clawfoot tub and stay there."

Good idea. She took off running. She made it as far as the steps when the sound of glass shattering spurred her on to greater speed. When she reached the top landing, she gasped, "Tripp, they broke a window. They'll be inside any second. Be careful when you get here. Better yet, stay out of sight and wait for the police."

"There's no way I'm going to hide in the bushes while someone is hunting for you. Do what I told you. I'll be there soon."

Abby crept into the bathroom, avoiding the creaky board just outside of the doorway. No use in giving the intruder a big, fat clue as to where she'd gone to ground. Considering how loudly her heart was pounding, that noise alone was likely to

give her location away. She froze as she was about
to climb into the old-fashioned tub. Didn't it always turn out badly for people in the movies when
they hid in the bathroom? Certainly, choosing that
as a hiding spot was almost cliché.

"Sitrep, Abby."

Tripp's terse order spurred her into making a
decision. "I want to hide in the sewing room.
There's more stuff in there I can use to defend myself. I'll try to lock the bathroom door to make it
seem like I'm in there."

After a brief silence, he whispered, "Fine. Just
get out of sight. Zeke and I have turned the corner
to the house, and I can see flashing lights headed
your way. No sirens, though. Smart thinking on
Gage's part. No use in warning the bad guy that
help is on the way."

"All I care about is that they hurry. Stay safe,
Tripp. I'm going to quit talking now."

The silence outside of her haven continued.
While she was grateful, it made the suspense worse
and didn't keep her from jumping when the board
outside of the bathroom door suddenly creaked.

"You might as well come on out. I know you're
in there."

What the heck? For some reason, she'd assumed
the intruder would be male, although Damon Wray
was the only man who might be coming after her
right now. The last she'd heard, he was still occu-
pying one of Gage's cells. Hysteria left her wanting
to snicker about how much the well-dressed man
would hate wearing a hideous orange jumpsuit.
She had far more important things to be thinking

about right now, starting with why Madam G would break into her house in the first place.

The floorboard across the hall by the bathroom creaked. "If I have to shoot the lock to get in, there's always the chance a ricochet will hit you. We wouldn't want that, would we?"

Well, duh. Nobody ever wanted the shooting to start.

Abby moved deeper into the sewing room in search of a weapon. She picked up the biggest pair of scissors she could find and gripped them like a knife. As an added precaution, she disconnected the call and sent Tripp a short text instead: **Madam G has a gun!**

He didn't reply for what seemed like a long time. **Warned Gage.**

"Abby, I don't have time to play games. That idiot Damon is a coward at heart. I'm quite sure he will start singing like a canary to the cops any minute now. Before that happens, I have to clean up this mess and get out of town. I'll give you to five to open the door. After that, I start shooting."

So Damon had been in on it all along. Abby set the scissors down long enough to send another text to tell Tripp what she'd heard. She'd just hit SEND when several shots rang out. Madam G must have blasted open the lock on the bathroom door, because she called out, "Clever ploy, Abby, but hide-and-seek was never my favorite game. I am good at it, however. It's part of my gift."

Apparently so was insanity.

She listened hard, hoping to figure out where Madam G was headed next. It sounded as if she was checking out the bedroom across the hall. There was a door to the attic from there, so hopefully the crazy woman would waste some more time poking around in there before heading back in Abby's direction.

No such luck. The board by the bathroom creaked again all too soon as the woman continued to prowl through the house. Abby took shelter behind the large metal shelving unit that jutted out into the sewing room near the door. It was piled high with fabric of all kinds that Aunt Sybil had collected over the years. Madam G would have to walk past it when she entered the room. It would take some effort to push it over on the woman, but Abby was pretty darn sure that the adrenaline high she was riding at the moment would give her the added strength she needed.

The footsteps came closer. "You're out of hiding places, Abby. Come out so we can have an intelligent conversation. I'll even tell you where we've stashed your buddy Dayna. You'll want to reach her before the food and water run out. Josiah's cabin is both remote and primitive. You strike me as an intelligent woman. Too smart to try to blackmail us like that Larabie woman did. Can you believe she was stupid enough to hide the evidence in her own workshop? Before she died, she admitted she'd sent a backup copy to Dayna to give to the police."

She sighed. "Unfortunately, Damon has proven to be remarkably incompetent. He took that nitwit Jenny along for backup, but Dayna caught them breaking into her house to look for the letter. After he drugged her, I came to get her out of there. He admitted he couldn't find the letter and claimed she might have given it to you. He used her phone to lure you to her place. Imagine his surprise when the homicide detective showed up first."

Her evil cackle made Abby's skin crawl. "I actually didn't believe she'd given you the letter. Otherwise, your cop buddies would've already been hot on our trail. Still, I need to know for sure. If you care about what happens to your friend, start talking."

It was tempting to obey just in case Madam G really would let Abby rescue Dayna. But the woman was up to her ears in two murders and a kidnapping, not exactly the kind of résumé that inspired trust. Besides, there was no use to risk getting shot just before the good guys arrive.

Instead, she peeked out between two stacks of fabric. Madam G, well-groomed as always, had just stepped into the doorway. The only part of her outfit that seemed out of place was the gun in her right hand, but it was doubtful she would appreciate any fashion advice at the moment. Instead, Abby held her breath and waited for the woman to come farther into the room. Three more steps should put her in perfect range of the shelves.

Counting down in her head, she set the scissors within easy reach and positioned her hands to get ready to shove. *Three, two, one . . . Shove!*

At first the heavy shelves moved in slow motion, but her second push turned the tide. Stacks of fabric slid off to land on Madam G as the shelves picked up speed. Their impact had her flinging her hands in the air to bat them away. Too late she realized the real danger was the steel shelves that were toppling over and about to land right on top of her.

The names she called Abby as she was knocked to the floor would've made a sailor blush, but words couldn't kill. Bullets could, so Abby scrambled over the tangle of fabric and sheet metal to stomp on Madam G's arm until she released the gun.

Over the woman's wailing about her wrist being broken, Abby heard the clomp of big feet heading up the stairs. "In here, Gage! I've got her weapon."

By the time the rescue party appeared in the doorway, Abby was across the room in the easy chair by the window. She'd traded the gun for her weapon of choice, figuring the scissors wouldn't go off accidently and hurt someone. She'd set the gun on the windowsill behind the chair. Even if Madam G had managed to free herself, she would have to get past Abby and her scissors to reach it. She knew Gage and Tripp wouldn't let that happen.

For now, she did her best to catch her breath and not worry about how long it was going to take her to restore order to Aunt Sybil's fabric stash. That was a problem for another day. For now, she smiled as Tripp shoved his way past Gage and climbed over every obstacle in order to reach her.

He lifted her out of the chair long enough to sit down himself and then settle her in his lap. Zeke wasn't far behind. Then the three of them huddled together as Madam G was unburied, handcuffed, and hauled out of the room by two of Ben's associates.

Ben came in as the woman was led out. He joined Gage in studying the colorful piles of calico and batiks for the longest time before finally approaching Abby. He pulled out his notebook and pen. "Kudos to you, lady. Not sure I would've ever thought of weaponizing a shelving unit. Sorry I missed it. Want to give me the highlights?"

Abby felt a momentary surge of pride in her ingenuity, but the adrenaline was already wearing off. Sensing the crash was on its way, she let the story all pour out. As soon as she told them Dayna was being kept in Josiah's cabin, both Gage and Ben promised to send someone to retrieve her. Abby ran out of breath and energy pretty much at the same time.

Tripp held her close for a few more seconds. "We probably need to get out of here so the crime scene folks can do their thing. Want to head downstairs to the kitchen so I can make a cup of my special tea?"

"For me or for you?"

He huffed a small laugh as they both stood up. "I haven't decided yet."

Chapter 28

All in all, it had been a busy couple of days since Madam G was taken down by fat quarters and shelving, starting with Dayna's rescue. After spending one night in the hospital, she was doing better than expected. Abby had invited her to move in for a while, but Dayna had to go straight home. She insisted returning to work would help her get back to normal. Besides, all the bad guys were in jail.

Abby was just as relieved by that fact as Dayna. That didn't keep her from twitching a bit when the front doorbell rang. Tripp, who was studying in the dining room, called out, "I'll let them in."

Aunt Sybil would never have entertained company at the kitchen table instead of in the dining room. She also wouldn't have let someone else greet her guests. But she would've understood that this was Abby's home now and she had her own way of doing things.

Gage, Ben, Dayna, and Tripp all filed into the

kitchen. Gage handed her a bottle of wine and sniffed the air. "Something smells good."

"I kept things simple. It's just chili and sour-dough bread."

Tripp pulled out Dayna's chair for her. "She also bought two of Frannie's pies for dessert."

That had Ben rubbing his hands together in greedy anticipation. "Bring it on! I've been living on fast food and frozen dinners while we got everything wrapped up."

"Then get seated, and I'll serve up the chili. We can talk afterward."

By unspoken agreement, they kept the dinner conversation light. Abby was glad she'd made a double batch of the chili, because the three men devoured two bowls apiece. Ben claimed only the promise of dessert kept him from asking for a third.

Gage had his own suggestion. "Let's save the pie until we finish recapping everything. Then we can celebrate closing several cases in short order."

Ben looked longingly at the pie on the counter, but he finally agreed. "That will keep us from being too long-winded. All I ask is that the audience save their questions and comments until the end."

Everyone laughed at that, but the smiles faded quickly as Ben launched into his summary. "The good news is that Damon Wray finally cracked and told us everything."

Abby blurted out, "Madam G figured he'd start singing like a canary."

At Ben's admonishing look, she mimed zipping

her lips. He picked up where he'd left off. "As we suspected, it was all about Josiah. The fight between him and Damon Wray was far more serious that we knew. Not only was he going to fire Damon as his agent, he was having his attorney take legal action to audit the sales he'd handled for Josiah. Not only would they learn that he'd been lying about how much he got for Josiah's work, but also that he'd sold more pieces under Josiah's name than he'd actually made. That's where Jenny came in."

He paused to sip his coffee. "I don't know if she had illusions of grandeur or if she really was as talented as she claimed. However, her uncle pretty much told her that she wasn't good enough to make it on her own. Damon took advantage of her determination to show Josiah he was wrong by having her create pieces that he marketed as Josiah's. They split the money between them."

Gage took over. "Josiah jettisoned Madam G about six months back. Damon and Jenny were right about that. When she kept trying to rekindle their relationship, Josiah made it all too clear that wasn't happening, and in the most cruel way possible. He laughed and told her that no amount of hair dye and Botox would ever make her attractive again."

"What a jerk!"

Dayna slapped her hand over her mouth at her outburst, but Gage only nodded. "Yeah, he wasn't a very likeable guy. That doesn't justify murder."

Ben picked up the story again. "The details about this next part are still a bit hazy. Damon and Madam G wanted Josiah to pay for destroying their lives and hatched the plot. Damon staged a fight with Josiah, and stormed off so everyone would think he'd left the fair. He actually ducked into Madam G's tent to change clothes. Evidently she routinely closed down for an hour every day at the same time to renew her spiritual energy, so no one would think anything of her disappearing for a short time."

Abby didn't know about the others, but the story sounded more like the script for a TV movie. Ben continued his narrative. "She called Josiah and claimed that she'd slashed his tires in retaliation for everything he'd said to her. He shut down the booth and took off to deal with the situation. Of course, she was nowhere to be found. Instead, she and Damon were waiting for him when he returned to his booth. Damon knocked him out and then killed him."

Abby shivered. A crime of passion might be understandable, but this entire operation sounded pretty cold-blooded to her. When neither man said anything for several seconds, Dayna risked another question. "What about Wendy? How did she get drawn into this?"

"Bad luck and greed. We think she was coming back from the dumpsters on the next aisle over when she saw Madam G and Damon sneaking out of Josiah's booth."

Ben gave Dayna a sympathetic look. "One of the other vendors said Wendy told her that she was going to toss your box of pottery. I'm sorry."

"Don't be. I'd pretty much written it off when I broke her teapot."

"We know what happened next because she

wrote everything down. Evidently, she peeked into Josiah's booth and spotted his dead body. She went into panic mode, packed up, and took off. Like I said, then she got greedy and tried to blackmail Damon and Madam G."

Ben pulled out his notebook and flipped through several pages. "According to Damon, he would've paid Wendy off and hoped for the best. After all, she was committing a crime herself. That only lasted until he learned Wendy had written out everything that had happened as sort of insurance so they wouldn't come after her."

"Only they did."

Gage's expression had turned grim. "They broke into her home looking for the letter. When they didn't find it, Damon hid in her workshop and waited until she made the mistake of coming back home. In his efforts to subdue her, she got cut on a piece of broken pottery. He promised to help her if she handed over the envelope, which she did. Instead of taking her to the hospital, he took her to Josiah's cabin and locked her inside."

Abby couldn't remain silent any longer. "So he's the one who killed her."

"No, he insists that was Madam G. When she found out Damon was holding Wendy prisoner, she decided to clean up his mess. After she killed Wendy, she forced him to sneak the body into the fair in the dark of night. She also insisted he rough her up just enough so we'd believe Wendy's killer had attacked Madam G and left the body as a warning. The head injury was also her excuse for not knowing what happened. Damon also made the threatening call to Abby. It appears Madam G planned to use the séance to focus all of our attention on Damon and Jenny."

Ben pocketed his notebook. "So, Abby, you were right about the envelope being important. Damon handed it over to Madam G at the fair. It wasn't until she finally read it, that they figured out that Wendy had also sent a copy to Dayna. We don't know why she chose you."

The woman in question shuddered. "It was in the mail when I came home from the fair in Snowberry Creek, but I didn't open it right away. When I did, I immediately left a message for Ben that I had important information for him, but then Damon showed up. Trying to stall for enough time for Ben to arrive, I hinted I'd already given the letter to Abby to pass on to her cop buddies. Meanwhile, he forced me to swallow some pills. I don't remember anything after that until I woke up in that cabin."

Abby picked up the story from that point, ending with her big calico takedown of Madam G. The situation hadn't been funny at the time, but they were all laughing by the time she was finished. After the pie made the rounds, Gage and Ben said their good-byes, claiming they still had work to do. Evidently, paperwork didn't write itself. Dayna didn't stay much longer.

Tripp turned off the porch light and locked the door. The quiet settled around them as Tripp leaned against the wall and stared down at her. When he didn't say anything, she asked, "Something on your mind?"

"Yeah, but I'm not sure this is the right time to bring it up."

Okay, that sounded ominous. She took a step back. "Now you're scaring me. Just tell me."

He studied her face for several seconds and then nodded. "We've been dancing around a certain subject for a while now."

Although she suspected she already knew the answer, she asked, "That subject being?"

"Us. I spend almost as much time over here as I do in my own place. Neither of us seem to have any interest in dating anyone else. And before you point out that no one else has asked you out, you should know that both Liam and Ben were interested. I warned them off."

He what? Maybe she should've been mad, but right now she was far more interested in where this conversation was headed. "Go on."

"I want to make it official that we're a couple, one with long-term intentions."

He pushed off the wall and closed the distance between them. Then he reached in his pocket and pulled out a small box. Abby's heart skipped a beat as he opened the lid and held it out for her inspection. "This diamond came from my grandmother's engagement ring. She left it to me a few years ago. When the time feels right, we'll pick out a new setting for it. How does that sound?"

"That sounds perfect." Then she gave him a teasing smile. "One question, though. When that time comes, will you finally tell me what you're majoring in?"

He laughed and pulled her into his arms. "We can save that for the honeymoon."

Epilogue

Abby woke up smiling. She and Tripp had spent the evening talking about anything and everything. Well, except about his college major. She suspected they'd be laughing about that subject for some time to come.

She'd just finished breakfast when the phone rang. "Hi, Bridey. What's up?"

"Abby, I need a favor. A huge one."

The worry in her friend's voice was sounding alarms. "Anything, you know that."

"The baby and I are both fine, but my blood pressure is up higher than the doctor likes. If I'm not careful, I could end up on complete bedrest. He recommended I stay off my feet as much as possible. That's when I thought of you."

"Okay."

"My staff is capable of running the shop out front. What they can't do is all the baking, but you could. I'll even share the gooey butter cake recipe."

Abby laughed. "It's a deal. Just tell me when to be there."

"Would tomorrow morning work? I usually start work at five a.m."

That was an ugly thought, but there was no way Abby could turn her down. "I'll be there."

"There's more, though. I'd already been thinking about cutting back on my hours when the baby comes, but I didn't see how that was possible. It was Seth who suggested I ask if you'd like to become my business partner long term. Covering for me now would let you test the waters and see what you think. No pressure. I mean that."

Abby considered the idea and found she didn't hate it. "Okay. Let's see how it goes, and then sit down and discuss the possibilities."

They discussed the logistics for another couple of minutes before hanging up. Then Abby plopped down in her favorite chair and stared at Zeke. "Well, boy, in the past twenty-four hours, I've ended up with an almost-fiancé and a new job. I don't know about you, but I can't wait to see what happens next."